Under the Millionaire's Influence
by Catherine Mann

ɔ ʔ ʎ ɕ ତ

"This is a no-strings offer."

David felt the need to make the statement, even when the heat between them continued to flare. "We're going to land, have a quick lunch on the way to the gallery and then look at some artwork before supper. If after supper you want to go straight to your room alone, that's your call."

He meant it. No matter how much he wanted to be w_____ _____ _____ r not at all. "V_____ _____ _____ us for you to _____ _____ _____ you to someth_____ _____ _____ thing."

She sta_____ _____ _____ on for a long drone of the private jet's engines before finally nodding. "I trust you."

"Good. Good."

He was glad she did, because staying strong against the temptation of sleeping in the room next to Starr would be total torture. He wasn't so sure he'd just made the wisest move.

The Millionaire's Indecent Proposal

EMILIE ROSE

Under the Millionaire's Influence

CATHERINE MANN

MILLS & BOON

Pure reading pleasure

*First published in Great Britain 2008
by Harlequin Mills & Boon Limited,
Eton House, 18-24 Paradise Road, Richmond, Surrey TW9 1SR*

The publisher acknowledges the copyright holders of the
individual works as follows:

The Millionaire's Indecent Proposal
© Emilie Rose Cunningham 2007
Under the Millionaire's Influence © Catherine Mann 2007

ISBN: 978 0 263 85901 0

51-0508

*Printed and bound in Spain
by Litografía Rosés S.A., Barcelona*

THE MILLIONAIRE'S INDECENT PROPOSAL

by
Emilie Rose

Dear Reader,

What could possibly be more delicious than a sexy, French chocolatier? I had more fun writing Franco Constantine than I have had with any hero in a very long time. Franco is a true sensualist – a man who believes he knows what he wants and how to get it. I am so glad Stacy Reeves came along to show him the error of his thinking. :)

Throw in a vicarious vacation in magical Monaco and writing this story was an absolute pleasure. I've been fascinated with Monaco since my school days when I begged my parents to allow me to go to Amherst College in Massachusetts, the alma mater of Prince Albert of Monaco. I was convinced I could make him my prince if only I could meet him. Fate had other plans. I attended college near home, but I did indeed meet my prince.

Happy reading!

Emilie Rose

PS Don't miss the next instalment of my MONTE CARLO AFFAIRS series – *The Prince's Ultimate Deception* hits the shelves in June 2008.

EMILIE ROSE

lives in North Carolina with her college sweetheart husband and four sons. Writing is Emilie's third (and hopefully her last) career. She managed a medical office and ran a day-care home, neither of which offered half as much satisfaction as plotting happy endings. Her hobbies include quilting, gardening and cooking (especially cheesecake). Her favourite TV shows include *ER, CSI* and Discovery Channel's medical programmes. Emilie's a country music fan because she can find an entire book in almost any song.

Letters can be mailed to:
Emilie Rose
PO Box 20145
Raleigh, NC 27619, USA
E-mail: EmilieRoseC@aol.com

Bron, Juliet, Sally and Wanda,
you know this book would not have happened
without you. Thanks, ladies, for keeping me
on the road.

MJ, thanks for the spark that gave me Franco.

Prologue

"Must you marry every woman you sleep with?" Franco Constantine demanded of his father. Furious, he paced the salon of the family chateau outside Avignon, France. "This one is younger than me."

His father shrugged and smiled—the smile of a besotted old fool. "I'm in love."

"No, Papa, you're in lust. Again. We cannot afford another one of your expensive divorce settlements. Our cash reserves are tied up in expanding Midas Chocolates. For God's sake, if you refuse to have a prenuptial agreement, then at least sign everything over to me before you marry her and jeopardize our business and the family properties with mistake number five."

Armand shook his head. "Angeline is not a mistake. She is a blessing."

Franco had met the misnamed harpy at lunch. She was no angel. But he knew from past experience his father would not listen when a woman had him trans-fixed. "I disagree."

Armand rested a hand on Franco's shoulder. "I hate to see you so bitter, Franco. Granted, your ex-wife was a selfish bitch, but not all women are."

"You're wrong. Women are duplicitous and mercen-ary creatures. There is nothing I want from one that I cannot buy."

"If you'd stop dating spoiled rich women and find someone with traditional values like Angeline, you'd find a woman who would love you for yourself and not your money."

"Wrong. And if your paramour loves you and not your wealth, she'll stick by you once you've divested yourself, and I won't have to borrow against our estate *again,* close stores or lay off workers when your ardor cools and her lawyers start circling."

"If you want to control the Constantine holdings so badly, then marry."

"I won't endanger the family assets by marrying again."

"And what of an heir? Someone to inherit all this when you and I are gone?" Armand's sweeping gesture encompassed the chateau which had been in the family for hundreds of years.

Something in his father's tone raised the hackles on the back of Franco's neck. "Is Angeline pregnant?"

"No. But son, you are thirty-eight. I should be bouncing grandbabies on my knee by now. Since you're not willing to provide heirs to our estate then I think perhaps I should. Angeline is only thirty. I could have several more sons and daughters by her before I die."

"You can't be serious. You're seventy-five."

His father speared him with a hard glance. "If you marry before my September wedding, I'll sign everything over to you. If you do not…" He extended his arms and shrugged. "I'll take matters into my own hands."

Franco could easily find a woman to marry. Any number of his acquaintances would agree, but the stench of his ex-wife's betrayal still clung to him. He'd been a young love-struck fool, blind to Lisette's faults and her treachery. He would never let a woman dupe him like that again. Marriage was out of the question.

He stood toe to toe with his father. "If I find one of these mythical paragons and prove she's just as greedy as the rest of her sex, then you will sign the Constantine properties over to me without a parody of a marriage on my part."

"Prove it how exactly?"

How indeed? "I'll offer her a million euros for the use of her body for one month without the pretense of love or the possibility of marriage. That amount is but a fraction of what each of your divorces has cost us."

"I accept your terms, but don't try to weasel out of this by finding an impossible woman. She must be one who you find attractive and beddable, and who you would be willing to marry if she cannot be bought."

A woman who could not be bought. No such animal existed.

Confident he would win, Franco extended his hand to shake on the deal. Victory would not only be sweet, it would be easy, and his father's most recent parasite would not get the chance to sink her fangs in the family coffers and suck them dry.

One

"*Le chocolat qui vaut son poids en or,*" Stacy Reeves read the gilt script on the shop window aloud. "What does that mean?" she asked her friend Candace without looking away from the mouthwatering display of chocolates on gold-rimmed plates.

"Chocolate worth its weight in gold," a slightly accented and thoroughly masculine voice replied. Definitely not Candace.

Surprised, Stacy pivoted on her sandaled foot. Wow. Forget chocolate. The dark-haired blue-eyed hunk in front of her looked good enough to eat.

"Would you care for a piece, mademoiselle? My treat." Monsieur Gorgeous indicated the shop door with his hand. A silver-toned, wafer-thin watch winked beneath his suit sleeve. Platinum, she'd bet, from the affluent look of what had to be a custom-tailored suit.

Nothing from a department store would fit those broad shoulders, narrow hips and long legs so perfectly.

Never mind that she'd probably dream of licking chocolate from the deep cleft in his chin tonight, Stacy had learned the hard way that when something looked too good to be true it was. Always. A seductively sexy stranger offering free gourmet chocolate had to be a set-up because sophisticated guys like him didn't go for practical accountants like her. And her simple lilac sundress and sensible walking sandals weren't the stuff of which male fantasies were made.

She glanced up and down the Boulevard des Moulins, one of the principality of Monaco's shopping streets, searching for her friend. Candace was nowhere in sight, but she had to be behind Mr. Delectable's appearance and offer. Her friend had joked about finding husbands for each of her bridesmaids before her wedding in four weeks time. At least Stacy had thought she was joking. Until now.

Stacy tilted her head, considered the man in question and gave him a saccharine smile. "Does that line usually work for you with American tourists?"

The corners of his oh-so-tempting lips twitched and his eyes glinted with humor beneath thick, straight eyebrows. He pressed a ringless left hand to his chest. "You wound me, mademoiselle."

With his fantasy good looks he had to have an epic ego to match. "I sincerely doubt it."

She scanned the sidewalks again looking for her MIA friend. Anything would be better than embarrassing herself by drooling over something she couldn't have. Namely *him* or the five-dollar—make that euro—per-piece candy.

"You are looking for someone? A lover, perhaps?"

Lover. Just hearing him say the word, rolling that *R,* gave her goose bumps.

"A friend." One who'd been right behind her seconds ago. Candace must have ducked into one of the quaint shops nearby, either to purchase something wedding-related or to spy if she was the one responsible for this encounter. After all, stopping by the chocolate shop had been Candace's idea.

"May I assist you in locating your friend?"

He had the most amazing voice. Deep and velvety. Was the accent French or native Monégasque? Stacy could listen to him talk for hours.

No. She couldn't. She was here with Candace, the bride-to-be, and two other bridesmaids to help prepare for Candace's wedding the first weekend in July, not to have a vacation romance.

"Thanks, but no thanks." Before Stacy could walk away, Candace popped out of the shop next door waving a scrap of lace.

"Stacy, I found the most exquisitely embroidered…" She trailed off as she spotted the Adonis beside Stacy. Surprise arched her pale eyebrows. "…handkerchief."

Maybe this wasn't a set-up. Stacy rocked back on her heels, folded her arms and waited for the inevitable. Candace had naturally white-blond hair and big baby-blue eyes. Her innocent Alice-in-Wonderland looks tended to bowl men over. No doubt this guy would fall at Candace's dainty feet. Stacy had never had that problem and that suited her fine. *Forever* wasn't in the cards for her. She'd never trust a man that much.

"Mademoiselle." Tall, Dark and Tempting bowed slightly. "I am trying to convince *vôtre amie* to allow me to gift to her *un chocolat,* but she questions my intentions. Perhaps if I buy you both lunch she will see that I'm quite harmless."

Harmless? Ha! He radiated smooth charm in the way that only a European man could.

A cunning smile curved Candace's lips and her eyes narrowed on Stacy. Uh-oh. Stacy stiffened. Whenever she saw that expression, someone was getting ready to try and pull a fast one on the IRS, and that meant trouble for Stacy, their accountant. "I'm sorry, Monsieur…? I didn't catch your name."

He offered his hand. "Constantine. Franco Constantine."

Recognition sparked in Candace's eyes, but the name meant nothing to Stacy. "I've been looking forward to meeting you, Monsieur Constantine. My fiancé, Vincent Reynard, has spoken of you often. I'm Candace Meyers, and this is my one of my bridesmaids, Stacy Reeves."

Mr. Wonderful's considerable charms shone back on Stacy with the heat of the noonday sun. He offered his hand. Darn protocol. She'd been warned during the hours-long etiquette session delivered by Candace's soon-to-be sister-in-law that the inhabitants of this tiny country were quite formal and polite. Refusing to shake his hand would be an insult.

Franco's fingers closed around Stacy's. Warm. Firm. Lingering. His charisma spread over Stacy like butter on hot bread. *"Enchanté, mademoiselle."*

She snatched her hand free and blamed the spark skipping up her arm on static electricity caused by the warm, dry climate. A predatory gleam flashed in his eyes, and warning prickles marched down Stacy's spine. Dangerous.

He turned back to Candace. "May I offer my congratulations on your upcoming nuptials, Mademoiselle Meyers? Vincent is a lucky man."

"Thank you, monsieur, and I would love to accept

your luncheon invitation, but I'm afraid I'll have to decline. I have a meeting with the caterer in an hour. Stacy, however, is free for the rest of the afternoon."

Stacy's jaw dropped. She snapped it closed and glared at her friend. Embarrassment burned her cheeks. "I am not. I'm here to help you plan your wedding. *Remember?*"

"Madeline, Amelia and I have everything under control. You have a nice lunch. We'll catch up with you tonight before we go to the casino. Oh, and monsieur, the hotel has already received your RSVP to the wedding and the rehearsal dinner. Merci. Au revoir." Candace waggled her fingers and departed.

Stacy considered murder. But she'd read that Monaco had a truly impressive police force. There was no way she could get away with strangling the petite blonde in broad daylight on a crowded street, and rotting away in a European prison wasn't exactly the financially secure future she had planned for herself.

A plan now in jeopardy.

Worry immediately weighted her shoulders, but she slammed the barriers in place. *Stop it. This is Candace's month. Don't ruin it for her.*

But Stacy wasn't the type to hide her head in the sand. She knew she had some difficult days ahead. *Not now. You have a more urgent problem standing in front of you.* She blinked away her distressing thoughts and examined the man problem. She hadn't missed Candace's not-so-subtle hint that Franco Constantine was close enough to the Reynards to have been invited to the intimate rehearsal dinner for only a dozen or so guests.

In other words, *play nice.*

Franco grasped Stacy's bare elbow as if he knew making a fast escape topped her to-do list. She felt those long fingers clear down to her toes, and it rattled her that an impersonal touch from a stranger could wreak havoc on her metabolism.

"If you will give me but a moment, Mademoiselle Reeves, I must speak to the shopkeeper, and then I am at your disposal."

He escorted Stacy inside the chocolate shop. The heavenly aroma was enough to give her a willpower-melting sugar rush. After greeting the clerk, Franco commenced a conversation in rapid-fire French…or something that sounded like French.

Stacy shamelessly eavesdropped while perusing the offerings in the glass cases, but she only managed to translate every tenth word or so. Despite the money-back guarantee on the box of *Speak French in 30 Days* CDs she had listened to during the month prior to leaving Charlotte, North Carolina, she wasn't prepared for natives speaking the language at Grand Prix speed.

She caught a hint of crisp, citrus cologne and the hair on the back of her neck rose. Without looking over her shoulder she knew Franco stood immediately behind her. After bracing herself against his potent virility, she turned.

"Mademoiselle?" He held a sinful morsel aloft. What else could she do but take a bite? Her teeth sank into dark chocolate and a tart cherry. Her eyes closed and she fought a moan as she chewed. Ohmigod. Yum. Yum. *Yum.*

Cherry juice dribbled on her chin, but before she could wipe it away Franco's thumb caught it and pressed it between her lips. Knowing she shouldn't, but unable to think of a way to avoid it, Stacy swallowed and then darted out her tongue. The taste of blatantly sexy male combined with the most decadently rich chocolate she'd ever sampled slammed her with sexual arousal like nothing she'd ever experienced.

She dragged a sobering breath through her nose and

struggled to fortify her quaking ramparts. Before she could make her excuses and bolt, Franco lifted the second half of the candy to her mouth. She tried to evade his touch, but his thumb grazed her bottom lip, and then, holding her gaze, he lifted the digit to his mouth and licked the remaining confection from his skin with one slow swipe.

Her pulse stuttered. *Gulp.* Seduction in a suit. The chocolate hit her stomach like a wrecking ball, and the desire in Franco's eyes rolled over her like a heat wave, intensifying the disturbing reactions clamoring inside her.

"Shall we dine, mademoiselle?" He offered his arm in a courtly gesture.

There was no way she could go to lunch with him. Franco Constantine was too…too…too *everything*. Too attractive. Too confident. And judging by his apparel, too rich for her. She couldn't afford to become involved with such a powerful man. If she did, she could very well repeat her mother's mistakes and spend the rest of her life paying for it.

She backed toward the exit. "I'm sorry. I just remembered I have a…a dress fitting."

She yanked open the shop's glass door and fled.

Stacy slammed into the luxurious four-bedroom penthouse suite she shared with Candace, Amelia and Madeline at the five-star Hôtel Reynard. There were perks in having a friend marrying the hotel chain owner's son.

All three women looked up from the sitting area.

"Why are you back so soon?" Candace asked.

"Why did you throw me at that man?" Stacy fumed.

Candace tsked. "Stacy, what am I going to do with you? Franco is perfect for you, and the sparks between the two of you nearly set the shop's awning on fire. You should have had lunch with him. Do you know who he is? His family owns Midas Chocolates."

"The shop?"

"The globally famous company. Godiva's number-one competitor. We have a store in Charlotte. Franco's the CEO of the whole shebang and one of Vincent's best friends. He happens to be absolutely yummy."

No argument there. "I'm not looking for a vacation fling."

Madeline, a nurse in her early thirties, swept her long, dark curls off her face. "Then let me have him. From Candace's description before you arrived Franco sounds beyond sexy. A short, intense affair with no messy endings sounds perfect, and I won't have to worry about getting dumped because we'll be leaving after the wedding anyway."

A vacation affair. Stacy couldn't imagine ever being so nonchalant about intimacy. Intimacy made her feel vulnerable which is probably why she avoided it 99 percent of the time. In her nomadic life she'd never had a friendship that lasted more than a few months until she and Candace had bonded over an IRS audit three years ago when the large accounting firm Stacy worked for had assigned her to Candace's case. Having a friend was a new experience—one Stacy liked—even if she did sometimes feel like an outsider with this trio of hospital workers. Madeline and Amelia were Candace's friends, but Stacy hoped they'd be hers too by the time they left Monaco. Otherwise, if Candace moved away after the wedding Stacy would have no one. Again.

But the idea of Madeline with Franco made Stacy uneasy, which was absolutely ridiculous considering she'd spent less than ten minutes in the man's company, and she had no claim on him. Nor did she want one. Could she have a vacation romance? No. Absolutely not. It just wasn't in her cautious makeup.

"So, is he sexy?" asked Amelia, the starry-eyed romantic of the group.

The women's expressions told Stacy they expected some kind of response. But what? She knew nothing about girl talk. "Yes. B-but in a dangerous way."

"Dangerous?" the three parroted in unison, and then Candace asked, "How so? Franco seemed perfectly civilized to me and very polite."

None of these women knew about Stacy's childhood. And she didn't want to share the shameful details. Not now. Not ever. From the time Stacy was eight years old she'd known she and her mother were running from something every time they packed up—or not—and moved to a new city. Stacy hadn't figured out from what or whom until it was too late.

She swallowed the nausea rising in her throat. "Franco Constantine exudes power and money. If things went wrong between you, he could afford to track you down no matter how far you ran."

The women looked as if her answer made no sense to them. But it made perfect sense to Stacy. Her father had been a wealthy man. When he'd abused his wife the authorities had looked the other way, and when she'd run he'd used his resources to track her down. It had taken him eleven years to get even.

Wealthy, powerful men bent the rules to suit their needs, and they considered themselves above the law. Therefore, Stacy did her best to avoid them.

Franco Constantine definitely fell into the Avoid column.

* * *

Franco studied Stacy Reeves from across the casino. She was perfect for his purpose, exactly the type of female his father had described. And he would have her. No matter the cost. With women there was always a cost. The question was, would she be worth it?

Without a doubt.

In all his thirty-eight years he'd never had such an instant visceral reaction to a woman before. Not even to his ex-wife. From the moment he'd caught the reflection of Stacy's expressive eyes in the shop window this morning he had wanted her to look at him the way she looked at the chocolate. Ravenously.

The contrast between her demure dress, the reserve she wore like a cloak and those hungry eyes had intrigued him. The touch of her tongue on his finger had electrified him. If she could arouse him with such a small gesture, then he couldn't wait to experience the results of a more intimate encounter.

A quick call to Vincent had garnered him a few pertinent details about Mademoiselle Reeves and had confirmed that she was suitable for his needs. Yes, playing his father's game would indeed be pleasurable.

Franco ordered two glasses of champagne and made his way toward her. She stood back from the roulette table in the Café de Paris, observing the trio of women she'd come in with, but not participating in the gambling. In fact, she hadn't made a single wager since she'd arrived half an hour ago.

Tonight she'd twisted her shoulder-length chestnut hair up on the back of her head, revealing a pale nape, a slender neck and delicate ears he could not wait to nibble. Her floor-length gown—a sleeveless affair the color of aged ivory—gently outlined her curves but unfortunately covered her remarkable legs. She'd draped a lacy wrap over her shoulders and strapped on high-heeled gold sandals.

Elegant. Subtle. Desirable.

Mais oui. They would be magnificent together. Anticipation quickened his blood as he reached her side. He paused long enough to savor her scent. Gardenias. Sultry, yet sweet. *"Vous êtes très belle ce soir, mademoiselle."*

She startled and turned. "Monsieur Constantine."

"Franco." He offered a flute and ignored her stiff, unwelcoming posture. Her blue-green eyes, as changeable as the Mediterranean, were more azure than they'd been earlier in the day. What color would they be when they made love? He had every intention of finding out.

After a moment's hesitation she accepted the drink. *"Merci, Mon—"*

He covered her fingers with his on the fragile crystal, stilling her words. He wanted to hear his name on her lips. "Franco," he repeated.

Her lips parted and the tip of her tongue glided over her plump cherry-red flesh. He nearly gave in to the need to taste her, but he restrained himself with no small effort. She was skittish. He had to move slowly if he wanted to successfully close this deal.

"Franco." She gave his name the French pronunciation not the nasally American one he'd grown to hate during his graduate studies in the U.S.

He touched the rim of his glass to hers. *"À nous."*

She blinked and frowned. "I'm sorry?"

"To us, Stacy." She hadn't given him leave to use her name, and he was taking liberties—the first of many he intended to take with the alluring American.

Her eyes darkened and rejection stamped her fine features, but her cheeks pinked. "I don't think—"

"Monsieur Constantine," a feminine voice interrupted.

He reluctantly released Stacy's hand, and forcing his lips into a polite smile, turned to the trio of women. *"Bonsoir, mesdemoiselles."*

Vincent's fiancée introduced her friends, and while etiquette decreed Franco greet each lady, every fragment of his being remained focused on the woman who would soon be his lover. He noticed each nervous shift of Stacy's body, heard the sounds of her silk dress sliding over her skin the way his hands soon would, and he relished the catch of her breath as he deliberately brushed against her when he motioned for a waiter. He ordered beverages for each of the women and then held Stacy's gaze as she lifted her flute to her mouth. He mimicked her actions, wishing it were her warm lips against his instead of the cool glass.

The brunette Madeline sidled closer, making her interest known with her direct stare and come-hither stance while the auburn-haired Amelia blushed and looked away from the other woman's bold behavior. Both women were attractive, but he only had eyes for Stacy. Eventually, the trio turned back to the roulette wheel, affording him the privacy with his quarry he craved. Or as much privacy as one could have in a crowded casino.

"Have you wagered?" He knew she hadn't. He'd been watching.

"No."

He reached in his pocket, retrieved a handful of chips and offered them to her. "Try your luck?"

Her mouth opened, closed, opened again. "That's ten thousand doll—euros."

"Oui."

Wide-eyed, she backed away. "No. No, thank you."

"You wish to play for higher stakes? We can go to the Salon Touzeta, if you like."

"That's a private room."

"*Oui.*"

She looked at her friends, as if hoping they'd rescue her, but the wheel held their attention. "I don't gamble."

The more she refused, the more he wanted her. Was she playing hard to get to torment him or to raise her price? Very likely both. But he would win. Since his wife's betrayal he always did. "You owe me the pleasure of your company at a meal."

Wary eyes locked with his. "Why me? Why not someone who's interested and willing?" A slight tilt of her head indicated her brunette companion.

He shrugged. "Who knows why a body sings for one and not the other?"

Her lace wrap slipped from her shoulder. Franco lifted his hand and dragged a knuckle along the exposed skin of her upper arm. Her shiver before she stepped out of reach gratified him. She would be a responsive lover. "Have dinner with me, Stacy."

"I don't think that's a good idea."

"Have dinner with me," he repeated. "If you choose not to see me privately again afterward, then I will accept your decision."

Her chin lifted. "And if I refuse?"

Enjoying her cat-and-mouse game, he smiled. Her breath caught audibly. *Bien.* The attraction wasn't one-sided. "Then you and your friends will be seeing me quite often."

Slightly imperfectly aligned white teeth captured her bottom lip. How had she escaped the American obsession with a perfect smile? "One dinner. That's it?"

"*Oui, mademoiselle.* Because I can take no for an answer when the woman really means it."

Her shoulders squared. "I mean it."

He could not prevent a small smile. "*Non.* Your mouth says one thing, but your beautiful eyes say another. You want to have dinner with me."

Her cheeks flushed and her kissable lips compressed. She nodded sharply. "One dinner and then you leave me alone."

A surge of adrenaline shot through him at the small success. He touched his champagne flute to hers. Victory was within his grasp.

"*À nous*, Stacy. *Nous serons magnifiques ensemble.*"

Two

Nous serons magnifiques ensemble.

"We will be magnificent together." Stacy groaned and tossed her French-to-English-to-French dictionary on the coffee table. Her flushed skin and restlessness had nothing to do with the morning sun streaming through the hotel sitting room's open curtains or her eagerness to get out and see more of Monaco. The blame for her twitchiness could be placed solely on the desire in Franco's eyes last night when he'd said the mysterious phrase before taking his leave.

She'd dreamed about him, about those hungry eyes and that deeply cleft chin. No surprise there, since the man's blatant sexiness was an assault on her senses.

Franco Constantine was pursuing her and she had no idea why. The country was full of more beautiful, more sophisticated and more available women, but for some incomprehensible reason he wanted *her*. And, like it or not, as foolish as it might be—and it was incredibly foolish—she was attracted to him too. Scary, heady stuff. Her instincts told her to blow him off, but his friendship with Vincent made that tricky. Stacy couldn't afford to be rude and risk upsetting Candace.

Stacy shifted uneasily on the sofa. Surely she could manage a meal with him without getting in over her head? One dinner and then he'd promised to leave her alone. She'd eaten with a number of clients who'd implied they wanted her handling more than their books, and she'd resisted easily enough. Of course, she'd never been tempted like this. Franco was beyond her experience, and she couldn't help feeling as if she'd made a deal she would regret.

The door to Madeline's bedroom opened and the brunette shuffled into the sitting area. Her gaze roamed over the coffee carafe Stacy had ordered from room service and Stacy's empty cup. "My God, how long have you been up?"

"A few hours. My body clock is confused."

"So are you and Franco going to hook up?"

Stacy's blouse and pants abraded her suddenly warm flesh. "We're going to have dinner and then he's all yours."

Her skin prickled anew. Why did that bother her? Franco was too rich and powerful for her and far out of her league, but that didn't mean the other woman couldn't enjoy him.

"No thanks. I met someone after you came upstairs last night, and man oh man, is he *hot*." Madeline poured herself a cup of coffee.

This was the girl talk Stacy didn't do so well. Where were the boundaries? What was she supposed to ask? What topics should she avoid? She settled for a non-committal, "Oh?"

"Oh yeah." Madeline smiled as she sipped. "He's going to act as my tour guide after we kill our diets this morning sampling the different wedding cakes the hotel chef has prepared."

Amelia glided silently into the room. "Did I hear you say you're going out today? Me too, if for no other reason than to avoid Toby Haynes."

"Who?" Stacy asked. The name sounded vaguely familiar.

Amelia grimaced. "Toby Haynes, the race-car driver for the NASCAR team Reynard Hotels sponsors. It was a fire in his pit that burned Vincent."

"Speaking of Vincent, I guess you've both met the groom since he was a patient at the hospital where you work?" Stacy hadn't—just one more reason she felt like the outsider in the group. Story of her life.

"Yes and his cocky Casanova driver is here in Monaco and determined to be a pain in my backside," Amelia grumbled.

"Perhaps you and I could do the tourist thing together," Stacy suggested somewhat hesitantly. These women barely knew her and might prefer to spend their time with someone else.

"Sounds great. I'll get dressed." The suite doorbell chimed. Amelia, already on her feet, answered. When she turned around she held a beautiful bouquet of gardenias. "They're for you, Stacy."

Stacy's heart stalled. No one had ever sent her flowers. She accepted the fragrant arrangement, extracted the card and read the slashing black script. Tonight. 20:00. Franco.

"Who are they from?" Amelia asked.

Stacy couldn't find her voice. Were the gardenias a coincidence or had he actually noticed her perfume?

Madeline read the card over Stacy's shoulder. "Her

delicious chocolatier. Monaco operates on military time. He's picking you up tonight at eight. *Bon chance, mon amie.*"

Stacy forced an unsteady smile. She'd need more than luck to resist the sexy Frenchman.

Madeline rose, stretched and yawned. "Amelia, make sure Stacy has something suitably sexy to wear. And Stace, tuck a few condoms in your purse. Be prepared."

Prepared for Franco Constantine? Impossible.

Thanks to Candace and Amelia, Stacy was as prepared as she possibly could be for her evening with temptation in the form of Franco Constantine, minus the condoms which she most definitely would not need.

After sampling enough wedding cakes to send her blood sugar into orbit, she, Candace and Amelia had attempted to walk off the calories by touring La Condamine, the second-oldest section of Monaco, this morning, and then exploring the wonderful shops on the Rue Grimald in the early afternoon. Afterward the women had returned to the hotel and turned Stacy over to the spa staff for a facial, a manicure and a pedicure.

Stacy stood in front of the mirror and smoothed her hands over the gown they'd found in a European designer clothing outlet. Claiming it would be perfect for the rehearsal dinner, Candace had overridden Stacy's polite refusal and insisted on buying it for her. The sapphire fabric skimmed Stacy's figure without clinging, and the halter top gave her enough support that she didn't need a bra. She felt worlds more sophisticated in this gown than in anything she'd ever owned.

The phone rang and Stacy nearly jumped out of her gold sandals. Her suitemates were out. She crossed her bedroom and lifted the receiver. "Hello."

"*Bonsoir,* Stacy," Franco's deep voice rumbled over her. "I am in the lobby. Shall I come up?"

Her pulse fluttered like the flag over the prince's palace in a stiff breeze. Franco in her suite? Absolutely not.

"No. I'll come down." She hung up the phone and pressed a hand over her pounding heart. "One dinner. You can do this."

She draped her lace wrap over her shoulders, grabbed her gold clamshell evening purse and headed out the door. Her stomach stayed behind as the elevator swiftly descended from the penthouse to the lobby level. The doors opened and there he was, a six-foot-something package of irresistible—correction, completely resistible—male. Franco leaned against a marble pillar looking as rich and sinful as the chocolate he'd fed her. Stacy inhaled slowly and then moved forward on less-than-steady legs.

Franco spotted her and straightened. A midnight-blue suit and a shirt in a paler shade emphasized his eyes as his appreciative gaze glided from her upswept hair to her newly polished toenails before returning to her face. Every cell in her body quivered in the wake of the leisurely visual caress. He took her hand and bent over it, brushing his lips against her knuckles in a touch so light she could have imagined it. The whisper of his breath on her skin made her shiver.

He straightened and his intensely blue eyes burned into hers. "*Vous enlevez mon souffle,* Stacy."

There was no way she could translate even the simplest sentences when he looked at her or touched her that way. "I'm sorry?"

"You take my breath away."

"Oh." *Oh? That's it? That's the best you can come up with?* She tugged her hand and after a moment's resistance he released her. "Thank you. And thank you for the flowers. They're lovely. But you shouldn't have."

"I could not resist. Their fragrance reminded me of you." He offered his elbow. Stacy couldn't think of a courteous way to decline. Reluctantly, she threaded her hand through his bent arm and let him escort her from the cool interior of the hotel into the warm evening air. The lights of Monaco twinkled around them in the falling dusk. He paused outside the entrance. "The restaurant is only a few blocks away. Shall we walk? Or would you prefer a taxi?"

"You didn't drive?" She'd pictured him as the powerful-sports-car type, the kind who careened around the hairpin turns at breakneck speed like a Grand Prix driver.

"I drove. My villa is in the hills overlooking Larvotto. Too far to walk. But there is no parking near the restaurant."

She and Candace had taken the bus to Larvotto beach yesterday before she'd met Franco. In a country covering less than one square mile how likely was she to be able to avoid him until the wedding once this obligatory date ended? The odds weren't in her favor. "Let's walk."

A breeze stirred her hair. He caught a stray strand and tucked it behind her ear. The stroke of his finger on the sensitive skin along her jaw made her hormones riot and her pulse leap. "I would like to show you the view of Larvotto from my terrace. *C'est incroyable.*"

No matter how incredible the view she had no intention of seeing it. *Get this date on an impersonal footing.* "How is it that you know Vincent exactly?"

A knowing smile curved his lips, as if he knew she wanted to tread safer ground. He turned and led her down the sidewalk. "We shared an apartment during graduate school."

She frowned up at him. "But didn't Vincent go to MIT?"

"*Oui.*"

"You lived in the States? No wonder your English is so good." They turned the corner and the smell of Greek food from a nearby sidewalk café permeated the air. Her mouth watered and her stomach rumbled, reminding her that she hadn't eaten since the cake overdose this morning.

"Midas Chocolates distributes product on six continents. It pays to be fluent in several languages. Interpreters are not always available or reliable." He turned down a narrow alley she would have missed and stopped in front of a salmon-pink building with a red tiled roof. The only signage was the address in brass script above an unremarkable wooden door. "Here we are."

"This is a restaurant? It looks like a private residence." She'd hoped for something less intimate, like one of the numerous cafés lining the streets. She still couldn't get over how people brought their pets into restaurants. Stacy pulled her arm free on the pretext of adjusting her wrap and instantly missed his body heat even on this sultry night. *Get over it.*

"It is a secret kept by the locals. Good food. Good music. Exceptional company."

She cursed the flush warming her skin. The man issued compliments too easily, and she didn't intend to be swayed by his glib tongue. She'd been burned by insincere flattery once before. The humiliating aftermath wasn't something she wanted to relive.

He opened the door with one hand. The other curved behind her waist, palm splayed. She could feel the imprint through the thin fabric of her dress as he guided her forward. She hurried inside only to stop suddenly in the tiled foyer.

This must have been someone's home once, but now a maître d's stand occupied the niche beneath a curving staircase. The dining rooms Stacy could see to the left and right were furnished with half a dozen widely spaced, candlelit tables draped in white linens. Crystal and silver glinted in the flickering light, and music played quietly in the background. Intimate, but not unbearably so. Some of Stacy's tension eased. She could handle this.

But internal alarm bells rang as the hostess led them upstairs and finally stopped in a small private room with only one table. This very likely had once been a bedroom. Any plans Stacy might have had to keep this meal impersonal by watching the other patrons or trying to translate their conversations evaporated. The same music she'd heard downstairs drifted through exterior doors left open to a wrought-iron railed balcony. A gentle flower-scented breeze stirred the sheer curtains and made the candle flames dance.

Franco seated her. She startled when his fingertips brushed her upper arms, dragging her wrap back so that it bared her shoulders. He draped the lace over her chair, and then sat at a right angle to her, his knee touching hers beneath the table. She shifted away from the contact, but that didn't stop the buzz of awareness vibrating through her.

An older man entered. He and Franco held a rapid-fire discussion Stacy couldn't understand, and then he departed. "Was that French?"

"*Non.* Monégasque, the local dialect. It's a combination of French and Italian."

"Is that what you were speaking at your shop the day we met?"

"*Oui,* but French is the language spoken most often in Monaco. Do you speak French?"

"A little. I had the required two semesters in college and then I listened to some instructional CDs before coming here."

He covered her hand with his on the table and stroked his thumb over the inside of her wrist. Her pulse bolted like a startled rabbit. "You may practice on me, if you wish."

The spark in his eyes said she needn't limit her practice to the language. Stacy pulled her hand free and tangled her fingers in her lap. Looking away, she chewed the inside of her lip and tried to ignore the tension knotting low in her belly.

Their server returned with a tray of tiny stuffed tomatoes and mushrooms, poured the wine and departed even though they hadn't ordered yet.

"There aren't any menus?"

"*Non.* Trust me. You will not be disappointed."

Trust. He couldn't possibly know how difficult it was for her to trust anyone but herself. "What if I have food allergies?"

"Do you?"

"No," she admitted, feeling slightly ashamed for being difficult. She sipped her wine, sampled a crab-stuffed tomato and struggled to find a topic that would dilute the romantic atmosphere. "I was surprised to discover that Monaco relies heavily on French laws, including the French wedding ceremony and that they've removed the promise of fidelity from their vows. Why is that? Can French men not be faithful?"

Franco sat back, the smile slipping from his face. "I was faithful to my wife."

That doused the warmth in her belly. "You're married?"

"Divorced." And bitter by the sounds of that one bitten-off word. "You?"

"I've never been married." She'd never even been in

a long-term relationship. She'd had one clumsy encounter in high school and a brief intimate relationship with a guy from work. She shoved the bad memories back into their cave. "How long were you married?"

"Five years."

"What happened?" None of her business really, but she'd never met a divorcé who didn't want to talk about the unpleasant experience, and dull as it may be, hearing about someone else's dirty laundry was better than having Franco focus his seductive charms on her.

He shrugged, but the movement seemed stiff instead of casual. "We wanted different things."

"Do you have any children?"

"Non."

Had she imagined his hesitation? "Do you keep in touch?"

"I have not seen Lisette since the divorce."

"And you're okay with that?"

"Absolument."

Absolutely. She studied Franco, trying to gauge his sincerity. His direct gaze showed no doubts, no prevarications.

Her father hadn't willingly let go. Had that been because he'd loved her mother so much or because he'd considered her a possession, as the therapists had said? Stacy shook off the questions to which she'd never have answers and focused on her date. "Have you always lived in Monaco?"

"Non. I grew up outside Avignon, France. My family home is still there. I relocated my residence and Midas Chocolates headquarters here eight years ago after my divorce." His expression turned speculative. "You are trying very hard not to enjoy our evening, Stacy. Why is that?"

He read her too easily. "You're mistaken."

"Then prove me wrong by dancing with me."

When he put it that way how could she refuse? "I'm not much of a dancer."

He rose, pulled back her chair and offered his hand. "*Pas un problème.* I will guide you. Relax. I am not going to devour you before dessert."

But after dessert, then what? She wanted to ask, but she was too overwhelmed by his proximity to form the words. He laced his fingers through hers and rested their joined hands over his heart. She could feel the steady thump against her knuckles. He looped his other arm around her waist, spreading his palm over the base of her spine and pressing his chin to her temple. He held her as close as a lover with his thighs brushing hers. *Too close.* She tried to retreat, but the muscles hidden beneath his expensive suit flexed and held fast.

Her breath quickened. His scent, a blend of tangy lime and something totally masculine filled her nostrils. Her mouth dried and her skin steamed. She could barely hear the music to which he swayed over her thudding heart. Regardless of how unwise it might be she could feel herself weakening and wanting to give in to the desire that welled inside her each time he was near.

Pressing her palm against his lapel, she angled her upper body away from his. The move had the unfortunate consequence of aligning their faces. His mouth was much too near. If she rose on her tiptoes she could—

No. She couldn't.

"Where is the music coming from?"

His indulgent half smile sent a spiral of need through her. "There is a string quartet on the terrace."

He danced her through the open doors and then raised his arm for her to spin, but instead of letting her turn a full circle he caught her with her back to his chest and held her facing the flower-filled courtyard below the balcony.

Stacy gasped at the hot length of him spooning her back and then she lifted her gaze from the couples whirling around the flagstone dance floor and the air left her lungs in a long, appreciative, "Wow."

The rocky terrain of Monaco spread out in front of her. One thing about having a country clinging to the side of the mountain was that no matter where you looked you had a postcard-worthy view. Lights twinkled on the landscape like constellations blanketing a clear night sky, and in the distance she could see a brightly lit cruise ship anchored in the harbor. "It's beautiful."

His breath stirred the hair at her temple a second before his lips touched her skin. "And so are you."

He cupped her shoulders and turned her to face him. His palms glided down her arms and then he grasped the railing on either side of her, caging her between a twenty-foot drop and temptation. Either one could leave her broken. The warmth of the iron railing pressed her back, but the heat of his hips and thighs against hers set her afire. He feathered a kiss on one corner of her mouth and then the other. Teasing, fleeting, tantalizing kisses. Insubstantial and unsatisfying.

Her insides quivered and she wanted more. She wanted him to kiss her—to really kiss her—in a way she'd never wanted any man before, and that was dangerous territory. It had to be Madeline's talk of a vacation affair making Stacy yearn for what she couldn't have.

"Come home with me tonight, Stacy. *Je veux faire l'amour avec toi.*"

I want to make love with you. Blood rushed to her head and then drained with dizzying speed to settle low in her belly. She closed her eyes, bit her lip and shook her head. "I can't."

But she wanted to. She really, *really* wanted to. Sex had never been the exciting event for her that everyone claimed it was. She had a feeling it *would* be with Franco, but he was exactly the kind of man she'd sworn to avoid.

"*Non?* Because even though your mouth tells me no, this—" his head bent and his lips scorched a brief kiss over the frantically beating pulse in her neck "—this says yes."

Torn between desire and common sense she pressed her palms against his chest and prayed for the strength to keep refusing. A flash of movement beyond his shoulder caught her eye. She sent up a silent thank-you for the reprieve. "The waiter is back."

Ever so slowly Franco straightened, but the banked fires in his eyes promised "later." He released his hold on the railing beside her, stepped back and gestured for her to precede him into the room. Her legs were almost too weak to carry her.

Close call. Good thing this was their one and only date because she doubted she could continue saying no.

And saying yes would be far too dangerous.

"What is it you want, Stacy?"

Stacy's yearning expression as she gazed at the moonless midnight sky hit Franco with the impact of a sailboat boom. Whatever it was she wanted, he wanted to give it to her. Within reason, of course. And he would reap the rewards for his generosity.

She stopped in the corner of Hôtel Reynard's garden. "What do you mean?"

Why her? Why did this woman arouse him so easily? He didn't have the answer to the question he'd been asking himself since seeing her outside Midas yesterday, but he would find it. Sipping from her soft, fragrant skin at the restaurant tonight had only whetted his appetite. "What is it you wish for when you look upon the stars?"

"What makes you think I'm wishing for anything?"

"Your eyes give you away."

She bit her lip and hesitated. "Financial security."

"Money?" He almost spat the word. It always came down to money, but he had expected Stacy to at least make an attempt to hide her greed. Disappointment dampened his satisfaction over being right about her. Had he believed Stacy was different from any of his father's ex-wives or from his own? *Non*. Life had taught him a hard lesson. All women were the same. Yes, they came in different sizes, shapes and colors, but the craving for money is what made their mercenary hearts beat. And Stacy's greed played directly into his hands.

"My mother struggled to make ends meet when I was a child. Sometimes she had to choose between rent and food. Until I landed the job with the accounting firm I wasn't in much better shape, and now I—" She turned her back abruptly and dipped her fingers into the fountain. "I don't ever want to be in that position again."

"Your father?"

Her spine stiffened and her hands fisted. "Not part of the picture."

The personal insights—of which she'd shared few during dinner—softened him and he couldn't afford sentimentality. Time to close the deal. "And if I could offer you that financial security?"

"What do you mean?" She frowned at him over her shoulder. "Are you offering me a job?"

He joined her beside the fountain. "I am offering

you a million euros to be my mistress for the remainder of your time in Monaco. One month, is it not?"

Shock parted her lips and widened her eyes. "You're joking."

"*Non.* I realize you have obligations to Candace and Vincent, but the remainder of your time would be mine. There will be no declarations of love. No false promises. Just passion and for you, profit. *Tu comprends?*"

She shook her head as if confused. "No, I don't understand. Are you offering to pay me to sleep with you? *Like a prostitute?*"

"In France, being a man's mistress is a respected position."

"I'm not French. And sex for money is still sex for money. I'm not for sale, Monsieur Constantine. Not by the hour. Or the week. Or the month." She hugged her wrap closer and backed away without taking her gaze from his.

He pursued for each step she retreated. Nothing worth having ever came easily. And contrarily, while he respected her for not accepting his first offer, her avarice angered him. She wanted him and she wanted the money. The flutter of her pulse, the rapidity of her breathing and those very expressive eyes gave her away. Why deny it? Why deny them both?

"Why not profit from the chemistry between us, Stacy? You would be doubly rewarded. With the pleasure I can give you and with the financial security you crave."

She reached the end of the path both figuratively and literally. A low stone wall blocked her escape. Franco had restrained himself all evening, but he no longer could. He lifted a hand and stroked his knuckles along her cheekbone. "I promise you pleasure, Stacy."

She inhaled a ragged breath, but she didn't jerk away.

He slid his fingers into her silky hair and held her captive as he lowered his head to sample the mouth he'd craved for hours. Her lips were as sweet and soft as he'd imagined—more so. But she stood stiffly in his embrace with her mouth closed and her arms crossed in front of her, clutching the wrap.

Franco wasn't willing to accept defeat. He dragged his fingertips over the clasp of her dress at her nape and down the ridge of her spine. She shivered and her lips parted on a gasp. He swept inside. She tasted delicious, and he couldn't help delving deeper. Pulling her closer, he eased his hand beneath her wrap and caressed the satiny skin of her back.

The tension drained from her rigid muscles on a sigh and she curved into him, nudging her soft breasts into his chest and touching her tongue to his. Her palms flattened against his ribs and then slid to his waist. Victory surged through him, mixing with the desire already pumping through his veins. He stroked downward, curving his hand over her rounded bottom and pulling her flush against his erection.

She stiffened and jerked out of his arms. Her delicious breasts rose and fell rapidly, the tight nipples like tiny pebbles beneath her bodice. "No. I— You— No. I can't. I won't."

But he could see the indecision in her eyes. Whether she wanted to admit it or not, his proposition tempted her. "I will give you twenty-four hours to reconsider. *Au revoir.* Sleep well, *mon gardénia.*"

He would not.

Three

A knock on the bedroom door jarred Stacy from her dream of a deep, velvety voice whispering illicit suggestions to her in French. Groggily, she sat up, finger-combed the hair from her eyes and tried to banish Franco Constantine from her mind. "*Oui?* I mean, come in."

The door opened and Candace breezed in. "*Bonjour.* You're a sleepyhead this morning."

Stacy glanced at the clock. Ten. She'd overslept, but thanks to the thoughts tumbling through her head after Franco's insulting offer, she hadn't fallen asleep until after four. She couldn't believe she'd actually lain awake debating the pros and cons of accepting and mentally converting euros to dollars. Worse, each time she'd dozed off she'd relived his reason-robbing kiss. "Sorry."

"No problem. But I need you to rise and shine. Vincent called. He heard about a villa that's about to come on the market, and he wants me to check it out. I need a second opinion and I know I can count on you to be practical." She perched on the edge of Stacy's bed. "Property sells fast here because there's such a high demand and a limited selection. Vincent's stuck at the new hotel site in Aruba until they work out this labor problem, and he's afraid we'll miss out on a good thing if we don't act fast."

Stacy shoved back the covers. "Then the move to Monaco is definite?"

Candace sighed. "It appears so. Vincent lives here for part of the year when he's not traveling for the hotel, but he says his condo overlooking the port in Fontvieille isn't big enough for three."

Surprise superseded the sinking feeling over the confirmation that Stacy's only friend was moving away. "Three?"

Candace winced. "Oops. I didn't mean to let that slip."

"You're pregnant?"

"Yes. Almost eight weeks. So it's a good thing we're getting married soon, isn't it?"

"I guess so." Stacy rose, but hesitated. "Should I offer my congratulations?"

"Absolutely," Candace said with a grin. She snatched Stacy into a bouncing hug and then released her. "I'm so excited I'm about to burst, but could you not tell anyone? We're not ready for Vincent's family to find out yet. I really shouldn't have said anything. I've been lucky so far because my morning sickness isn't so bad that I can't hide it or claim it's pre-wedding stress, and I can blame the need for naps on our late nights."

"You can trust me to keep your secret."

Trust. There it was again. That word. The one Stacy struggled with. "Give me thirty minutes to shower and dress."

She headed for the bathroom, shed her gown and stepped into the glass shower stall and then dunked her face under the hot spray to wash the grogginess away. The shower pelted her overly sensitized skin, dredging up remnants of dreams best forgotten.

Maybe a short-term affair was the best she could hope for given her trust issues. Should she reconsider Franco's offer? It wasn't as if he'd follow her across the Atlantic to try to force her to come back to him when he wasn't in love with her. And he'd stated up front that all he wanted was a month of her time.

But sex for money is still sex for money.

She lathered, rinsed and then shoved open the etched-glass shower door to glare at the wet woman in the steamy mirror. "I can't believe you are still debating this."

Would you have slept with him if he hadn't sprung this on you? Maybe. Probably. Because when he'd kissed her, saying no had been the last thing on her mind.

She snagged a towel and scrubbed briskly. "Let it go. You're grossly underqualified to be anyone's mistress."

But a million well-invested euros could set you up for life. No more worries about poverty. No more living paycheck to paycheck. And you won't have to panic if you can't find another job right away.

"No. Too risky. I don't have to see him again until the wedding. Forget his obscene offer. Forget him." With that settled she nodded at her reflection and reached for her makeup bag.

Twenty minutes later she zipped on another one of the sundresses she'd bought before getting laid off, this one a knee-length mint green number, stepped into her walking sandals and then yanked open the door to the sitting room and spotted the one man she'd hoped to avoid. Her stomach plunged. "What are you doing here?"

Franco set down his coffee cup and rose from the sofa. His gaze raked her from head to toe in a long, slow sweep, and Stacy couldn't stop hers from doing the same to him. She hadn't seen him in casual clothing before. His white short-sleeved shirt exposed the thick biceps his suits had only hinted at and his belted khakis revealed a flat stomach and narrow hips. A swimmer's body.

"*Bonjour,* Stacy. I am your chauffeur today."

She caught herself watching his lips move as he spoke and remembering how they'd felt against hers, and then his words sank in. Alarm clamored through her. She looked from Franco to Candace sitting in a chair. "What?"

Her friend smiled smugly. "Didn't I mention that Franco is the one who told Vincent about his neighbor's decision to sell?"

"No. You didn't. So you have your second opinion. You don't need me."

"Are you kidding? No offense, Franco, but you're a man. I need a woman's opinion."

He shrugged his wide polo-covered shoulders. "None taken."

Stacy wanted to lock herself in her room. Part of being able to resist his indecent proposition depended on not having temptation shoved in her face at every turn.

"Please, Stacy," Candace wheedled.

Stacy stifled a grimace. How could she refuse when Candace and Vincent were treating her to a month in paradise? Even if she had a sneaking suspicion the request for those consecutive weeks off might have contributed to her getting laid off. "All right."

Franco's broad palm gestured to the tray of pastries on the table. "We will wait for you to eat."

If she put food in her agitated—compliments of Franco—stomach she'd be sick. Stacy poured a glass of orange juice, guzzled it with inelegant haste and then returned her glass to the tray. "I'm ready."

Franco's knowing look made her twitchy. Stacy kept her gaze averted from him as he escorted them downstairs and outside. She could feel his steady regard as they waited for the valet to bring his car around, and when Candace became distracted by something in the hotel gift shop's window and wandered a few yards away he took advantage by moving closer. Stacy's senses went on red alert.

"You slept well?" he asked quietly.

"Of course," she lied without lifting her gaze above the whorl of dark hair exposed by the open neck of his shirt.

"I did not. Desire for you kept me awake. Each breeze through my open window felt like your lips upon my skin."

Her breath caught and her pulse stuttered. She glared at him. "You said I wouldn't have to see you again if I had dinner with you."

"*Non.* I said you wouldn't have to see me alone, *mon gardénia.*"

"Stop that. I am not your anything."

"But you will be." The certainty in his voice rattled her already fragile composure. "I cannot wait to have you in my bed, Stacy."

Were Frenchmen born knowing how to talk a woman out of her clothes? "Don't hold your breath."

An expensive-looking black sedan—Maserati made sedans?—rolled to a stop in front of them. The valet hopped out and circled the car to open the doors for the women while Franco moved to the driver's side. Stacy stepped toward the back, but Candace cut in front of her. "You sit up front. The hairpin turns make me nervous, and my stomach would appreciate the back seat. It's a little dicey this morning," she whispered the last phrase.

No fair playing the morning-sickness card. "Fine."

Stacy slid into the leather passenger seat beside Franco. Even with the console between them in the spacious interior, his presence overpowered her. His hand seemed larger on the gearshift just inches from her knee and his shoulders immense in the enclosed space. She inhaled his cologne with every breath.

He turned his head and their eyes met for heart-stopping seconds. "Fasten your seat belt, Stacy."

She complied with unsteady hands, and then Franco drove away from the coast and wound his way up the rocky mountainside. Although the steep drop-offs had Stacy clutching the sides of her seat, she had to admit the view was breathtaking.

"Do you see Larvotto?" he asked a few moments later. The blue-green Mediterranean glimmered beyond the three crescents of beach.

"Yes," Stacy answered when Candace didn't, and then she twisted in her seat to see her friend's pale face. "Franco, could you open the windows a bit?"

"Bien sûr." He quickly checked the rearview mirror and then the windows silently lowered. Slowing the vehicle, he turned down a tree-lined street which appeared to have been chiseled from the mountainside. "Candace, *tu va bien?"*

"Ah…*oui.* I'm fine." She clearly wasn't. "Are we close?"

He stopped the car in the quiet roadway. "We are here, but my house is two doors over if you need to lie down."

"No. I'll be better once I get out of the car. I keep remembering Princess Grace drove off one of these roads and died."

"Not this one." He turned into a driveway leading to a cream-colored stucco house with a red tiled roof that looked like something from a Mediterranean vacation guide. Stacy climbed from the car and immediately turned to check on Candace.

"Who would have believed pregnancy would give me vertigo?" Candace whispered. She linked arms with Stacy and followed Franco down the stone path to the front entrance. He pulled a key from his pocket and unlocked the door.

Stacy balked. "There's no real estate agent?"

"*Non*. My neighbor has only recently decided to sell. He is abroad, but left me a key."

He gestured for them to precede him. Stacy let Candace go first. Franco caught Stacy's hand and held her back. Her heart stuttered. Was he going to badger her about his offer? Or kiss her again?

"Is this part of the pregnancy?" he asked.

She blinked. "You know?"

"*Oui*. Vincent asked me to keep an eye on her, so you will be seeing a lot of me, Stacy."

Not good news when her plan to resist him was already on shaky ground. She tugged her hand free before the heat of his palm against hers melted her resistance. "She claims the pregnancy is giving her vertigo."

He looked adorably confused. *"C'est possible?"*

"I have no idea. I know nothing about being pregnant."

He nodded and then escorted her inside. To Stacy, who'd lived in low-budget accommodations all her life, the home looked like something from the *Architectural Digest* magazines her accounting firm—*former* firm—kept in the waiting area. Talk about lifestyles of the rich and famous…. She couldn't even begin to guess how many millions of euros this place cost.

She trailed after Candace who'd apparently recovered enough to examine one gorgeous room after another in the spacious home. When the women returned to the living room where Franco waited, he pushed open the door to the terrace behind the house. Candace wandered off to explore every nook and cranny of the gardens.

Stacy stayed on the flagstone patio, letting her eyes devour the flower-filled landscape. She had only vague memories of the landscaped yard of the house she'd lived in until she was eight. The places she and her mother had lived afterward had been barren and devoid of color. One day, Stacy vowed, she'd own a home a fraction as beautiful as this. One terrace of the two-level lot held a large pool, and another, a maze of roses. Living here would be a fantasy come true. And the view—

"C'est incroyable, non?" Franco said directly behind her seconds before his muscular frame spooned her back. His arms surrounded her and his fingers laced through hers on the iron railing, holding her captive when she would have ducked away.

He had to stop doing that. Every feminine particle in her urged her to lean into him and relish in the novel sensations he sent bubbling through her, but her survival instincts screamed *Run, danger ahead.* The emotional push-pull left her breathless and disoriented.

"But my view is better. You will see," he added in a deep voice that stroked her skin like a caress, peaked her nipples and made her quiver. "Come, we must go. Candace looks in need of a chaise and a cool drink."

He stepped away, taking his body heat with him and leaving Stacy surprisingly chilled in the warm late-morning air. How could she be so affected by a man she barely knew?

Candace had indeed paled as she slowly climbed the

stairs to the main patio. Stacy crossed to her side, but her friend waved away her concern as they returned to the car.

Stacy struggled to fortify her resistance to Franco as they pulled onto the road, but her internal alarms shrieked when he slowed the vehicle and turned into a driveway two doors down. "Is this your house? Why are we coming here?"

"Did I forget to tell you Franco invited us for coffee?" Candace asked from the back seat.

Stacy turned to scowl at her. "Yes. You did."

"Oops." There was no *oops* about it. The bride was matchmaking and not at all subtly.

"How kind of him." Not kind. Manipulative.

The satisfied smile playing about Franco's delectable lips made Stacy seethe. He'd wanted her in his home and he'd manipulated circumstances to make it happen. The man was set on seduction, and she had a sinking feeling he wasn't thwarted often or easily. And then she spotted his house and gasped.

The large two-story rectangular villa had been painted a buttery yellow. The trim on the second-floor balcony and around the arched windows gleamed white in the morning light. "Palladian style, right? How old?"

"Correct. The original structure was built in 1868. It has been renovated many times. Most recently by me. You have studied architecture, Stacy?"

"No. I just like to read."

Candace scooted forward. "Stacy's a bit of a history buff. She devoured any research material on Monaco and the Mediterranean she could get her hands on before our trip."

A blush warmed Stacy's cheeks. "Your home's beautiful, Franco."

"*Merci*. Wait until you see the inside. And the gardens,

of course. They are lovely by moonlight." His gaze held hers and last night's invitation lingered in his eyes. She would have seen his gardens by moonlight if she'd come home with him after dinner. She still could if she became his mistress.

Her heart accelerated and her mouth dried. "Too bad we'll miss that."

The twitch of his lips as he climbed from the car said he hadn't missed her sarcasm, and then Candace poked Stacy's shoulder. "Cut it out."

Stacy twisted in her seat. "Quit matchmaking."

The car doors opened. Franco stood in the driveway. "Mesdemoiselles?"

He helped them from the car and then turned toward the house. Stacy caught herself admiring the fit of his trousers over the tight globes of his derriere as she followed him up the stone walk toward the covered front entrance. European men wore pants that fit—none of that super-baggy stuff American guys currently favored. The fitted style certainly suited Franco.

After unlocking the tall arched door he motioned for them to enter with the sweep of his arm. Candace led the way. Stacy reluctantly followed with Franco on her heels. She couldn't help feeling that by entering his domain she was crossing a point of no return.

Her first impression was one of high ceilings and sun-drenched spaces rolling on and on in acres of cool, glossy white marble floors. Wide arches divided the individual rooms, but the glass-paned doors to each stood open. To her left a suspended staircase circled upward, and in front of her a pair of round marble columns separated a foyer bigger than her den back home from a living room larger than her entire apartment.

She glanced at Franco and found him watching her intently. "Welcome to my home."

"It's um…" Gorgeous. Huge. Intimidating. "Very nice."

The million euros he'd offered her should have been a clue to Franco's wealth, but she'd had no idea he was filthy rich. Most women would find his affluence a turn-on. But for Stacy it had the opposite effect.

"We will have refreshments on the terrace." He led them through the living room. Stacy trailed Candace past the dark wooden tables that interspersed the black leather sofas and chairs. Woven carpets in shades of ivory, black and red dotted the floor.

Red. Like blood on the white floor. She shuddered and skirted around the rugs.

Curved floor-to-ceiling French doors punctuated the exterior wall revealing an expansive patio that put the last home's to shame. Franco opened one of the doors. His bare forearm brushed Stacy's as she passed through. Accidental? Doubtful. Awareness trickled over her. She moved into the sunshine to bake the goose bumps away.

Candace crossed directly to the swimming pool located at the far end of the stone terrace and leaned over the railing. "Stacy, you have to see this. The pool pours over the side of the patio in a waterfall."

"It empties into a whirlpool below," Franco told her and then he moved closer to Stacy, dipped his head until his breath teased her ear. "Half of the spa is concealed beneath the house by the falling water. I would like to make love to you there."

Stunned by his sneak attack, Stacy struggled to catch her breath and formulate a prickly reply, but her brain refused to cooperate. Her heart raced and her palms moistened. Her skin flushed hot and then cold when she realized that in the split second before reason intervened she'd wanted to make love with him too.

That kiss clearly addled your thinking.

"Make Candace sit and rest," he murmured quietly along with a brief, but electrifying caress over the curve of her waist. "I will return with refreshments momentarily." He went inside.

Shakily, Stacy crossed to the railing. Not because she wanted to see the whirlpool below and visualize the decadent scene Franco had planted in her head. No, definitely not that. She looked because the view of Monte Carlo and Larvotto Beach from Franco's patio was more beautiful than any of the postcards she'd bought as souvenirs of her trip.

To her right a stone staircase wound down to the lower level of the terraced yard. Trees and flowers dappled the lush slope of green grass with shadows and brilliant splashes of color. And fight as she might, Stacy couldn't prevent her gaze from dropping to the exposed half of the spa.

Why not? You want to.

She'd have to be crazy to risk it. From what she'd seen of his home Franco had to be ten times wealthier than she'd suspected. *And ten times sexier. He arouses you with nothing more than words. Why not give those big hands a try? It's not like you're ever going to let yourself fall in love with anyone. So why hold out?*

"Amazing, isn't it?" Candace interrupted Stacy's illicit thoughts. "I can't imagine living like this."

Stacy pushed aside the tantalizing images. "Neither can I. It must be a real power rush to have enough money to buy whatever you want. We should find a shady spot to sit and wait for Franco."

"He knows about the baby, doesn't he? Did you tell him?" Candace asked as they strolled toward the shady covered loggia.

"Yes, he knows. Vincent told him."

"I should have guessed Vincent would. He's very protective, and he would trust Franco not to betray our little secret." Candace plopped onto a rattan lounge chair covered by a deep white cushion, lay back and closed her eyes. "Wouldn't it be great to live in paradise like this only two doors apart?"

Stacy chose a chair. She couldn't relax in Franco's home—not with him stalking her like a predatory beast. And then Candace's meaning sank in. "There's nothing like that between Franco and me."

"Oh please. He undresses you with his eyes whenever he thinks I'm not looking. You can't tell me you haven't noticed."

Stacy *had* noticed, and she was ashamed to admit the desire simmering in Franco's gaze sent a reciprocal surge through her. At least she assumed that achy, itchy tension was desire. No one had ever made her feel as attractive or feminine in her life, and she'd certainly never looked at a man and wondered how his hands would feel on her body. What would it be like to experience that kind of passion? Did she dare risk it?

"Sex is all he wants."

"Honey, that's all any man wants at first." Candace yawned.

"True. But I'm not looking for a husband."

"Then why not do as Madeline suggested and enjoy what Franco's offering? Other than Vincent, Franco is unquestionably the sexiest man I've ever met. My God, his accent just melts me, and you have to admit he's not hard on the eyes. You'll never get a chance to live like this again. I confess I'm thoroughly enjoying the five-star treatment. But I wish Vincent was here."

Stacy wanted to tell Candace about Franco's insulting proposition, but she didn't dare because telling her friend meant confessing how tempting Stacy found the offer. "Doesn't Vincent's wealth ever…concern you?"

Candace rolled to her side and met Stacy's gaze. "You mean do I worry that he'll use his money and influence to hurt me? No, I don't. I trust Vincent. Stacy, you haven't said much about your past, but from the bits you've let slip I'm guessing some rich guy did a number on you. Whoever he was, you can't let him screw up the rest of your life. Not all rich men are jerks. And you know, I don't think you've dated or gotten laid since I met you. Aren't you overdue?"

"I've dated." Twice, in three years. Pitiful. But sex? No. She needed more than a couple of dates to let her guard down with someone. If she ever could. And now that she thought about it, she probably never had, which was very likely the reason her last brief relationship had ended.

"Stacy, you've heard my sob story about the visiting surgeon who wooed me, bedded me and then returned home to the wife and kids I didn't know he had. Loving and losing that jerk burned me, but then I met Vincent and realized that sometimes you have to trust your heart and move on or be stuck in the past forever." Candace yawned again. "Do you mind if I close my eyes until Franco gets back?"

"No, go ahead." Questions and doubts tumbled through Stacy's mind. Was she stuck in the past? Had she given her father and that one tragic night too much power over her life? Or was she merely being prudent? If she didn't face her fears would she continue running from them indefinitely? Running, the way she and her mother had done for eleven years of Stacy's life. After losing her mother, Stacy had sworn she'd stop running and put down roots.

Roots a million euros could buy.

She stared at the pool and the water pouring over the ledge. She'd said no to Franco's proposition and she'd meant it. Deep in her heart she knew sleeping with him for the money was the wrong thing to do, but her practical side couldn't completely dismiss the idea of a lifetime of financial security in return for a month of intimacy with a man she desired like no other.

The mental debate circled her thoughts like an annoying, persistent mosquito no matter how often she swatted it away. Was Franco's offer too good to be true or was this an opportunity to put her past to bed and secure her future?

Trusting him when she barely knew him went against everything her mother had taught her about being wary of strangers. If only she had more time to discover whether power and money had corrupted Franco, but he'd given her only twenty-four hours to make a life-altering decision. Half of those hours had already passed.

The rattle of crockery drew her gaze to Franco crossing the terrace with a tray in his hands. His biceps bulged under the weight. He paused, his gaze landing on Candace. "She sleeps?"

Candace didn't stir. Stacy shrugged. "I guess so."

He nodded toward the house, turned and retraced his path. Stacy hesitated, but then rose and followed. Franco's kitchen was a combination of old-world charm and modern convenience—a cook's dream of dark cabinetry, glossy countertops and top-of-the-line appliances.

The aroma of freshly brewed coffee filled the air. He set the tray on the table. "You did not eat breakfast. You must be hungry."

She studied the array of fruits, cheeses and chocolates. He also had a coffee carafe, a pitcher of orange juice and a couple of bottles of sparkling water. "Your housekeeper did this?"

"You think I am not capable of feeding my guests?"

"I don't know you well enough to know what to think." And therein lay the crux of her dilemma. Part of her wanted to explore the way he made her feel and part of her wanted to play it safe.

"My housekeeper comes twice a week. The rest of the time I fend for myself. Eat, please. Or would you prefer I feed you?" He lifted a candy. "These are the chocolate-covered cherries you enjoyed the day we met. I would like to taste it on your tongue."

Her breath snagged. She staggered back a step, but that wasn't nearly far enough. She needed a break from his overwhelming charisma because she was perilously close to caving. "I need the restroom."

"*Bien sûr.* This way." He popped the chocolate into his mouth and led her down a hall, through a set of arched double doors, and he then stepped aside and gestured to another door. *"C'est là."*

Stacy stood frozen in what could only be Franco's bedroom. A huge wooden bed covered in a red-and-gold nubby silk spread dominated the otherwise black-and-white space. "You, uh…don't have a guest bathroom?"

"Of course, but I wanted to see you in my bedroom, and I wanted you, *mon gardénia,* to imagine yourself in my bed and in my bath with my hands and my mouth on your skin. As I have done."

The tantalizing vision exploded in her mind in vivid

Technicolor, and a fine tremor rippled over her. Her heart hammered and her mouth dried.

Franco didn't attempt to touch her or coerce her by using the desire clearly visible in his blue eyes. He'd simply stated his wishes and left the rest to her.

One step and she'd have financial security for life and a lover who might possibly make sex enjoyable rather than endurable. And when she left there'd be an ocean between them.

She closed her eyes and inhaled deeply.

Play it safe? Or risk it all?

Four

"Okay. You win, Franco. I'll be your mistress for a month. But I have conditions," Stacy added before Franco could speak. She dodged when he reached for her. There was no way she could think with his hands on her.

Cynicism replaced the triumphant spark in his eyes. He leaned against the doorjamb and folded his arms over his broad chest. Cocky. Arrogant. Male. "And they are?"

She had to be insane to agree to this, but if she hoped to survive it then she had to maintain some control and keep the affair on a business footing. What she needed were boundaries and rules. Safeguards. With her heart racing, she dampened her lips.

"I don't want Candace, Amelia and Madeline to know about the money." Or any chance of friendship would be destroyed. She wasn't even sure she could respect herself once this was over. She hadn't had to go hungry or bail on a landlord in the middle of the night since her mother's death, but the memories of the hunger pains and furtive escapes of her childhood lingered. And then there was her current employment—*un*employment—status to deal with once she returned home. She'd had excellent reviews at work, but still, the job market was tight and hers wasn't the only company downsizing. Add in a dwindling saving account and…

Focus on the future. With careful investing you'll never be poor or homeless again.

He inclined his head. "Anything else?"

"I won't spend the night." Call her crazy, but she didn't want to let her guard down enough to literally sleep with him.

A single dark eyebrow lifted. *"Non?"*

"No. My duty is first and foremost to Candace. We begin most days going over the wedding planning stuff. My time with you can't interfere with that."

"I shall return you to the hotel before your morning meetings."

Suddenly, she felt dirty. "When and how will I get paid?"

His nostrils flared and his generous lips thinned. "Your bridesmaid duties will end when Vincent and Candace depart on their honeymoon trip following the reception. You are scheduled to leave Monaco the next day, *oui?*"

"Oui. I mean, yes."

"You will spend your last night in Monaco with me. The entire night, Stacy." It was an order not a question. "In the morning I will give you a cashier's check and drive you to the airport, but should you not fulfill any part of our agreement, then no money."

Her breath hitched and her pulse thumped as loudly as the helicopter taxi they'd taken to Monaco from the Nice-Côte d'Azur airport. "And if you decide to end it early?"

A muscle in his jaw bunched and then his lips curled in a slow, devastatingly sexy smile. "I assure you I never finish anything prematurely."

It took a second for his meaning to sink in and when it did her cheeks caught fire. "But if you do?"

"You will be paid."

"Okay." Now what? Did they shake hands over the deal or—

Franco captured her elbows and tugged her forward. His mouth slanted over hers in a hard kiss as if she'd angered him. Stacy stiffened as second, third and fourth thoughts descended like an avalanche. She was on the verge of pulling away and cancelling their arrangement when his lips softened and parted. The fingers grasping her arms loosened and swept up to sift through her hair and cradle her head in his hands.

His mouth lifted, realigned and returned, seducing a response from her with long, luxurious turn-her-muscles-to-mush kisses. She tasted a hint of dark chocolate on his tongue. Chocolate and Franco, a hot and heady combination. His hands painted warm stripes down her back, over her hips and then around to her waist, before rising until his thumbs rested just below her bra.

Her breasts ached in anticipation of his touch, and desire simmered inside her. She couldn't believe her body could respond with such abandon when she knew Franco was using her. She'd been used before. But she wasn't a lonely seventeen-year-old trying to fit in at her third high school anymore. She wouldn't expect love or forever this time, so she wouldn't be hurt.

"Hey guys, where'd you go?" Candace's voice called out from somewhere in the house.

Franco slowly lifted his head, his lips clinging to

Stacy's for several heartbeats. His passion-darkened gaze speared hers. "Tonight we begin."

She couldn't find her voice, but she managed a stiff nod.

Dear God, what had she done?

She'd agreed to trade sex for security. She couldn't help feeling she'd sold her soul to the devil, and she hoped she didn't live to regret it.

Anticipation made Franco edgy. He hated it. He was, after all, a man of thirty-eight and not a boy of eighteen. His hormones did not seem to know the difference tonight.

Impatience urged him to take Stacy directly to his bedroom, to strip away her modest black dress and cover her ivory skin with his hands and mouth, but her pale, anxious expression cooled his ardor. Standing in his foyer, she looked torn between running back into the night and fulfilling her end of the bargain no matter how unpleasant.

Where was the passionate but reserved woman he'd left at the hotel mere hours ago? The one who'd kissed him with such fervor this morning that only her friend's untimely interruption had prevented him from consummating their agreement against his bedroom door? He wanted that passionate woman back. And he would have her. Stacy would be warm and pliant in his arms and his bed before the night ended. And he would win. The woman. And the contest with his father.

He pitched his keys onto the credenza, halted behind her and curved his hands over her shoulders. She startled. "May I take your wrap?"

"Oh, um, yes, sure." She darted a quick, nervous glance at him and tension tightened inside him as an unacceptable thought pierced his conscience.

"Stacy, are you a virgin?" He'd had lovers, dozens of them, but no virgins. Experienced women understood that all he wanted was the transitory pleasure of their bodies. An innocent might expect more.

Color rushed to her cheeks and she ducked her chin. "No. But I…this…is new to me. I don't know where to begin."

His clenched muscles loosened. Nerves he could handle. Regrets and crying, he could not. He had intended to satisfy his hunger for Stacy first tonight and then his less demanding appetite for dinner afterward, but perhaps he would alter his strategy. Dinner first. Pleasure later. Anticipation would only heighten the senses. "Leave that to me."

Franco stroked the lace down her arms, caught her elbows and pulled her back against his front. Her bottom nudged his thighs. The urge to thrust his growing arousal against her gnawed at him, but he would coax Stacy until she was breathless and eager for his possession, as she had been earlier. He nuzzled through her silky hair and sipped from the warm, fragrant juncture of her neck and shoulder. She shivered.

Bien, the responsive woman still lurked beneath her pale and tense exterior. He encircled her with his arms and spread his palms over the slight curve of her abdomen. "I will ensure your pleasure tonight, *mon gardénia.*"

A little *hic* of breath lifted her breasts, and though he wanted to cup her soft flesh in his hands and stroke his thumbs over the tips pushing against the fabric of her dress, he could wait. But not long.

"We will dine on the terrace." He released her and led her through the living room, draping her wrap over the back of a chair as they passed. On the patio he seated her, lit the candles he'd placed in the center of the table and then poured the cabernet franc. After removing the lid covering the crudités and setting it aside, he sat and lifted his glass. *"À nous et aux plaisirs de la nuit."*

She made a choked sound. "I'm sorry?"

"To us and the pleasures of the night," he translated.

"That's what I thought you said," she muttered into the bowl of her glass and took a healthy sip of wine.

He removed a small box from his suit pocket and placed it on the table in front of her. He had planned to give her this after savoring her delicious body, but why wait? Stacy needed coaxing, and in his experience jewelry always made women more amenable. "For you."

The line formed between her eyebrows. "You don't have to buy presents for me."

He would make sure she wore it when she met his father. He shrugged. "Open it."

She set aside her wine, hesitantly opened the box and stared. Seconds later she snapped the lid closed and shoved the box toward him. "I can't accept that."

He stilled. "You don't like diamonds?"

"Of course, but—"

"You have a diamond bracelet?"

"No." She closed her eyes, swallowed and then met his gaze. "Franco, we already have a deal. Can we just stick to it?"

He masked his surprise and puzzlement. He had never had a woman refuse his gifts before—especially not expensive jewelry. "Perhaps I wish to see you wearing the diamonds. And nothing else."

"Oh." Her cheeks flushed. *"Oh,"* she repeated and fiddled with the stem of her glass for a moment before looking at him through her thick lashes. It was a worried glance rather than a flirtatious one. "Diamonds do it for you, huh?"

He reared back. "No, diamonds do not *do it for me*. I merely wished to give you a gift."

"And I'm telling you that you don't have to."

What game was she playing? He examined her face, her guileless eyes. Was her innocence an act? It had to be. Otherwise she never would have accepted his offer. He rose. "I will return momentarily with dinner."

In the kitchen he mechanically plated the smoked mozzarella with sundried tomatoes and peppercorns in a puddle of olive oil while mulling over Stacy's refusal. She had to have an ulterior motive. He retrieved the filet *barole* from the warming oven, divided it onto dishes and poured the cognac and mushroom sauce over it.

Was she after a bigger prize? Perhaps a diamond ring instead of a bracelet? If so, she would not get one from him. He would never marry again. His one and only failed marriage had taught him that women were selfish creatures. Nothing mattered except their wants. *Nothing*.

Not even life.

His throat tightened at the memory of the babe his wife had carelessly discarded without his knowledge or consent. Had there not been complications with the abortion, causing the doctors to hospitalize Lisette and call Franco to Paris, he would never have known her "shopping trip" was a lie or that she had conceived his child—a child she did not want. And then there were his father's costly divorces. Stacy was no different from any other greedy woman. She had revealed her true nature by accepting his terms. He set his jaw.

Non. He did not trust women. He enjoyed them *briefly* and then he moved on. But he was a generous lover both in bed and out. Stacy would have no complaints.

Stacy was not at the table when he carried the tray outside. He scanned the dimly lit terrace and found her in the shadows by the railing overlooking the garden below. Or perhaps she studied the whirlpool. His arousal stirred in anticipation.

After placing the meal on the table he joined her. "Dinner waits."

She turned slightly. A gentle breeze lifted tendrils of hair. "I'm sorry, Franco. I didn't mean to hurt your feelings by refusing the bracelet. I just don't think we should try to make this into something it's not."

Again she surprised and perplexed him. "What would that be?"

"A relationship."

His thoughts exactly, but hearing her voice them disturbed him in an inexplicable way. "We are going to be lovers, Stacy. We will have a relationship, albeit a temporary one. And if I choose to buy things for you then I do so because it pleases me, not because I expect more from you than our original agreement. Now come. We will eat and then we will pursue our mutual pleasure."

Would she be worth a million bucks?

Stacy's stomach clenched. She had absolutely no appetite and her taste buds had deserted her, but she forced down another bite of tender steak to drag out the meal as long as possible. Throughout dinner she'd watched Franco's hands as he cut his meat or cradled his wineglass, and her mind had raced ahead. Those hands would soon be on her. Cupping her flesh. Stroking her skin. Was that anticipation or dread making her dizzy?

What if after they did this Franco decided she wasn't worth the money? After all, she wasn't experienced. She could count her intimate encounters on one hand, and her knowledge was limited to the basics—which in her opinion were overrated. If he expected anything like the fancy stuff she'd read about in the women's magazines she'd borrowed from work, then he'd be disappointed.

Franco placed his knife and fork on his empty plate. "The food is not to your liking?"

Chew. Chew. Chew. Gulp. "It's delicious. Did you cook?"

His knowing eyes called her a liar. "No. It is catered. Perhaps your appetite lies elsewhere."

Her fork slipped, the tines screeching across the china. She winced. Franco had probably never encountered a more gauche female. He was sexy and sophisticated down to the soles of his shoes and she was…not. So why had he chosen her?

She abandoned her utensils, blotted her mouth with her cloth napkin and then knotted her fingers in her lap. "I guess I'm just not very hungry."

"I am ravenous." He abruptly pushed back his chair and stood. "But not for food."

Stacy's heart stalled and then raced, but Franco reached for their plates instead of her, piled them on the tray and carried them toward the kitchen.

Time's up. Time to deliver your end of the bargain.

Stacy slowly exhaled and then lurched into action, nearly overturning her glass in the process. She gathered the stemware and then followed Franco inside, wishing she'd drunk more than one glass of wine. If she had, maybe she wouldn't be so nervous. But she'd never acquired a taste for wine. She preferred girly drinks with umbrellas, and she drank precious few of those because she kept herself on a strict budget. Unfortunately, sobriety left her tense and clear-headed enough to doubt her sanity in accepting his proposition. Besides, getting drunk would be stupid. She needed to stay in control.

Whatever had possessed her to believe she was quali-

fied to be Franco's mistress? How could she satisfy a
worldly man like him? And how could she become
intimate with a man she barely knew? Franco wasn't
much of a talker. If he'd shared half as much conversation as he had lingering, desire-laden, toe-curling
glances, then she could write an in-depth biography
about him. But he hadn't. Then again, neither had she.

*Details aren't necessary. This isn't about friendship
or forever.*

Stacy stiffened her spine. She could get through
this. She'd survived attending fourteen schools in ten
years, her mother's shocking and unexpected death
and her father's betrayal. Four weeks as Franco's
plaything would grant her the economic freedom to
buy a home and to stop feeling like a visitor in her own
life—a visitor who might have to pack up and leave at
any moment.

But thinking about the money made her feel a little
like a hooker. A lot like one, actually. So she shoved
those thoughts aside and tried to focus on the man.
About how sexy and desirable Franco made her feel…

When she wasn't thinking about the money. She
winced.

Franco deposited the tray beside the sink and then
took the goblets from her and set them on the counter.

"Let me help you wash those," she offered, hoping
to buy time.

"The dishes can wait. I cannot."

Before Stacy could do more than blink, Franco's
arms surrounded her and his mouth crashed onto hers.
Possessive. Hungry. Demanding. He cupped her
bottom, pulling her flush against the length of his hot
muscle-packed body, and his tongue found hers,
stroking, tasting, tangling. Arousal simmered beneath

Stacy's skin, but it couldn't completely overcome her stomach-tightening trepidation or doubts.

Franco was a wealthy, powerful man who had the money to buy whatever he wanted—including her. Would he play by the rules? She was on foreign territory here—both in Monaco and in this affair. Who would protect her if this turned ugly?

She pushed against his chest, breaking the kiss. "Wait."

"For?" His barely audible growl swept across her damp lips, and his passion-darkened eyes bored into hers.

She licked her lips and tasted him. "What if I don't meet your expectations?"

"I find that unlikely." His hand covered her breast, his thumbnail unerringly finding and caressing her nipple with a back and forth motion.

Tendrils of sensation snaked through her defenses. She had to stay clear and focused. Letting go meant becoming vulnerable. Perhaps she should just take care of him? But how? Drop to her knees and take him in her mouth? If so, she had a problem, because her one and only experience with that in high school had not gone well. She shuddered.

He gripped her upper arms and set her from him. "Stacy, what game are you playing?"

"I'm not playing a game. I just…" She bit her bottom lip. "We don't know each other very well."

"What is there to know except the pleasure we can give one another?" His fingers threaded through her hair, tugging gently and tipping her head back. "Have you never experienced immediate attraction for someone you have just met and let passion lead?"

"Uh…no."

His eyes narrowed suspiciously. "How old are you?"

"Twenty-nine. But I, um…"

"You haven't had many lovers."

Was it obvious? Heat scalded her cheeks. She wanted to hide her face, but his grip on her hair prevented it. "No."

His nostrils flared. "I will teach you what pleases me, and I will satisfy you, *mon gardénia*."

He stated it with surety and she wanted to believe him, but why would he bother? He'd bought her whether she liked sex with him or not. "If you say so. You probably should have asked about my sexual experience before offering your bargain."

"Ce n'est pas important."

Not important? How could her lack of experience be unimportant?

He released her hair and laced his fingers through hers. "Come. The kitchen is not the best place for our first time."

Nerves twisted tighter in her stomach with each step. She knew where they were headed long before they reached the carved double wooden doors. His bedroom. Once inside the large chamber he faced her. "I have pictured you here. Sprawled on my sheets. Naked except for the flush of passion on your skin."

She wheezed in a breath at the sensual image his words painted and blurted, "Do you have condoms? Because I'm not on the pill."

"And even if you were, the pill is not protection against sexually transmitted diseases—of which I have none," he stated matter-of-factly.

Her discomfort with the current conversation further illustrated her lack of qualifications to become Franco's mistress. A more experienced woman could probably have this preliminary chat without as much as a blush. But not her. She shifted on her feet. "Me neither."

"I have protection." He turned her toward the bed,

reached for the zip of her dress, swiftly pulled it down to her hips and then flicked her bra open.

Oh God, were they going to just do it? She shouldn't be surprised or disappointed. Despite what the magazines said, in her experience, that's the way it happened. Rushed, fumbling hands followed by awkward contact and grunting. At least it would be over soon.

Air cooled her skin and then warm hands slipped inside the gaping fabric of her dress to trail down her spine with a feather-light touch. Goose bumps rose on her skin and her toes curled in her pumps.

Franco's thumbs worked upward from her lower back, massaging her knotted muscles all the way to her neck. His fingers drew ever-widening circles over her shoulders, down to her waist and back again. Her eyelids grew heavy and she shivered as unexpected pleasure rippled over her.

A hot, open-mouthed kiss on her nape surprised a gasp from her, and then her dress and bra fell from her shoulders. Startled by the swift disrobing, she grabbed at her clothing, but too late. The garments puddled around her ankles. She crossed her arms over her chest, covering her breasts.

"*Non.* Do not hide."

Her eyelids jerked open. She found her gaze locked with Franco's in the large gold-leaf mirror hanging over the dresser. Slowly, painfully, she lowered her hands and fisted her fingers beside her. Her heart pumped harder as his gaze devoured her breasts, her black hipster panties and then her legs. In her opinion, her body was okay, her breasts merely average, but if Franco was disappointed in what he'd bought he didn't show it.

Behind her, he discarded his coat and tie, tossing both toward a chair without breaking her gaze. His belt whistled free and then thumped into the chair. Each movement stirred the air around them and teased the fine hairs on her body. He unbuttoned his cuffs and then his shirt and tugged his shirttails free, but didn't remove the garment. Part of her wanted to turn and examine him as he had her, but the governing part of her stood transfixed, muscles locked and rigid.

"*Tu es très* sexy, Stacy." His hands, shades darker than her pale skin, curved around her waist.

Her lungs failed, but whooshed back into action when his palms splayed over her belly, one above her navel and one below. An unaccustomed urge to shift until his hot hands covered more intimate territory percolated through her, but she remained as still as a statue.

"Your skin is like ivory. You do not sunbathe?" he whispered against the sensitive skin beneath her ear a second before his lips made electrifying contact.

"I d-don't have the time. When I'm not working I volunteer my time mentoring at-risk teens." Kids who were lonely outsiders like she'd been.

His gaze searched hers for a moment and then lowered to the tiny birthmark above her right hip bone. He traced the small reddish splotch with a fingertip. The delicate caress made her feminine muscles clench.

His mouth opened over her skin, laving her pulse point. At the same time he pulled her back against his bare chest. She hardly had time to register the heat of him seeping into her or the tickle of his chest hair before his hands swept upward. His thumbs stroked beneath her breast once, twice, three times. Her nipples tightened painfully. She mashed her lips on a whimper.

Involuntarily, her head tipped back against him. He trailed kisses down her neck, across her shoulder and back to her jaw. She shouldn't be enjoying this. She didn't know him and wasn't certain she could trust him, but the rasp of his hands across her skin aroused her unbearably.

And then he covered her breasts. His fingers tweaked her nipples and something inside her detonated, radiating a delicious sensation from her core. A moan slipped between her teeth.

Franco murmured words in French as he caressed her, words she was too distracted to translate. Stacy squeezed her eyes shut and struggled to maintain control, to remember this was a business transaction, and then Franco's hand slipped into her panties and his fingers brushed over her most sensitive spot. Her thighs automatically clamped together against the intrusion, but Franco continued to stroke. He delved into her wetness and plied it over her flesh again and again. Circling. Tormenting. Tempting her to let go.

His foot nudged hers apart, opening her for deeper access, and his fingers plunged inside her. Her lungs emptied. Warmth expanded in her belly and her body trembled with need—need she fought to restrain. He pulled her hips flush against his. The length of his erection nudging the base of her spine fractured what little control she had maintained. And then suddenly the tension snapped and orgasm washed over her in waves of pulsing heat, buckling her knees and making her clutch Franco's arms to keep from falling to the floor. His caresses slowed, easing her though the aftershocks buffeting her.

So that's what all the fuss is about.

Winded and stunned by the intensity of her response, Stacy forced her lids open and met Franco's gaze in the mirror. Questions filled his eyes and her skin baked with embarrassment. Feeling raw and exposed, she ducked her head. He must think her totally shameless.

But then shameless is what he'd bought.

Five

Franco could not believe the evidence before him, but the wonder on Stacy's face and her current embarrassment could only have one cause. "Your first orgasm?"

She winced and dipped her chin in the slightest of nods.

Franco swiftly withdrew his hands. Not because her revelation repulsed him, but because her confession sent a volatile cocktail of emotions through him. Anger rose swiftly toward those who'd misused her, and possessiveness wasn't far behind. Stacy would be his, *certainement,* but only temporarily. The third and possibly the most dangerous reaction was understanding. Inexperience, not manipulation, explained the mixed signals she'd been sending him. None of those responses had any place in this relationship.

"Stacy." He waited until she eased open her eyes again. "Your first, but not your last."

Her lips parted and then relief replaced the surprise

in her eyes. Had she thought he would reject her because her past lovers had been selfish bastards? She might be a pawn in the game with his father, but she would not suffer for it.

He turned her in his arms and covered her mouth, gently this time. Seducing instead of taking. Sipping, suckling her bottom lip and teasing the silken inside with his tongue instead of ravaging her as he'd done earlier.

He still desired her, still hungered for her, but for her sake, he would dull the sharp edges of his need and make this good for her. Good for both of them. By the end of their month Stacy would be a sexually confident woman. She would not forget the lessons he taught her. That other men would benefit bothered him marginally, but he brushed the concern aside.

Inexperienced or not, she accepted your proposition. That makes her like all the others.

Stacy clutched his waist, bunching his shirt in her hands. He wanted her hands on his skin. He released her long enough to rip off the garment and cast it aside.

Stacy's breath caught. Her pupils expanded as her gaze explored his torso, following the line of hair to his waistband. He captured her hands and spread them over his skin and then glided their joined hands over his burning flesh. Her fingers threaded through his chest hair, tugging slightly, and sending electrifying bolts of pleasure straight to his groin. Her palms dragged across his nipples. His whistled indrawn breath mingled with her gasp as hunger charged through him. He released her hands and fisted his by his side, fighting the need to crush her to him.

She tentatively traced the lines defining his abdominal muscles, and his flesh contracted involuntarily beneath her curious fingers. His control wavered like tall trees in the hot sirocco winds.

What is this? You are no boy.

And yet he trembled like one.

"Unfasten my pants," he rasped.

She hesitated and then slipped her fingers between fabric and flesh. His stomach muscles clenched and his groin tightened as she fumbled the hook free and then reached for his zipper. Franco gritted his teeth as she lowered the tab over his erection.

Perhaps all women are born knowing how to torture a man.

When she finished the task, she paused, bit her lip and looked up at him though her thick lashes. His control frayed.

Franco moved out of reach, ripped back the covers and sat on the edge of the bed. He swiftly removed his shoes and socks, letting his gaze rove over her as he did so. Stacy did not have the stick-straight model figure to which so many women aspired these days. Her breasts were exquisite, round, the perfect size to fill his palms, and tipped with dusty-rose aureoles which he could not wait to taste. Her waist and hips curved nicely. Who would have guessed that she hid such an alluring body beneath her sedate clothing?

"Remove your panties." He didn't dare touch her. Not yet.

Her breath hitched and then her thumbs hooked into the black, shiny fabric and slowly pushed it over her hips and thighs to encircle her ankles. She toed them aside and crossed her hands in front of her dark curls. He shook his head. "Let me look at you. Next time I will taste you."

Her eyes closed. She swallowed.

Franco extended his hand. "Come."

Watching him warily, Stacy shuffled forward.

"Sit." She turned as if she were going to sit beside him on the bed, but he caught her, pulling her toward him until her legs straddled his. She slowly sank onto his thighs, her knees flanking his hips on the mattress and her buttocks resting on his lap. The position left her breasts level with his mouth and her feminine core open and exposed.

She was his, his to do with as he wanted, and at the moment he wanted her hot and wet and writhing with pleasure in his arms. He would wipe away the memory of her selfish lovers.

Franco pulled a nipple into his mouth, sucking, laving and gently nipping until her panted breaths stirred his hair. He caressed her back, her buttocks, savoring the smooth texture of her skin, the scent of her filling his lungs and the taste of her on his tongue. *"Touche-moi."*

She lifted her hands to his shoulders and then tangled her fingers in the hair at his nape.

He groaned against her breast. Need urged him to grind his hips against hers, but he settled for reaching between them to stroke her slick folds. Her short nails dug into his skin and a quiet whimper slipped free.

By the time he finished with her, she would not be shy about expressing her passion, he vowed.

His thumb found a rhythm to bring her satisfaction while he feasted on one nipple and then the other until she shuddered against his palm as *le petit mort* rippled over her. Not a moment too soon. Franco was about to erupt.

He stood abruptly, lifting her and then laying her on the bed. Just as he'd envisioned, only a passionate flush covered her skin. He swiftly removed his pants and briefs and reached into the bedside drawer for a condom. Lips parted and eyes wide, Stacy watched his every move as he donned protection. The color on her cheeks deepened and spread to her kiss-dampened breasts, and desire hammered insistently inside him.

He knelt between her legs, finesse and patience long gone, and cupped her buttocks in his hands. "Guide me inside, Stacy."

She curled her fingers around his length. He slammed his eyelids closed, clenched his teeth and stiffened his spine against the exquisite agony of her touch. She steered him toward her entrance and, muscles rigid and trembling with the effort to go slowly, Franco eased into her tight core one excruciating inch at a time. Restraint made his lungs burn and sweat bead on his skin.

When she lifted her hips to rush him the rest of the way in his control snapped. Franco surged deep, withdrew and plunged again and again and again. He fell forward, catching his weight on arms braced on the pillow beside her head. Stacy's back bowed, her arms encircled him, and her breasts teased his chest. The scrape of her nails on his back stimulated him past sanity. He gazed into her eyes and saw desire and surprise as her breath quickened and her body arched.

Her muffled cry as she climaxed again combined with the contracting of her inner muscles to hurdle him over the edge. His roar echoed off the walls as desire pulsed from him.

He collapsed to his elbows, satisfied and yet at the same time unsettled. Gasping for breath, he searched for the cause of his disquiet. And then understanding descended like a guillotine. Quick. Sharp. Cold.

He had let sex with Stacy become personal. A mistake he'd learned to avoid long ago.

It could not—would not—happen again.

* * *

Even before her pulse slowed, Stacy had regrets. What had she done? She'd had sex for money. And she'd enjoyed it.

What did that say about her?

Nothing complimentary, that's for sure.

She closed her eyes tightly and tried to distance herself from the lean, hard body of the man above her. *Inside her.* But she couldn't block out the comfortable weight of him pressing her into the mattress, his scent or the aroma of sex.

Franco rolled away to sit on the edge of the bed with his back curved and his elbows on his knees. Her sweat-dampened skin instantly chilled without the heating blanket of his body, but he was sitting on the covers. Feeling exposed and vulnerable, she crossed her ankles and hugged her arms over her breasts.

He rose and his pale backside mesmerized her. As much as she hated herself at the moment, the ashes inside her sparked to life at the sight of corded muscles rippling beneath the sleek, tanned skin as he shoved his fingers through his hair. The movement drew her gaze to the breadth of his shoulders. Had she made those scratches? Embarrassment flamed her face.

"Would you like to shower?" he asked in a flat, un-readable voice, without turning.

She blinked and looked away. "No. Thank you."

She wanted a shower. But not here. Not now. What if he decided to join her? He'd bought her. Did that mean she'd forfeited the right to say no? She hadn't yet come to terms with the pleasure he'd wrung from her tonight, so she wasn't ready for another intimate encounter. She had to keep this affair impersonal, because opening up to more than that would make her vulnerable.

But there had been nothing impersonal in what they'd just shared. At least not on her part.

Sex for money. She clutched the thought close—like a talisman. As ugly as it sounded, it was safer than trusting her heart to a man like Franco Constantine. A man with more money and probably more power than her father.

The moment he disappeared into the bathroom Stacy vaulted from the bed and snatched up her clothing. Her hands trembled so badly it took three tries to fasten her bra. In her haste she pulled her panties on wrong-side out, but she didn't dare take time to remove them and put them on again. She wanted to be dressed before Franco returned. Dressed and ready to leave.

She stumbled over her shoes—she couldn't even remember removing them—and shoved her feet inside, and then snatched up her dress and dragged it over her head. The zipper stuck in the middle of her back. Frustrated tears stung her eyes as she tugged in vain. She bit her lip, blinked furiously and willed them away.

Gentle hands nudged hers aside. Stacy nearly jumped out of her pumps. She hadn't heard Franco return. His knuckles brushed against her spine, raising goose bumps as he fiddled with the zipper, freed the fabric and pulled up the tab.

Stacy stiffened her resolve and met his gaze in the mirror. His broader naked form framed hers. Her hair was a mess and her lips were swollen, but she didn't care. "I want to go back to the hotel."

His jaw shifted. All signs of passion had vanished from his face, leaving his features hard and drawn. "I'll drive you."

"I'll wait in the living room." She bolted.

"Stacy." His voice halted her on the threshold.

Reluctantly, she turned. Her breath caught at the sight of Franco in all his naked glory standing with one knee cocked and his torso slightly angled in her direction. The man had a body worthy of the beefcake calendar someone had given Candace at her bridal shower. His chest was wide and covered with dark curls, the muscles clearly defined, but not bulky like a body builder's. A line of hair led to a denser, darker crop surrounding a masculine package any centerfold would be proud to claim, and his legs were long and strong.

"Are you all right?" The question seemed forced.

Physically? "Yes."

Mentally? She was a wreck. She'd never felt more alone or confused or ashamed of herself. She needed to reassess. Maybe financial security wasn't worth it. On the other hand, she'd enjoyed sex for the first time in her life. But sex with a man she'd known only three days. Brazen, that's what she'd been.

"I will be with you in a few moments," Franco said, reaching for his shirt.

Stacy nodded and fled. Agitated and anxious, she paced the length of the living room, skirting the red rugs and ending at the kitchen archway. She needed to do something to channel her thoughts and nervous energy. Her gaze lit upon the dirty dishes. Seconds later she had them submerged in a sink filled with hot soapy water. She scrubbed the fine china probably harder than she should have.

Franco had turned cold immediately after he'd…finished. Had she turned him off with her fumbling and inexperience? What if he drove her to the hotel and told her to forget the deal? At this moment she wasn't sure that wouldn't be a good thing. She wasn't sure about anything except that she needed to be alone.

She cleaned the second plate, rinsed and dried it and then tackled the stemware.

"Que fais-tu?" Franco asked from behind her, startling her into almost dropping the last glass.

She didn't turn. "I'm washing the dishes."

"My housekeeper comes tomorrow."

She finished drying the wineglass, set it on the counter and carefully folded the damp towel, delaying facing him until the last possible moment. When she did she focused on the cleft in his chin rather than his eyes. "It's done."

"You are my mistress, Stacy, not my maid."

Mistress. Her mother would have been appalled. Her mother, who'd always told Stacy the right man would treat her like a princess. Her mother, who'd led a secret life Stacy hadn't known about until the investigation into her mother's murder had revealed details of a life that looked like a fairy tale to outsiders, but had actually been a nightmare.

"Am I? Still?"

Franco closed the distance between them. He'd dressed in the clothing he'd worn earlier, but without the tie or jacket, and he'd left the top few buttons of his shirt open. Her traitorous nipples tightened at the memory of those dark, wiry curls teasing her breasts.

He reached out and lifted her chin, forcing Stacy to look into his eyes—eyes that no longer burned with passion, but were completely inscrutable instead. "Unless you find my touch repugnant, and I don't think you do, *mon gardénia,* then our agreement stands."

She couldn't speak and didn't know what she'd say if she could find her voice. Did she want the affair to continue? His fingers stroked down her neck, making her pulse leap and her skin tingle. Apparently, no matter what her brain said, her body was all for the affair.

He withdrew his hand. "Come. I'll drive you to the hotel."

"You look shell-shocked."

Stacy pivoted and found Madeline behind her in the hotel lobby. "Hi."

"Was that Franco I saw leaving?"

"Yes." After a silent ride from his home, Franco had insisted on walking her inside. Stacy hadn't invited him upstairs.

"Okay, Stace, what gives?"

"Nothing. I…we had dinner." He hadn't kissed her goodnight, and she didn't know whether that was good or bad.

"Uh-huh, and what else?"

Her cheeks burned. She wished she and Madeline were closer, because she needed to talk to someone, and she was certain the more experienced woman would be able to help her unravel her tangled and conflicting emotions.

"Stacy, did he hurt you?"

"No, no, it's nothing like that. We should go up. It's late."

"It's barely midnight, and we're not going upstairs until you tell me what has you fluctuating between blood-red and hospital-sheet white." Madeline hooked her arm through Stacy's and half led, half dragged her toward the bar.

Within minutes Madeline had snagged them a secluded table, an attentive waiter and a couple of fruity cocktails. "Drink and spill."

Stacy didn't know where to begin or how much to share with this woman whom she'd only met a week ago.

"Okay, let me start. You slept with him and…" Madeline prodded.

Stacy choked on her drink. "How did you know?"

Madeline shrugged. "Was it good? Because I'm going to be seriously disappointed if a guy as sexy as Franco Constantine was a lousy lay."

Lousy lay. The words echoed in Stacy's head, an unpleasant blast from the past, compliments of the high-school jock who'd wooed her until she'd surrendered her virginity. She'd thought being a popular guy's girlfriend would win her acceptance in a new school, but afterward he'd dumped her and told all his friends she was a lousy lay. That was the first time Stacy had welcomed her mother's decision to relocate.

Madeline gripped her hand. "You've gone pale again. Start talking, Stace, or I'm calling the cops, because I'm starting to think he forced you do something you didn't want to do."

"No, don't. There's no need for that. Yes, we slept together and no, it wasn't lousy. He didn't hurt me or force me. I promise." Uncomfortable with the confession, she shifted in her seat.

"Did he dump you?"

"No."

"Then what's the problem?"

She hesitated and then confessed in a whisper, "I barely know him and I had sex with him."

"So?"

So she felt like a tramp. Worse, she'd made a bargain with a man who had the power to make her repeat her mother's mistakes. Not one of her finest decisions.

"You weren't a virgin, were you?"

"No."

"Then I'm not seeing a problem. It was good, right?"

Stacy could feel a blush climbing her neck as she nodded.

"And what's wrong with being with a guy who makes you feel good as long as he's not diseased, married or committed to someone else?"

Stacy fidgeted with her napkin. "Nothing, I guess."

"Stace, there are plenty of guys out there who'll make you feel like crap. You have to grab the good ones when you can. And if it lasts, great. If it doesn't…well, you tried. As long as you're careful. STDs are ugly. Take my word on that. I see plenty of them in the E.R."

Madeline took a sip of her drink and then continued, "It's a double standard, you know? Guys are expected to be experienced and good in bed, but women are supposed to virtuously wait for Mr. Right. How will we recognize him if we don't look around? And what happens when our Mr. Right turns out to be a total jerk?"

Stacy vaguely remembered Candace mentioning a nasty breakup in Madeline's past. She tentatively covered Madeline's hand offering support, but at the same time Madeline's words lifted a load from Stacy's shoulders.

An affair with Franco wouldn't hurt anyone as long as she remembered his passion-profit-and-no-promises offer was temporary and kept her heart safely sealed off. For the first time all night she smiled. "Thanks, Madeline. I needed to hear that."

"Hey, that's what friends are for."

Friends. Stacy savored the word and nodded.

When she left Monaco behind she'd have friends, good memories of sex instead of only bad ones, and for the first time in her life, she'd have a nest egg and soon, a home of her own.

And she'd be an ocean away from the man who threatened her equilibrium.

"Everybody needs to take a nap today," Candace said as she entered the sitting room for breakfast and their usual planning session Friday morning. She placed her cell phone on the coffee table. Candace was the only one of the women who had one that worked in Monaco. Their U.S. cell phones were useless here.

"Why?" Stacy asked.

"Because Franco's taking us to Jimmy'z tonight. He says the place doesn't start rocking until after midnight."

Franco. Stacy's heart skipped a beat. She'd wondered when she'd see him again. Wednesday night he'd left her with a vague, "I will be in touch."

Because she refused to waste a day in paradise sitting in her room and waiting for him to call, she'd spent yesterday exploring Monaco-Ville, the oldest section of Monaco, alone. Her suitemates had other commitments. She'd looked over her shoulder countless times as she watched the changing of the palace guard, wondering if she'd run into Franco, but he'd have no reason to visit tourist spots like the Prince's Palace or the wax museum. He'd probably seen it all before. Besides, he was probably at his office…wherever that was.

Filled with a mixture of anticipation and dread, she'd returned to the hotel late in the afternoon. But there'd been no message from Franco. Stacy had shared a quiet meal at a sidewalk café with Candace and then gone to bed early, only to toss and turn all night.

How could she miss a man she didn't even know? She blamed her uneasiness on not wanting to violate the terms of their agreement by being unavailable. It definitely wasn't a desire to see him again. The warmth between her thighs called her a liar.

"Typical of a guy," Candace continued, "he was stumped when I asked him what we should wear."

Stacy reached for one of her three guide books, looked up the club and read aloud, "'Jimmy'z—An exclusive dance club where the jet set hangs out. Dress code—casual to formal, but wear your designer labels.'"

Stacy didn't own any designer labels.

"You three can go shopping after we tour the Oceanographic Museum and the cathedral this morning," Candace said. "But I have an appointment with the stylist for a practice session on my wedding-day hairdo."

Madeline shook her head. "Not me. I have plans for later."

"Same here," Amelia offered.

Stacy couldn't afford anything new, and she refused to let Candace keep buying things for her. "I'll find something in my closet."

And just like that Franco undermined Stacy's concentration for a second day. Every tall, dark-haired man she spotted in the distance Friday morning made her pulse spike, and no matter how impressive the sights, she kept thinking about Franco and the night ahead. Had it not been for her lack of sleep for the past three nights she wouldn't have been dead to the world when the suite doorbell rang later that afternoon. Shoving her hair out of her eyes she stumbled groggily into the sitting room, opened the door to a hotel staff member.

"A package for Ms. Reeves," he said.

"I'm Stacy Reeves." She accepted the large rectangular pewter-colored box and the man turned away. "Wait. I'll get a tip."

"It's been taken care of, mademoiselle. *Bonsoir.*"

He turned away. Stacy closed the door and leaned against it, her exhaustion totally eradicated. Only Franco would send her something. She pushed off the door and carried the package into her room. With trembling hands she plucked at the lavender ribbon and opened the box.

A folded piece of ivory stationery lay on top of the lavender tissue paper. She lifted it and read, For tonight.

No name. No signature. But the handwriting was the same as that on the card included with Franco's flowers. Franco. She inhaled a shaky breath and pushed back the tissue paper to reveal a pile of teal garments, the same shade as the Mediterranean Sea outside the hotel windows.

She pulled out the first piece, a soft, silk camisole, and laid it on the bed. The second, a sheer, beaded wrap top, matched perfectly, as did the third, a handkerchief-hem skirt with the same beading on the edges as the wrap. She held the skirt against her body. It would be fitted from her waist through her hips, but the lower half would swish and swirl about her thighs as she moved. The perfect dancing outfit, and judging by the designer label, it probably cost more than her monthly rent and car payment combined.

And then her gaze caught on two more wrapped items in the bottom of the box. She unwound the tissue from the largest first and found strappy sandals to match the clothing. She slipped one on her bare foot. Perfect fit. In fact, everything looked as if it would fit. How had Franco known her sizes? Even she didn't know the European conversions. Had Candace told him? Or was he so experienced with women he could accurately guess their sizes just by looking at them. Probably the latter.

She opened the last package, gasped and dropped the

matching bra and thong in the exact same shade of teal on the bed. Heat rushed through her.

Franco was dressing her from the skin out. He'd bought the privilege to do so, just as he'd bought the right to undress her later if he chose.

Anticipation—or was it dread?—made her pulse race.

Six

A wiser man would choose another woman, Franco told himself as he entered Hôtel Reynard a few minutes before midnight. Stacy had made him feel more than sexual relief—a luxury he no longer afforded himself. It would not happen again.

He had ignored her yesterday just to prove he could, but he had failed miserably. She had invaded his thoughts like a fever. If the family estate and the company he had sweated blood over were not at stake, he would bid her farewell. But it had taken him two months after making the agreement with his father to find a woman who met both his and his father's criteria. Stacy came with the added benefit of leaving the country after the month was up. He would not have to deal with a clingy woman who refused to accept goodbye.

Nodding to the concierge, Franco stepped into the penthouse elevator and swiftly ascended. Tonight there would be no intimate conversations. He would dance with Stacy in the crowded, noisy club. Afterward he would send her suitemates back to the hotel in the limo and take Stacy to his villa where they would have sex. And then he would put her in a cab and send her back to the hotel. Alone.

He did not want to know her better—except intimately, of course. Nor did he want to discover what had made an attractive and intelligent woman completely unaware of her appeal, for she seemed to have absolutely no vanity.

The suite's doorbell chimed when he touched the button, and seconds later the wooden panel swung open. Stacy. She took his breath away. His gaze absorbed her, from her loose shining hair to the outfit he had chosen, down her lovely legs to her pink-painted toenails in the sexy heels.

"*Tu es ravissante, mon gardénia,*" he murmured in a barely audible—thanks to the annoying thickening of this throat—voice.

Her cheeks pinked and she dipped her chin. "Thank you. And if I look ravishing it's because of the lovely outfit. Thank you for that too. But you don't have to buy—"

"The color matches your eyes when you climax," he interrupted. Ignoring her shocked gasp, he reached for her right hand and bent to kiss her knuckles. At the same time he retrieved the diamond bracelet she had left behind from his pocket and fastened it on her wrist.

He straightened. "Are your suitemates ready? I have a limo downstairs."

"Is that Franco?" Candace called from within the suite.

Fingering the bracelet, Stacy stepped back, opening the door and revealing the trio of women. "Yes. He has a limo waiting."

"Then let's go," Madeline replied. "And Stace, if that's the kind of stuff you have stashed in your closet I'm glad we're the same size."

Stacy shot him a quick glance as if warning him not to correct Madeline. "I need to get my purse."

His gaze followed her as she walked away, the uneven hem of her skirt swinging flirtatiously above her knees. Knowing her buttocks were bare save the clinging fabric of her skirt and the thin ribbon of her thong made his blood pool behind his zipper. Nor could he take his eyes from her once she rejoined them. This fascination was not good. But it was temporary. He would get over it.

In the limo he settled beside her with the other women on the seat across from them. Stacy's scent filled his nostrils and her legs drew his gaze. His fisted his hand against the compulsion to smooth his palm up her thigh.

He belatedly remembered the role Vincent had asked of him. "I have a table reserved beside the dance floor. The rules are different here than in the States. Unattached men and women dance freely without partners. If you see someone you wish to dance with you make eye contact, and if the interest is returned you move toward each other on the floor."

"You mean the guys don't ask you to dance?" Amelia queried.

"Not verbally, no. The club is safe, but if you have problems come to me. Stacy and I will be nearby."

Stacy's eyes widened. She seemed to sink deeper into the seat as her companions' speculative gazes landed on her. She had not wanted her friends to know about the money, but hiding the affair would be impossible.

Franco nodded to Candace. "Vincent says you are only to dance with women or ugly men."

His comment brought a laugh and eased the tension. "The limo is on standby. If you wish to leave, use it. Don't get into cars with strangers."

A collective groan arose from the opposite bench and Madeline mumbled, "Not my father's favorite speech."

Franco shrugged. "Vincent charged me with your safety."

The limo pulled to a stop outside Jimmy'z. The women climbed out, Stacy last. Franco followed, his gaze on her shapely bottom. The men gathered near the entrance eyed the women, Stacy in particular. Franco rested a possessive hand on her waist and bent closer. "You will dance with no one but me."

She briefly closed her eyes and then nodded.

Inside, the hostess led them to their table. The club was dark and the music loud with a driving beat. Franco wondered what Stacy thought of the retro decor, but decided it did not matter. Knowing her tastes was not part of their deal.

He arranged for their drinks and waited with impatience he had no business feeling for Stacy to consume hers while the women chatted, pointed out celebrities and acclimatized themselves to the club. An hour later even the shy Amelia had deserted them for the dance floor. Franco extended his hand. Stacy bit her lip, hesitating before she laid her palm over his and rose.

Thankful that slow songs were few and far between at Jimmy'z, he led her onto the floor. The night would be long enough without the arousing slide of her body against his. Needing the physical exertion to expend some of his caged energy, he released her hand and found the rhythm of the beat. Stacy moved self-consciously at first, but soon either the gyrating crowd surrounding them or the alcohol relaxed her. The results devastated him. A slight sheen of sweat dampened her flushed skin, reminding him of her face just before *le petit mort*. He would have been better off if Stacy had remained stiff.

His gaze slid over her. When he had chosen her clothing he'd had no idea the effect she would have on his control and his carefully planned evening. Each pirouette flared her skirt almost to her bottom. He wasn't the only man to notice. A primitive urge to mark her as his surged through him.

He cupped a hand around her nape, pulled her close and pressed a quick, hard kiss on her lips. He said into her ear, "You dance like you make love. *Très* sexy."

Shock made Stacy stumble. Could the man read minds? Franco caught her quickly, pulling her flush against the hot length of his hard body. The contact was too intense, too arousing. She jerked back, her gaze slamming into his. Suddenly the air seemed loaded with sexual tension.

For the past two hours she'd been thinking he moved like an invitation to sin—an invitation she wanted to accept more and more with each passing second. She'd believed that after a night in his bed she couldn't—wouldn't—desire him again. Wrong. Her body, already warm from dancing, flushed with heat and pulsed with a sexual awareness with which she'd been unfamiliar until Franco.

Franco moved closer, his hand curving around her waist and his hips punctuating the beat in a purely sensual dance that made her feminine muscles clench in anticipation. A mating dance. Not graphic or crude. Just devastatingly, pulse-acceleratingly sensuous. And she wasn't the only woman to notice. Since they'd arrived, each time Stacy had glanced past the cobalt silk stretched across his broad shoulders she'd caught women glaring at her or ogling Franco's behind, and who could blame them?

More than one bold woman had sashaycd up to them on the dance floor and shimmied directly beside him as if trying to draw his attention. But Franco's gaze never strayed. His eyes had remained locked on hers or on the movement of her body with an intensity burning in the blue depths that made her feel incredibly attractive and yes, very desirable. Realizing she was proud to be the woman he'd chosen was a scary thought since the man *should* be her worst nightmare.

Her throat dried and her belly tightened. She blamed the discomforts on thirst and hunger. Nerves over this evening had ruined her appetite and she'd barely touched the dinner she and her suitemates had shared earlier. Hoping for a distraction, she dampened her lips and glanced toward their table, but her friends weren't there to rescue her.

Franco intercepted her look, caught her hand and led her off the dance floor without a word. He paused beside her chair, brushed stray tendrils of hair from her damp forehead and tucked them behind her ears. His fingertips lingered over her pulse points, no doubt noting the rapid tattoo not solely caused by the dancing, and then one hand traced her collar bone and dipped into the V of her top. Desire rippled over her, tightening her nipples and making her shiver.

"Another drink, *mon gardénia?*"

Maybe the alcohol was to blame for loosening her inhibitions and erasing her common sense. Whatever, she wanted him to kiss her instead of staring at her lips as if he would consume her were they not surrounded by people, and her response was both unacceptable and unwise, given what she knew of men in his position.

She cleared her throat and sat. "Water this time."

He signaled the waiter, ordered another round of drinks for their table and seated himself beside her.

Stacy gasped when his hand smoothed up from her knee and then her breath wheezed out again when his fingertips stroked along the sensitive skin of her inner thigh.

"You wish to go?"

She did. Oh boy, she did. What did it say about her that she couldn't wait to get back to his house, back to his bed? She waited until after the waiter deposited the drinks and left to reply. "We shouldn't leave before the others."

"Amelia has found someone. Madeline and Candace are coming this way."

Surprised that he'd kept track of her suitemates, she turned in her seat and searched the crowd until she located Amelia dancing with a tall, sandy-haired man. "Should we leave her with him?"

"Toby will take care of her."

"Toby? Toby Haynes? The race-car driver?"

"*Oui*, and Vincent's best man. He is also charged with your safety while you are in Monaco." He removed his hand as the women neared the table and Stacy immediately missed his touch.

Something is definitely wrong with you.

Madeline and Candace slid into their seats.

"*Merci*, Franco," Candace said. She and Madeline toasted him with their fresh drinks. "This has been a blast, but I wish Vincent were here."

Madeline scanned the crowd. "And Damon. I had hoped he'd join us tonight."

"Damon is your tour guide?" Stacy asked.

"Yes. But I guess he had to work tonight."

"Shall I call for the limo for you?" Franco asked.

"Yes," Madeline and Candace answered simultaneously.

"Excuse me." Franco left the table, headed onto the dance floor and spoke to Toby and then disappeared toward the club entrance.

Candace grinned mischievously. "I'll tell ya, Stacy, Franco is definitely a keeper. He has some seriously sexy moves, and if he's half as good in bed as he is on the dance floor, a girl could have a real good time."

Stacy's cheeks burned. She ducked her head and fiddled with her cocktail napkin. So this was girl talk. "He's a good, um…dancer."

"You're going home with him?" Madeline asked.

Stacy fought the urge to squirm in her seat. "Yes, but I'll be back for our morning meeting."

"The only thing on the agenda tomorrow is me tinkering with the rehearsal dinner and reception seating. No work for you, so stay as long as you like," Candace replied with a wink and a smug smile. "It's almost 3:00 a.m. I have a feeling we'll all be sleeping in."

Stacy had permission to spend the entire night with Franco. Did she want to? The swiftness of her answer surprised and alarmed her. She'd slid far too easily into the role of a rich man's mistress.

"Remove your clothing," Franco ordered in the darkness thirty minutes later.

Stacy's breath caught. She couldn't see anything, not even her hand in front of her face, and she didn't know where she was. Franco had led her into his home, and without turning on any lights, he'd guided her down a hall and a flight of stairs.

The click of her heels had echoed off the walls until

they'd stopped moving and now the eerie silence deafened her. Or maybe her thunderous heartbeat drowned out all sound.

Did she dare trust him? She found herself wanting to. Scary.

A mechanical whirl startled her, making her look to her right. The wall slid open like a curtain to reveal moon-washed gardens, the roar of a waterfall and a spa large enough to lie down in without touching the sides.

Half of the spa is concealed beneath the house by the falling water. I would like to make love to you there, Franco had said. Was it only a day and a half ago?

A thrill of anticipation raced through her. Anticipation. Something she'd never experienced in a relationship with a man before Franco.

Moonlight seeped around the cascading water to dimly illuminate her surroundings, and a gentle breeze wafted in, carrying the scent of flowers. The people of Monaco loved their flowers. Gardens and flower boxes abounded.

Stacy scanned the room filled with more exercise equipment than the gym in her apartment complex until she spotted Franco in the shadows. He flipped a switch and the whirlpool splashed to life, its water gleaming like bubbly champagne from the golden glow of lights beneath the surface.

With his gaze fixed on her he leaned against the wall, toed off his shoes and removed his socks. Mesmerized, she watched as he straightened and reached for the buttons on his shirt. It fluttered to the floor followed quickly by his pants and briefs. He stood before her like a finely chiseled statue. An incredibly aroused and well-endowed statue. His chin lifted. "Your turn."

She gulped and reached for the knot of her sheer wrap, but she was nervous, her fingers uncooperative.

She'd never stripped for a man before. Nor had she ever had one look at her the way Franco did with his gaze burning over her, his nostrils flaring, his fists clenched by his side. Finally, the knot gave way. She shrugged off the wrap and dropped it on a nearby weight bench.

Taking a fortifying breath, she reached for the back hook and zipper of her skirt. It swished down her legs. She stepped out of it and her shoes and turned to deposit both on the bench.

A warm hand covered her bottom, making her jump and gasp. Franco. She hadn't heard him cross the room. His other hand joined the first, stroking her buttocks, thighs and her belly, and molding her against him. The thong was no barrier to the heat of his lean flanks against her cheeks and the hard length of his erection against her spine. Desire made her dizzy.

What happened to maintaining a clear head and control?

He murmured something in French, something she couldn't translate, and then his fingers caught the hem of her camisole and whisked it over her head.

"Turn around," he ordered in a deep, velvety voice.

She pivoted on trembling legs. The sharp rasp of his indrawn breath filled her ears. He lifted a hand to outline the top of her demi-bra with a fingertip. Her nipples tightened and need twisted inside her as he retraced his path, this time delving below the lace and over her sensitive skin. How could he make her want like this?

"Take it off."

Stacy reached behind her, unhooked the bra and shrugged out of it. Franco's approving gaze caressed her breasts and then dropped to the tiny teal thong.

"And the rest."

She shoved the lingerie down her legs wondering

why she had not once considered saying no. And then she straightened. Franco tipped his head to indicate the spa. Stacy descended the whirlpool steps. The hot water swirled around her ankles, her calves, and once she reached the center of the small pool, her thighs. Franco joined her, reclined on the bench seat and extended his hand.

"Turn around."

She did and then he pulled her into his lap and flattened her back against his chest with his erection sandwiched in the crease of her buttocks. The water swirled between her legs and lapped at her breasts, but then Franco's caressing hands replaced it, massaging, tweaking, sweeping her up in a whirlpool of desire.

She let him have his way. He'd bought her, bought the right to use her any way he wanted. And she had to remember that, but it was hard to keep up the mental barriers when he touched her like this. Sure, he'd promised her pleasure, but did she really deserve it?

His teeth grazed the tendons of her neck. She shivered and tilted her head to give him better access. He stroked her breasts, her abdomen, her legs, nearing but never quite reaching the place where she needed his touch the most. She squirmed in his lap and bit back a frustrated whimper. He stood abruptly, lifting her with him, sat her on the cool tile edge of the whirlpool and then knelt between her legs.

Next time I will taste you, he'd said.

"Wait—" The touch of his tongue cut off her shocked protest with an intense burst of sensation. No man had ever licked her there. Franco laved and suckled, taking her to the brink again and again, but each time she thought she'd shatter he'd stop to kiss her thigh, nibble her hip bone or tongue her navel.

Frustration built until she unclenched her fingers from the rim of the tub and tangled them in his hair to hold him in place.

He grunted a satisfied sound against her and then found the heart of her again with his silken tongue. Seconds later climax undulated through her. Her cries echoed off the stone walls and her muscles contracted over and over, squeezing every last drop of energy from her until she sagged against Franco's bent head and braced her arms on his broad shoulders.

He straightened, reached behind her for a condom packet she hadn't even noticed and quickly readied himself. Cupping her bottom, he pulled her to the edge of the spa and plunged deep inside her, forcing another lusty cry from her lungs. She shoved her fist against her mouth.

Franco pulled her hand away. "I want to hear the sound of your passion. Better yet, I want to taste your cries on my tongue."

He covered her mouth with his.

She ought to be ashamed of herself, Stacy thought as she clung to him and arched to meet his thrusts, but she couldn't seem to rally the emotion with Franco pistoning into her core and bringing her to the brink of another climax. She yanked her mouth free and gasped for breath as her muscles tensed and she came again, this time calling out his name.

Franco plunged harder, deeper and faster until he roared in release, and then all was silent except for the rush of the water and their panting breaths.

He held her, or maybe she held him, as he sank back into the hot water, taking her boneless body with him. She drifted above him. The current swirled over her sensitized skin, teasing, tantalizing, slowing her return to sanity. Without Franco's arms to anchor her, she'd float away like a cork on the tide. She trusted him to keep her head above water.

Trust. The thought jarred her into planting her knees on the bottom of the tub on either side of Franco's hips and pushing him away so abruptly that she almost dunked him. How could she trust him? He was everything she'd sworn to avoid, but avoiding him was becoming the last thing she wanted to do.

To protect herself she'd have to learn everything she could about him. Did he have a temper? Any obsessions?

She'd learn—even if learning meant letting her guard down enough to spend the night.

"I'll call a taxi for you." Franco disentangled their bodies and stood. He stepped over the low wall separating the indoor and outdoor halves of the spa and ducked beneath the waterfall. The cooler water from the pool sheeted down on his head and splashed over Stacy's skin. Seconds later he climbed from the whirlpool.

Stacy rose on legs so rubbery it was a miracle they supported her, and wrapped her arms around her waist. "Candace said there's nothing on the agenda for tomorrow—today. I—I can stay."

Muscles rippling beneath his wet skin, he disappeared into an adjoining room without responding and returned moments later with a black towel around his hips and another in his fist. When she didn't take it from his outstretched arm he dropped it beside the spa. "I have other plans for the weekend."

Plans? With another woman? Stacy didn't care to identify the uncomfortable emotions stirring inside her. She had no claim on Franco's time. In fact, she should be glad he wanted to spend it elsewhere. But strangely, she wasn't.

"There is a change of clothing for you in the bathroom." A tilt of his head indicated the room he'd just vacated. He flicked a series of switches. The wall slid closed, the whirlpool stilled and silence and darkness descended on the room. Then overhead lights flashed on leaving Stacy feeling naked and exposed under his thorough perusal. Her damp skin quickly chilled.

"You may shower, if you like, and then join me upstairs." He gathered his discarded garments and left.

Dismissed. He'd had his way with her and now he was done. How could he be so conscientious of her satisfaction one moment and then such a cold bastard the next? Shame crept over her.

What are you doing? Falling for the first guy to give you an orgasm? So he's a good lover. He bought *you. Just because he's doing favors for Vincent and he watched out for your friends at the club doesn't make him a nice guy.*

And he has plans. *Plans that don't include you.*

Irritated with herself, Stacy climbed from the water, dried off and wound the towel around her nakedness. She grabbed her shoes and clothing from the weight bench and let curiosity lead her into a humongous tiled bathroom. A large glass shower stall took up one corner and a wooden sauna occupied the other. And was that a massage table? Did Franco have a personal masseuse?

A V-neck sundress in a muted floral print of blues and greens and a matching lightweight sweater hung in an open closet beside a white toweling robe. She ran her fingers over the dress's flirty ruffled hem. Silk, whereas her dresses were cotton. Designer instead of department store. Other than the sexy but impractical sandals in a box on the floor of the closet, the outfit was exactly the style she would have chosen for herself if she had an unlimited budget. Which, of course, she'd never had.

The dress tempted her, but she didn't want anything else from Franco, nor did she want to explain to her suitemates why he kept buying her presents.

Her reflection in the long mirror caught her eye. Ugh. Her makeup was ninety percent gone and her hair clumped in wet tangles over her shoulders. She dumped her clothes on the counter, washed her face in the sink and then finger-combed her hair as best as she could. She unhooked the diamond bracelet and left it on the long marble vanity and froze. Her heart stalled. *Her watch.* She hadn't removed it. Panic dried her mouth. Where had she misplaced it?

She backtracked, but didn't see it on the bottom of the spa or anywhere around the weight bench. It hadn't been expensive, but its value couldn't be measured in dollars. She remembered putting it on tonight. Wherever it was, she *had* to find it.

Maybe Franco could help. She returned to the bathroom and quickly yanked on her dancing outfit. The cool, sweat-dampened fabric made her grimace. After smoothing the wrinkles with her hands, she followed the direction Franco had taken earlier. The stairs led to a hallway, and while she would have preferred to explore this end of the house and perhaps learn more about Franco, she tracked his voice to the living room. With his back to her, he swore, dropped the phone on the cradle and shoved his hands through his damp dark hair.

"Is something wrong?"

He turned, his gaze narrowing over her choice of clothing. He'd changed into jeans and a black polo shirt. "The taxi is unavailable for an hour. I will drive you back to the hotel. Why are you not wearing the dress?"

"I told you. You don't have to keep buying me gifts. I accepted this one because I didn't have anything suitable to wear tonight, but otherwise…" She shrugged. "I don't need anything."

His lips compressed and a muscle in his jaw jumped. "And the bracelet?"

"I left it downstairs on the counter. It's beautiful, but not practical for an accountant. If I wore it to work people would wonder if I'd been embezzling from their accounts, and I never go anywhere dressy enough to need something like that."

Surprise flicked in his eyes. "You will continue to work when you return home?"

"Of course." As soon as she found another job. "Once I pay taxes on the money and buy a house there won't be enough left to live a life of idle luxury."

"Taxes? And what job will you list as a source for your income?"

Good question. She twisted the thin gold strap of her evening bag. "I haven't figured that out yet, but suddenly opening a bank account with more than a million dollars would red-flag the IRS. And I'm not stupid enough to keep that much cash lying around my apartment."

"Why not use an offshore bank?"

"Too cloak-and-dagger. I'd feel like a money launderer. Besides, not reporting the income would be illegal." Did he think she was crazy not to hide the money? She couldn't tell from his neutral expression. "Franco, I lost my watch. I didn't see it downstairs. Could you give me the number for the limo service, the taxi and Jimmy'z? I'll call to see if anyone found it. It wasn't expensive, but it was…my favorite. I need to find it."

"I will make the calls."

"Thank you." She agreed because the language barrier might be an issue, but then shifted in her sandals, reluctant for some stupid reason to see the night end. "I enjoyed tonight."

He folded his arms and leaned his hips against the back of the sofa. "You sound surprised."

She rubbed her bare wrist and wrinkled her nose. "I'm not a clubbing kind of person."

He studied her so intently her toes curled in her shoes, and then he reached behind him and lifted a small plastic shopping bag. "This is one gift I insist you accept. A cell phone. My numbers are already programmed into it."

She'd be at his beck and call. But that's what he'd bought. And the phone might come in handy when she needed to reach Candace or if one of the women needed to reach her. "Am I allowed to use it to call anyone else?"

"Not your lover in the States," he replied swiftly.

She took the bag from him and peeked inside to see a top-of-the-line silvery-green picture phone. "I meant Candace, Madeline or Amelia. I don't have a lover back home. If I did, I wouldn't be involved with you."

Again he looked as if he didn't believe what she said—a circumstance she was beginning to get used to. He pushed off the sofa. "Come."

She followed him outside and slid into the passenger seat of his car and waited until he climbed in beside her. "Why did you choose MIT?"

He didn't answer until he'd buckled his seat belt and started the engine. "They have an excellent Global Leadership program."

"Couldn't you get that at a university closer to home?"

He pulled onto the road and drove perhaps a half mile before replying. "My mother was from Boston and I was curious about her city."

Stacy jerked in surprise. "An American?"

Another long pause suggested he didn't want to share personal info. "Second-generation. She met my father while visiting her cousin in Avignon."

The lights of Monaco sparkled across the mountain-side in the pre-dawn hour. Stacy didn't think she'd ever tire of the view, but the insights into Franco fascinated her more. "Are you close to her? Your mom, I mean."

"She died when I was three," the brusque response seemed grudgingly offered.

"I'm sorry. It's hard to lose a parent." She still missed hers, and now that she knew why she and her mother had lived such a vagabond life, she could even accept, respect and forgive her mother's choices.

A streetlight briefly illuminated his tense face. "Yours?"

A gruesome graphic image flashed through Stacy's mind. She squeezed her eyes shut and forced it away. "She...died when I was nineteen."

"And she left you enough money to attend college?"

"No. I co-oped."

"What is that?"

"I worked part-time in my field with sponsoring companies and that meant I had to take a lighter load of classes. It took six years of going to school year-round, but I finished."

"Vincent did not tell me that."

"You asked Vincent about me? What did he say?"

"That he had not met you, but that you had...how did he put it? You saved Candace's bacon in a tax audit."

Stacy laughed and Franco's gaze whipped in her di-rection. He acted as if he'd never heard her laugh. Come to think of it, he probably hadn't. "Candace's was my first audit, and I went a little overboard in her defense. I think the IRS agent was glad to get rid of us by the time

I finished pointing out all the deductions Candace could have taken but hadn't."

Franco pulled the car into the hotel parking area, but not into the valet lane and stopped. He turned in his seat and studied her face in the dim light. "You enjoy your work."

"I love—um, my job." She'd barely caught herself before using past tense. Being laid off had been like moving to a new school and being rejected all over again. It had hurt—especially since she hadn't done anything wrong. "Numbers make sense. People often don't."

He pinned her with another one of his intense inspections that made her want to squirm. "I will be out of town this weekend. A car will pick you up at quarter to six Monday evening and deliver you to my house. My housekeeper will let you in before she leaves. Wait for me. We will have dinner."

And then sex? Her shameless pulse quickened. "I look forward to it."

And the sad thing was, that wasn't a lie, and Monday seemed a very long way away.

Seven

"I have found her," Franco said upon entering the chateau's study.

His father looked up sharply, set his book aside and rose from the sofa to embrace him. "Franco, I was not expecting you this weekend. If you had called I could have delayed lunch."

He hadn't known he was coming. This morning's urge to put some distance between him and Stacy had been both sudden and imperative. She had clouded his thinking with incredible sex and contradictory behavior. He needed distance and objectivity to decipher her actions.

"No problem. I will raid the kitchen later. Where is Angeline?"

"Shopping in Marseille."

Ah, yes. Exactly why he was here. To remind himself that a mercenary, self-indulgent heart beat at the core of every woman.

Take his mother, for example. Although his father had never spoken a negative word against her, Franco had been curious enough about the woman who had given birth to him to investigate her death. During one of his university vacations he had researched the police reports and the newspaper stories and discovered that his mother had enjoyed her status as a rich, older man's wife. She had often attended weekend house parties without her husband, and there she'd indulged. In booze. In cocaine. And who knew what else? At one such party, a chemical overdose had killed her at age twenty-six.

His father passed him a glass of wine. "So tell me about this young lady."

"She is an American accountant, a friend of Vincent's fiancée, and she claims she counsels troubled teens in her spare time."

"And?"

"I offered her a million euros to be my mistress for a month. She accepted." But she would not accept all his gifts. That did not make sense. Her honesty had to be a ruse. Who would report a million euros windfall to the tax man and forfeit almost half in taxes?

"She is attractive? Desirable?"

An image of Stacy rising like Venus from the churning waters of the spa flashed in his mind. Droplets had streamed down her ivory skin, clung to her puckered nipples and glistened in the dark curls concealing her sex. Before he had removed the first condom he had been ready to reach for a second. He'd had to dunk beneath the cooling waterfall to regain control. "That was our agreement."

"And yet you're here and she's…where?"

"Monaco. Vincent is pampering his bride-to-be and

her attendants with an all-expenses-paid month at Hôtel Reynard while they plan the wedding. Stacy is a bridesmaid."

"Ah, yes. Vincent is another one making his papa wait for grandbabies. Has he recovered from the accident?"

Vincent had come home with Franco several times during school vacations. Franco had also visited the Reynard home in Boca Raton, Florida. It had been Vincent who had suggested Franco relocate to Monaco for the tax advantages the principality could offer Midas Chocolates. "He is completely mobile now, and through surgeries and physical therapy, has regained 80 percent use of his right hand."

"And his fiancée does not mind the scars or the handicap?"

"She was his nurse in the burn unit. She has seen him look worse." And she had stood by him. Probably because Reynard Hotels was a multi-billion dollar corporation with ninety luxury hotels spread across the globe.

"I look forward to seeing him again and to meeting his bride. I also want to meet your…Stacy, you said? You'll bring her here."

The idea repulsed him. "I do not see the need."

"I do. And is she the kind of woman you would be willing to marry if she refused the money?"

Franco cursed the wording of his agreement with his father, but it would not become an issue. "It will not happen. She has already accepted."

"You seem very certain of that."

"I am."

"When is the money to be paid?"

"The day after Vincent's wedding."

His father turned away, but not before Franco caught a glimpse of a smile. "Just remember our agreement, son."

"How could I forget?"

How indeed? When he returned to Monaco, he would show Stacy the benefits of being a rich man's plaything. Before long she would greedily beg for his gifts instead of refusing them.

And then she would take the money and run.

Alone in Franco's house.

Stacy stood in the foyer after the housekeeper left. Uncertain. Uncomfortable. Undecided. She could be a polite guest and wait in the living room as directed or she could search for signs of obsession. Being a snoop wasn't honorable, but after what she'd learned about her father... She shuddered.

Knowledge was power and she needed all the knowledge she could get about Franco Constantine. Her safety depended on it.

She turned down the hall toward the master-bedroom wing. A twinge of guilt made her pause on the threshold, but she took a deep breath and marched in. The furniture surfaces were clear of clutter. No photographs or knickknacks gave a clue to the room's owner other than big, bold wooden furniture and luxurious linens. The classic landscapes on the wall also revealed little. She would not stoop to pawing through his drawers.

The view of Larvotto through the open drapes lured her, but she ignored it and cautiously opened a door to reveal a closet as large as her apartment bedroom. It looked like a *GQ* man's dream with clothing and shoes neatly aligned on the racks and shelves. There was no sign of a woman anywhere...except for the dress Stacy had left behind the other night hanging alone on an otherwise empty rod with the shoebox beneath it.

She closed the door, returned to the foyer and looked

out the window, but there was no sign of Franco's car. The opposite hallway beckoned. Just past the stairs to the basement she found an open door and looked inside. Franco's study. A large dark-wooden desk dominated the space and tall bookshelves lined the walls on either side of the double French doors opening onto the back patio.

A pair of photographs on one shelf drew her across the room. She lifted one of Franco and another man about the same age standing in front of a picturesque castle. Vincent Reynard. Stacy recognized him from the picture Candace had shown her, but the photo had been taken before the accident that had marred half of Vincent's face. Franco looked at least a decade younger than the man she knew, and his smile was genuine and devastatingly handsome instead of twisted and cynical. Fewer lines fanned from his eyes and none bracketed his chiseled lips. Had this been taken during their grad-school days? But the setting looked European instead of American.

Stacy returned the frame to the shelf. An older man stared out at her from the second photograph. His heavily lined face couldn't conceal the same classic bone structure and cleft chin as Franco. He had Franco's thick hair and straight brows, but his were snowy white instead of coffee-bean dark, and his eyes weren't nearly as guarded as Franco's. Was this Franco's father? She'd never know. And she was okay with that. Really.

Turning slowly, she scanned the tables, sofa and bar cart, but she found no sign of Franco's ex-wife. She returned to the entrance hall and eyed the staircase. Did she dare? What if Franco came home while she was upstairs? How would she explain her snooping without revealing that she'd visited her father's house after her mother's death and what she'd discovered had given her the willies? Franco didn't need to know her tragic past or that her father most likely had been mentally unbalanced. No one needed to know. It was hard enough to make friends without people wondering if she carried her father's defective genes.

Her futile search supported Franco's claim that he was over his wife and his marriage and that he'd moved here after the divorce…unless there was something upstairs. Not that Stacy really cared about his wife, but she wanted to make sure Franco wasn't the type to use his money and power in dangerous ways.

It's not as if you're the kind of woman a man can't forget, especially a man like Franco who must have far more glamorous women than you at his beck and call all the time.

That again raised the question of why he had chosen her?

The sound of a car in the drive made her heart stutter. She hustled to the window, looked out as Franco's black sedan rolled to a stop. Her mouth dried and something resembling anticipation shot through her.

How could she be eager to see him? He was using her.

And you're using him, so don't get sanctimonious.

He climbed from the vehicle. His gaze searched the front of the house and found her in the window. For a moment he paused with one arm braced on the top of the car and just stared at her. A lump rose in her throat and her heart beat like a hummingbird's wings. He bent and reached inside. When he emerged again and started toward the villa he carried a small white bag with pink ribbon handles that looked too feminine in his big hand.

Another gift she'd have to refuse?

And why did she keep refusing? The diamond bracelet alone could be pawned to pay off her car. But they'd agreed on a price for a service and to keep tacking on extras seemed unethical.... As if there could be anything more unethical than their current agreement. The irony of her situation didn't escape her. But she had to be able to live with herself after this affair ended, and that meant setting standards and sticking to them. It wasn't easy. There had been precious few gifts in her past. And she'd lost the most important one.

She rubbed her bare wrist and then wiped her palms over her pencil-slim skirt and opened the front door. If they were truly lovers this was the point where she'd rush down the walkway to embrace him and welcome him home. Instead, as he approached she stood frozen inside the door unsure exactly what he expected of her.

The closer he came the more shallow her breathing became. While her gaze fed on his lean dark-suited form, he inventoried her lavender blouse, navy skirt and sensible low-heeled pumps. Suddenly she felt dowdy, and she wished she'd slipped into the flirty and feminine sundress hanging in his closet. That she'd even consider dressing to please him rattled her. "Hi."

"*Bonsoir,* Stacy." His arm encircled her waist. He snatched her close, taking her mouth in a ravenous kiss that bent her backward. She clutched his lapels and held tight. Their thighs spliced and the heat of his arousal nudged her belly. His tongue stroked hers and hunger suffused her with embarrassing swiftness.

By the time he released her she was breathless and dizzy, with her pulse galloping out of control. She unfurled her fingers from his suit coat and sagged against the door frame. He swept past her, set the gift bag on the credenza and continued through the living room and toward the kitchen.

Stacy stared at the bag, her curiosity piqued. Maybe

it wasn't for her. After taking a few moments to gather her composure—and to battle the urge to peek into the bag—she closed the front door on the balmy evening and followed him.

Franco had removed his suit coat and laid it over the end of the center island. He held a martini shaker in his hands. The flexing and shifting of his muscles beneath his white shirt as he mixed the sloshing liquid filled her mind with images of those bare muscles bunching and contracting beneath his supple skin as he braced himself above her. She plucked at her suddenly sticking blouse and exhaled slowly.

He poured the contents into a glass and set it on the counter in front of her. Her eyebrows rose.

"You are surprised I noticed you never drink more than one glass of wine at dinner and you ordered fruity drinks at the club?" he asked as he opened a bottle of red wine with practiced ease.

"I guess I am."

He filled his wineglass and lifted it in a silent toast then nodded toward the martini. "Try it."

Stacy lifted the glass and sipped. Chocolate, cherry and vanilla mingled on her tongue. "Very good."

"It is made with Midas Chocolate liqueur." He reached into his inside coat pocket and withdrew a handful of gilt-edged cards which he placed on the counter. "*Le Bal de L'Eté* is this Saturday. I have tickets."

There were more than two tickets in the pile. "A summer ball?"

"*Oui*, it is an annual charity event to mark the opening of the summer season at the Monte Carlo Sporting Club. Europe's *l'aristocratie*, including royalty, attend. You and your friends might even meet the prince."

She gaped. "Of Monaco?"

"*Oui.*"

She'd heard it wasn't uncommon to see members of the royal family on the street or at sporting events, but to meet them… "Will either of the two long dresses you've seen me wear work?"

He shook his head. "*Non.* I will arrange for you—"

"Then I can't possibly go."

"—and your friends to have appropriate gowns," he continued as if she hadn't interrupted.

She sighed. He had her cornered and he knew it. "And if I refuse then Candace, Madeline and Amelia will miss the ball."

He shrugged. "*Tout a un prix.*"

Everything has a price. Yes, he did seem to live by that rule. But how could she deny the other women this opportunity to rub elbows with royalty? "You fight dirty."

"I play to win."

"Okay. On behalf of my friends, I accept." Jeez. That had sounded ungracious. But she hated being manipulated.

"*Bien.* And while you are in an accepting mood…" He left the kitchen and returned moments later carrying the bag. "For you." He held up a hand to stop her protest. "Open it before you refuse."

She reluctantly accepted the bag, withdrew a small box, opened it and gasped. *Her watch.* Hugging it to her chest, she ducked her head, blinked her stinging eyes and struggled to contain the happy sob building in her chest. He couldn't possibly know how much this meant to her. "Thank you."

"You are welcome. The limo driver found it. The band was broken. I had it replaced with a similar one."

"My mother gave me this when I graduated high

school. It was the last gift she gave me before she—" Her throat thickened, choking off her words.

Franco smoothed his hand from her brow to her nape. His fingers clenched in her hair and then stroked forward to lift her chin. "I am glad we found it. Now finish your drink and then go downstairs and remove your clothing. The masseuse will be here in ten minutes."

"Masseuse?" Stacy wasn't wild about the idea of someone else seeing or touching her naked body. She hadn't joined her suitemates in the hotel spa for sea-salt massages for that very reason. But she wouldn't mind Franco's hands on her. "You're not going to, um… massage me?"

A slow naughty smile curved his lips. "I am going to watch. And after she has turned your muscles to butter and departed, I am going to take you on the massage table."

The image he painted sent a shiver of arousal over her. Stacy realized she was beginning to like not only Franco, but this mistress stuff too.

And that was definitely not good news.

My God. He had almost hugged her.

Franco fisted his hands and watched the lights of Stacy's taxi disappear into the night. What kind of fool was he to be swayed by eyes brimming with tears and gratitude? And yet when Stacy had looked at him earlier tonight, clutching that cheap watch to her breast and smiling through tear-filled eyes, he'd almost succumbed to the urge to embrace her.

He did not hug or cuddle or any of those other relationship things that would lead a woman to expect more from him than he could give. And he did not trust tears. Tears were nothing more than a weapon in a woman's arsenal. How often had Lisette used tears to get her way during their marriage? After the abortion she'd tried to soften him by crying and claiming that he'd been spending more time at work than with her, and she'd been afraid he no longer loved her and would not wish to have a baby with her.

Regret crushed his chest in a vise. He *had* spent more time at work during that final year of his marriage. His father's latest divorce settlement had forced him to borrow against the estate, and that meant finding new sources of revenue to cover the debt. Franco had not explained that to Lisette which meant if he were to believe her story, he would have to accept part of the blame for the loss of his child. And that was a burden he could not bear.

Much better to remember that Lisette, like his mother, had been selfish. She'd made a decision she had no right to make without his input, and then she'd tried to place the blame on a scapegoat—him. And of course, there had been more to her story, as he'd discovered the day the hospital released her and his replacement had arrived to carry her to her new home.

He slammed the front door. Stacy Reeves was no different from any other woman. He simply hadn't figured out her strategy yet. But he would. In the meantime, he would make use of her beautiful body and then send her back to her hotel each night until he had his fill of her. And he would sleep alone—as he always did.

"Ohmigod, is that Prince William?" Amelia asked in a hushed voice on Saturday night.

Stacy followed Amelia's wide-eyed gaze over the glittering guests gathered in La Salle Des Etoiles in the Monte Carlo Sporting Club to the tall blond with an aristocratic nose. Stacy had never been a royal watcher. She probably wouldn't recognize a prince if he walked up and shook her hand, but that didn't dilute the excitement of being in the room with the kind of people who graced the pages of the magazines in her former employer's waiting room.

"It could be. Franco said there would be royalty here." In the minutes since they'd climbed from the limo and made their way inside Stacy had spotted at least a dozen American movie stars, two rock idols and a late-night talk-show host. She was so far out of her element it wasn't even funny.

"You want to tell me how you scored tickets for *Le Bal de L'Eté?*" asked Candace, looking stunning in a platinum satin dress. Vincent hadn't been able to get away from the job site to join them, but Candace had handled her disappointment well. "Vincent said they're almost impossible to get unless you're famous or one of the super-rich upper class."

Stacy glanced at her suitemates, each wearing an evening gown Franco had purchased. He'd given Stacy the name of an elite shop on Avenue des Beaux Arts and told her the proprietress would take care of them. "You'll have to ask Franco."

Amelia fidgeted beside her in pale-yellow tulle. "So is it getting serious between you two? Because from where I stand he's looking a lot like Prince Charming and the Fairy Godfather rolled into one very attractive package."

Stacy stroked her hand over the delicate floral beading on her turquoise dress and searched for an answer that wouldn't shock her friends. Telling them the driver had picked her up Monday, Tuesday and Wednesday evenings and delivered her to Franco's villa for sex and dinner probably wasn't the best response. Just thinking about those nights made her tingle.

But Franco had been out of town since Thursday

morning, and her body, which had happily gone without sex for so many years, was having withdrawals. *And withdrawal is all it is,* she assured herself. Just because he'd shown her facets of her sexuality that she'd never known existed didn't mean she was developing an emotional attachment to him. She hadn't missed him or anything mushy like that. Besides, his absence had allowed her to spend time with her suitemates.

She was actually beginning to feel like one of the group instead of an outsider. The bonds of friendship were forming, and tonight while they'd fussed over each other's clothes, hair and makeup in preparation for the ball she'd had a hint of what it might have been like to have sisters. But she wasn't comfortable enough yet to tell her suitemates the unvarnished truth. "Not serious, no. I'm just having a holiday romance as Madeline suggested."

"Are you sure it's not more than that?" Candace asked. "You certainly jumped on that gown the moment the shop owner told you Franco had suggested she help you choose something the color of your eyes."

Heat rushed to Stacy's cheeks. So she wanted to look attractive for him. What was wrong with that? She was beginning to realize he wasn't an arrogant ass even though he did a good imitation of one quite often by pulling away immediately after making love—having sex. But if he were truly a jerk he never would have had her watch repaired or treated her friends to this Cinderella evening. He'd shown his generosity in a dozen other ways outside of bed, like the museum and theater tickets that had been delivered to their suite Thursday morning, the basket of chocolates yesterday and the flowers today. He was showering her with gifts her friends could share—gifts she couldn't refuse without depriving her suitemates.

She shrugged. "He's paying for my gown. He ought to have some say about it."

"Uh-huh," Madeline said, her disbelief clear. She'd chosen a drop-dead-sexy black dress guaranteed to make heads turn, but Madeline seemed to be searching for someone in particular and was unaware of the attention her dress garnered. "Don't get your heart involved, Stace. Remember, we go home in two weeks."

Stacy nodded. How could she forget that in a matter of days she'd either leave Franco and the most sensual period of her life behind or discover she'd repeated her mother's mistake? The first filled her with regret, the second with stomach-twisting apprehension. She forced a smile. "Don't worry about me."

She scanned the crowd searching for Franco. He was supposed to meet them here tonight, but they were a little late arriving. Her gaze collided with his across the room and her stomach took a nose-dive to her sandals. He turned and spoke to the group he was with and then headed in her direction. Her pulse skipped erratically and her mouth dried.

He looked amazing in a tuxedo. Rich. Powerful. Sexier than any man in the room. And hers. For now. The thought filled her with pride…and doubts. Why her when, judging by the heads turning in his wake, he could have any of these more sophisticated women?

Desire flared in his eyes as he climbed the shallow stairs. His gaze lingered on her décolletage before gliding to her toes and back to her face, and then he took her hand in his and bent to brush his lips over her knuckles. He straightened and looked into her eyes. *"Tu es magnifique, mon gardénia."*

Before she could find her voice he turned toward her companions and bowed slightly without releasing her hand. "*Bonsoir,* mesdemoiselles. *Vous êtes très belle ce soir.* As before, the limo is at your disposal. You will forgive me if I steal Stacy for a dance."

He didn't wait for a reply, but tucked her hand in his arm and led her away. Stacy glanced over her shoulder at the women who offered her a trio of grins and thumbs-up.

On the dance floor Franco pulled her into his arms, leaving her with the sensation of being swept off her feet and into another world—a world in which she wasn't a lonely, staid and unemployed accountant. For a few moments she could pretend to be one of the beautiful, glamorous people who attended exclusive balls, traveled by limousine, rubbed elbows with royalty and captivated a millionaire.

But this wasn't real. She had to remember that.

She laced her fingers at Franco's nape, relishing his slight shudder when she inadvertently teased the sensitive skin with her nails. Each night he'd taught her something new about giving pleasure as well as receiving it. She loved knowing she had the power to make him tremble with desire, but the downside of learning her strength was that her fear of letting anyone get too close faded more with each intimate encounter. Keeping her walls strong wasn't as easy as before—especially when his touch made her feel so alive.

The muscular length of his thighs and torso brushed hers as he swayed to the music. He nuzzled her temple and inhaled deeply, his chest rising to tease her breasts through the thin fabric of her gown. "*J'ai manqué ton parfum.*"

She tilted her head back and studied him through her lashes. His passion-darkened eyes cut short any attempt at translating his words. Her skin prickled with awareness and desire smoldered within her. Only inches separated their mouths and the urge to rise on her toes and kiss him tugged at her, but this was his turf, not hers. She didn't know the rules here and until now had never been tempted to make a public display.

"What did you say?"

His lips thinned, as if he regretted speaking. Finally he said, "I have missed your scent."

Her heart stalled and her breath caught. "Me too—yours."

A muscle in his jaw bunched. His fingers flexed against her hips, urging her closer to his thickening arousal. A corresponding heat pooled low in her abdomen. "We must stay until Vincent arrives and then we go. I want you naked and hungry for me."

She gasped and jerked in surprise, but Franco held her close. "Vincent's coming? I should tell Candace. She'll be thrilled."

"It is a surprise. He should be here any moment." He tucked her head beneath his chin. "I must go to Avignon tomorrow. You will accompany me."

She wanted to see where Franco had grown up, but at the same time, her duty to Candace came first. "I don't know if I can, Franco."

"I have paperwork I must peruse. It cannot wait and neither can I." He smoothed a hand over her bottom. The song ended, but he made no effort to release her or leave the dance floor.

Stacy's pulse drummed in the silence. She glanced to where she'd left her suitemates, but they weren't there. "I'll have to check with Candace."

"I have already discussed it with Vincent. He has not seen his fiancée for a month, and he assures me he will not let her leave his bed for the next few days." A flame burned in his eyes. He tightened his arms and melded his hips to hers as the orchestra began another song. "I understand his needs."

She swallowed the lump rising in her throat. Franco wanted her and he made no attempt to hide his desire. What would it be like to have that forever?

Stop it. This isn't about forever—especially not with a man like him.

She tried to pull back, mentally, physically, but the steel band of Franco's arms held her captive. His hands and body subtly rubbed and nudged hers. The rich and famous faces around her blurred as she focused on the man who seduced her at every turn. Moisture gathered in her mouth and much lower. Dancing with him was like foreplay. Her arousal grew so intense she was tempted to find a coat closet and drag him inside. Her face burned and she buried her nose against his neck. How had he turned her from a sexually reticent woman into one who craved his touch so badly she was considering public indecency?

What seemed like eons later Franco said, "Vincent is here. Come."

She glanced toward the entrance and saw a handsome man with brown hair. He resembled the man in the photos she'd seen, and yet Franco led her in the opposite direction. That wasn't Vincent? But then the man in question turned his head to scan the room and Stacy saw the tight, burned skin on the right side of his face. Definitely Vincent. She caught her breath in sympathy. She couldn't imagine the pain he'd endured. Candace had told her about the series of surgeries he'd already undergone and those yet to come.

Franco shot her a hard look and his grip on her hand tightened. "His scars repel you?"

"Of course not. Besides, I knew what to expect.

Candace showed me a picture. She's very protective of him." And from the hard and cool tone of Franco's voice and the warning glint in his eyes, it seemed as if he might be as well. Loyalty to his friends was yet another interesting facet of Franco's personality, but reading him was like trying to decipher a foreign language. There were bits she couldn't understand. "Where are we going?"

"To retrieve his fiancée." They reached a group of women gathered on the far side of the room. "*Excusez-moi, mesdemoiselles.* I must borrow Candace."

Candace frowned. "Is something wrong?"

"*Non.* There is someone you need to see."

Candace noted Stacy's hand held tightly in Franco's and a smile curved her lips. "Having a good night?"

Stacy's face and neck warmed. "Yes."

"And it is about to get better," Franco muttered for Stacy's ears only, sending a flash fire through her.

He led them toward the entrance and stopped at the bottom of the stairs where Vincent waited with love in his eyes so intense Stacy's heart stuttered.

Candace spotted him, squealed and launched herself into his arms. Given Stacy's already erotic thoughts, witnessing their passionate kiss made her squirm and glance at Franco. His thumb stroked over the inside of her wrist and his eyes promised *soon.* Her pulse tripped.

The couple drew apart, hugged and parted again with blinding smiles. And then Vincent turned to Franco. The men embraced and exchanged a few words too quiet for Stacy to overhear in the noisy ballroom. The genuine affection between them surprised Stacy. To date, Franco had seemed somewhat aloof except when in seduction mode.

When they parted, Candace dragged Stacy forward. "Stacy, this is Vincent. Vincent, Stacy."

Vincent extended his hand. Ignoring the scars, Stacy shook it. From Candace she knew he'd come a long way in his recovery, but other people's squeamishness sometimes bothered him. "It's good to meet you, Stacy."

"You too, Vincent. And thank you for this once-in-a-lifetime vacation."

"You're welcome. Anything that keeps Candace from overdoing it with the wedding plans works for me." Vincent encircled Candace's waist and spread his left hand possessively over her still flat belly. The couple exchanged another intimate, love-laden glance.

What would it be like to have a man look at her that way?

The rogue thought staggered Stacy. Suddenly it hit her that she would never experience the bond that Candace and Vincent shared. Until now that hadn't concerned her. In fact, being alone and safe was a path she'd deliberately chosen, but now the solitary life she'd planned yawned ahead like a barren stretch of desert road.

Because of her bargain with Franco she'd soon have a home. But it would be empty.

She'd never fall in love.

Never experience the hope, joy and anticipation of having a child with someone she loved—all of the emotions written clearly on Candace's face.

Stacy would live alone. Die alone. And the world would be no different because of her time in it.

Sadness settled over her like a cold, wet blanket. Every lesson she'd learned to this point had made her afraid to let anyone get too close. But she'd found the courage to make friends. Could she also find the courage to allow a man into her life and into her heart?

Not a powerbroker like Franco. But maybe someone tamer. Someone less wealthy. Someone she could trust. If such a man even existed.

Eight

Stacy had shared intimacies with Franco that made her blush, and yet she still knew very little about him beyond the physical. She hoped a night in his family home would fill in a few of the blanks.

"Do you always buy your women?" she asked to fill the silence during the hours-long Sunday-afternoon car ride to Avignon.

Franco's jaw hardened and he shot her a chilly glance. "I have never offered a woman money for sex before you."

If that was supposed to make her feel special, it failed. "Good, because it seems a little like…prostitution."

"It is supply and demand. You have something I want and I am willing to pay your price. Relationships always come at a price, Stacy. If you do not believe that then you are deceiving yourself. I prefer to have the terms stated up front rather than be unpleasantly surprised in the end."

Would anyone willingly enter a relationship if they knew the costs going in? Stacy's fling with the high-school jock had cost her her self-respect, and her short-lived involvement with a coworker had diminished her confidence. But her mother had paid the ultimate price for loving the wrong man.

Stacy pushed the memories away and studied Franco's profile, the way he brushed his thick dark hair away from his brow, his straight nose, his sensuous lips and square chin. Beard stubble already shadowed the line of his jaw even though it was barely two in the afternoon. "As an accountant I often see the effects of costly divorce settlements. Is that what happened in your case?"

Seconds passed as Franco exited off the autoroute and onto a narrower road. She wondered if he'd avoid answering personal questions the way he usually did. She'd given up on getting an answer when he said, "Money was not the issue. My wife had an abortion. I did not know she was pregnant or that she did not want children."

No wonder he was bitter. "I'm sorry. Did you want a large family?"

"It was assumed I would provide heirs."

"You still could."

"I will not marry again."

She felt a quick stab of…something. Regret? Of course not. It didn't matter to her if Franco didn't want another wife. What he did once she left Monaco was none of her business. And she wanted it that way.

A few minutes later he turned down a long, straight tree-lined driveway. When they reached the clearing at the end of the drive Stacy mouthed a silent, "Wow."

The white stone structure with its round twin towers flanking opposite corners looked like something from a fairy tale. Flags bearing coats of arms fluttered from the conical spires. It looked familiar and then she placed it as the building in the background of the picture of Franco and Vincent in Franco's study.

"You grew up in a castle?"

"*Un château.* There is no moat, drawbridge or curtain wall."

Castle, chateau, whatever. "No wonder you were able to get tickets to the ball. You're one of them. The aristocracy."

A twinge of envy stirred inside her—not for his wealth, but for the childhood he must have had. "You and your siblings must have loved playing here."

"I am an only child."

"Me too." As a child she'd longed for someone to play with, and as a teen she'd just wanted to belong somewhere and to have someone to confide in. Always being the new kid and an outsider had been difficult.

The cobblestone courtyard circled a round multi-tiered fountain. Wanting to absorb every detail, she barely waited for the car to come to a stop before she shoved open the door and leaped out. Moments later Franco joined her beside the gurgling water. "How long has the chateau been in your family?"

He shrugged. "A few hundred years."

"A few hundred *years?*" Stunned, she faced him. "Do you have any idea how lucky you are?"

"How so?"

Regretting her revealing outburst Stacy bit her lip and stared at the parapets and then panned the acres of emerald lawn. "You've always had a home to go to. A place where you belonged."

"You did not?" he asked quietly.

"No." She turned toward the trunk. "Let's get the luggage. I can't wait to see the inside of the chateau."

He caught her arm in a firm, but not painful grip. "Explain."

She didn't want his pity, but if her past could keep him from taking this spectacular place for granted then what would it hurt to tell him? "My mother left my father when I was eight. After that we never lived in any one city for more than a year."

"They divorced?"

"No. He refused to grant her a divorce, so she ran away."

"Why did she run?" He drew mind-numbingly erotic circles on the inside of her bicep with his thumb.

"According to the diaries I found after she…died, my father was physically abusive. She wrote that she left the first time he struck me. I don't recall being hit, but I do remember my mother sending me to my room whenever my father started yelling. And I remember the fights and arguing and the sound of my mother crying. I remember kissing her boo-boos." The last phrase came out in a strangled whisper as the past descended over her like a dark, oppressive cloud.

He muttered something she suspected was a curse. "Why did she not have him arrested?"

Feeling chilled despite the sunny day and warm temperature, Stacy pulled away and hugged herself. "She tried once, but my father was wealthy and powerful. He had friends in high places and the hospital records of her injuries mysteriously disappeared, so the charges were dropped. In her diary she claims reporting him only made him angry and vindictive."

"You said earlier that your mother had to choose between food and rent. Could she not demand monetary support from your father?"

"No. She wrote that the one time she called for help he threatened to kill her if he ever found her." The memories rose up to choke her and a shudder slithered through her. She'd never confessed the full extent of her past to anyone. She didn't know why she wanted to now except perhaps she wanted Franco to understand why financial security was so important to her. For some reason it was important that he know greed hadn't been the motivating factor in accepting his proposition. "One day he did."

A moment of shocked silence stretched between them. "*Mon dieu.* What happened?"

"I came home from my first class in night school and found my mother and a man I didn't recognize dead in our apartment. The police identified him as my father. He'd found us with the help of a private investigator. The CSI guy said my father shot my mother and then himself."

She squeezed her eyes tight against the memory of red blood pooled on the white kitchen floor and having to walk through it to see if her mother was still alive, and then rib-crushing panic when she realized she wasn't.

Franco yanked Stacy into his arms and hugged her tight enough to squeeze the breath from her lungs. One big hand rubbed briskly up and down her spine. His lips brushed her forehead. She leaned into him, absorbing his strength and accepting comfort in a way she'd never allowed herself before, but then she gathered herself and withdrew, because leaning on him was a habit she couldn't afford. But she instantly missed his embrace.

The empathy in his eyes made hers sting with unshed tears. "So now you know why I accepted your proposition. I want a home. Nothing as grand as this. But a place that's all mine."

"What of your father's estate? If he had wealth, then why did you not inherit?"

A question she'd asked herself countless times

until she'd learned the truth. "He left everything to his alma mater."

"And you did not contest his will or file a wrongful death suit?"

She shifted on her feet and studied the sunlight reflecting off the windows of the chateau. "No. Either would have cost money I didn't have. And I couldn't risk running up years of legal fees and then losing and being in debt."

"Stacy, no court in the States would have denied your right to his estate after what he took from you, and a lawyer would have accepted you as a client with payment contingent upon a settlement."

She dug the toe of her sandal into the gravel drive and debated full disclosure. What did she have to lose? She lifted her gaze to Franco's. "Immediately afterward, I wondered if I could have stopped him if I'd been at home, and I said as much to the police detective. He told me that from the extra bullets in the gun and the photographs of me in my father's rental car, they suspected he had intended to kill me too."

The ultimate betrayal. A parent who wanted her dead.

"By starting school and changing my schedule I wasn't where he thought I'd be." She walked to the back of the car, struggled to regain her emotional footing and waited for Franco to open the trunk.

"After that I didn't want anything from him except answers which he couldn't give me. The executor of the estate let me walk through my father's house before the auction. Mom's makeup table looked like she'd gone out for the day and would return any minute, and all the clothing she'd left behind hung in the closet even though she'd left eleven years before. My room was the same. It was like a shrine to an eight-year-old girl. It creeped me out."

"And you had no one to turn to?"

"No one I trusted." *Trust.* There was that word again. She realized she was beginning to trust Franco and that couldn't be good. He was rich. She hadn't seen signs of him abusing his power or the law, but she'd known him less than two weeks.

"You have accomplished much by moving on instead of letting your past destroy you." The approval in his voice wrapped her in a cocoon of warmth.

"I didn't want my mother's sacrifice to be in vain. She left to protect me."

He stroked his knuckles along her cheekbone. "You have done her proud."

His words were a soothing balm she hadn't known she needed, and the tenderness in his eyes made her yearn for something, but what exactly, she wasn't sure. She stepped closer.

"Franco, Franco, Franco," a childish yell splintered the intimate spell. Stacy flinched and backed away. Close call. She couldn't afford to become dependent on him or his approval.

Franco lowered his hand and turned to the small boy bolting from the chateau. The child raced down the walk and launched himself at Franco who caught him, swung him in the air and then hugged him while the boy talked far too fast for Stacy to translate the words. Franco replied in the same language, his voice low and tender.

Stacy couldn't help but stare. Franco looked relaxed and happy. A wide smile transformed his handsome face into a knee-meltingly gorgeous one. If he ever looked at her that way she'd completely forget about his wealth and all the other reasons why he was the wrong man for her.

Who was the boy? Franco had said he and his wife

hadn't had children and yet the affection between the two was unmistakable. She guessed the child to be about six or seven.

Franco set the child on the ground and ruffled his dark hair. "Stacy, this is Mathé. Mathé, this is Mademoiselle Reeves. Speak English for her, please."

Mathé's small left hand clutched Franco's larger one as he shyly mumbled a hello and quickly shook Stacy's hand. Big brown eyes peeked at her before turning back to Franco with idolization shining in their depths. "Are you staying?"

"*Oui*, for the night. Go tell your *grandmère* we will need two rooms." The boy rushed off.

Stacy's gaze followed him back to the house. "He's cute."

"The housekeeper's grandson. He has lived here with her since his mama ran off with her lover and left him behind three years ago." The bitterness in his voice raised a number of questions.

"He's about the same age your child would have been."

Doors slammed in Franco's expression. Any remnants of his smile vanished. He extracted their suitcases and slammed the trunk. "Do not try to paint me as a hero or a sentimental fool. I am neither."

"Whatever you say. But he's clearly thrilled to see you."

"I spend time with him when I can. He has no father and mine is too old to keep up with him."

"*Entrez-vous?*" An older man called from the open front door. Stacy recognized him from the photo in Franco's study.

"*Oui*, Papa. We are coming." Franco carried the luggage toward the house. Stacy followed. "I have come to look over the documents you had drafted."

"You are staying the night?" Stacy thought he asked.

"Oui."

Her French had improved tremendously in the past two weeks, but Stacy quickly lost track of the heated rapid-fire conversation that followed. Whatever his father said turned Franco's face dark with anger.

Franco turned to her. "It appears my soon-to-be stepmother has decided to redecorate the house. All of the bedrooms except for mine and Papa's have been stripped."

"We could go to a hotel," she suggested.

"Not necessary. Stacy, is it? I am Armand Constantine. Welcome. Come in." He extended his hand. "It is not as if you and Franco are not already sharing a bed. I am old, but I am not old-fashioned or easily shocked."

Embarrassment sent a scalding wash across her skin. "It's nice to meet you, Monsieur Constantine."

She shook his hand and followed him inside. The detailed plasters, gilt-framed artwork and period furniture in the entrance hall screamed history—a history Stacy had never had as her father's house had been built after Stacy's birth. A wide staircase worthy of a romantic Hollywood movie soared upward from the center of the grand hall.

"Franco, show Stacy upstairs and then bring her to the salon for refreshments."

Franco remained motionless for several seconds and then nodded stiffly and climbed the stairs. Stacy followed, her eyes drinking in the original oils on the walls, the beautiful antiques and the endless halls. Finally, Franco shoved open a door and walked into a round room that looked as if it belonged to a teenage boy.

She quickly averted her gaze from the double bed covered in a blue spread. Her pulse skipped erratically at the thought of sharing the narrow mattress with him.

Sleeping with him—something she had yet to do. "Your bedroom's in a tower."

"Oui." The clipped word drew her gaze from the boyish decor to his face.

"I guess your stepmother didn't get to your room yet?"

"My room is off-limits to her as it has been to each of my father's four wives." He dumped their bags on a large wooden trunk beneath one of the five windows punctuating the walls.

"He's been married four times?"

"Five if you count my mother. He likes to fall in love. Unfortunately, he falls out of it rather quickly. But not before each of my stepmothers has her turn at emptying the bank accounts and erasing all traces of the previous Madame Constantine from the chateau."

No wonder he thought every woman had a price. She'd learned more about Franco in the past half hour than she had in the previous two weeks. She'd thought the chateau meant Franco had enjoyed the stability and permanence she'd lacked, but apparently not if he had revolving stepmothers and his home was always being torn apart.

Shelves loaded with sports memorabilia lined the walls. The trophies and ribbons drew her to the side of the room. Bicycle racing. Swimming. Rowing. That explained those wide shoulders and muscular legs. She'd never lived anywhere long enough to join a team, and at one time she'd condemned her mother for that. Stacy had lost count of the times during the past decade she'd wished her bitter words back.

She dragged her fingers along the spines of a series of books on car racing. Franco's cologne teased her nose a second before the heat of him spooned her back and his hands settled at her waist. She leaned into him.

"I took Vincent to the Monte Carlo Grand Prix after our grad-school graduation twelve years ago. He became hooked on fast cars. When he returned to the States he convinced his father to sponsor a NASCAR team."

And last year he'd been badly injured at a race.

Stacy turned. Franco stood so close their hips and thighs meshed and she could see the tiny strain lines radiating from his eyes and lips. "You can't blame yourself for his accident. Candace said it was a freak event. Something about an equipment failure."

He hesitated. "There is a price for each choice we make."

"*Tout a un prix,*" she quoted his earlier words back to him. Everything had a price. Including her.

Would the price for this affair end up being more than she could bear?

Franco needed to get away from Stacy. *Now.*

He had broken a rule and hugged her. How could he not? She might have tried to act unaffected while telling her grisly tale, but the tremor in her voice and the deathly pallor of her face had given her inner angst away. If she was acting, she was the best damned actress he had ever seen.

But if she was telling the truth then not only had her mother walked away from money, but Stacy had as well. She could not possibly be that different from other avaricious members of her sex. Could she? Had she not already hinted that a million dollars would not be enough to give her a life of leisure?

But she plans to go back to work. She did not ask for more.

What was it about her that made him talk? He had revealed things about Lisette and Vincent that he had never shared with anyone. If he did not leave now then there was no telling what she would extract from him.

He put necessary inches between them. "I must read over the documents and spend an hour with Mathé. Can you amuse yourself?"

"Of course," Stacy replied without hesitation.

"If you are genuinely interested in history then you may explore the house. The wives are allowed to change the linens, but not the furniture or the architecture."

Excitement flared in Stacy's eyes. Any of his other lovers would have pouted if he tried to ignore them, and then they would have cajoled or attempted to seduce him into entertaining them. If he had brought his lovers here, that is. And since Lisette, he had not. Stacy would not be here if not for his father's insistence on meeting her. Franco would not put it past the old goat to have stripped the rooms himself to force Franco to share his bedroom and his bed.

"Your father won't mind if I snoop around?"

"*Non.* Papa knows the history of the house and the furnishings. I will see if he can accompany you."

"I don't want to be any trouble." She fussed with a button on her blouse and Franco struggled with a sudden urge to strip the garment from her. He had escorted her from his bed to a taxi less than twelve hours ago, and yet his desire for her had not diminished with exposure. If anything, his craving for her had intensified. Not a positive circumstance. "Your father wasn't expecting me, was he?"

"He asked to meet you."

Her eyes widened. "You told him about me? About us?"

"*Oui.*"

"The whole truth?"

"I do not lie." Her gaze fell and her cheeks darkened.

From embarrassment? Was she ashamed of the bargain they had made? Franco reached out and tucked a stray lock of hair beneath Stacy's ear. "Tonight, we will do something I have never done."

Her pulse quickened beneath his fingertips. "What's that?"

"I have never had a woman in my boyhood bed. Fantasies, *oui*. But flesh? *Non*."

Her gaze darted to the object in question behind him and the tip of her tongue dampened her lips. He could not resist bending down to capture and suckle the soft, pink flesh. Stacy leaned into him, curling her fingers around his belt and rising on her toes. Her breasts pressed his chest with tantalizing softness.

She had come a long way as a lover. In a short time she had become less reticent about her pleasure, but she had yet to initiate any contact. He was on the verge of saying to hell with the documents and tumbling her onto the sheets when she pulled away. Blushing, she ducked her head as if her ardent response embarrassed her. "Go. I'll be fine."

He didn't want to leave her, and for that very reason he escorted her to the salon where his father waited with refreshments, then walked out and locked himself in his father's study.

The documents transferring ownership of the Constantine holdings to Franco, less a lifetime annuity for his father, were straightforward. His father had agreed to sign the papers the day Stacy returned to the States with her million. Franco delayed as long as he possibly could, rereading the document and then playing with Mathé before going in search of Stacy two hours later.

He found her in the nursery, sitting in an old rocking

chair with her head tipped back and her eyes closed. Her slender fingers caressed the worn wooden arms.

His mood lightened at the sight of her. And what nonsense was that? Why did Stacy affect him so strongly? Was it because she did not try to work her wiles on him? Or did she have him completely fooled? Was her air of innocence the bait in her trap?

"Que fais-tu?" he asked, more harshly than he had intended.

She startled and her lids flew open. "I'm imagining what it would be like to rock your baby in the same chair that your mother and grandmother used. It must be comforting to know that generations of ancestors have sat here and had the same hopes and fears for their children. Any child would be fortunate to have roots that deep, Franco."

An image of Stacy rocking with a dark-haired baby at her breast—his baby—filled his mind. He rejected the possibility. No matter how logical her motivations, he'd bought her, and he could not respect a woman he could buy. "I doubt my mother ever rocked me in that chair. She was not the loving type. I had a series of *bonnes d'enfants.*"

"Nannies?"

He nodded.

"My mother was wonderful. We moved a lot and she worked most of the hours in the day, but I always knew she loved me." Stacy rose, hugged herself and walked to the window. The curtains had been removed, leaving the wide casement bare to the evening sun. "She was my best friend even though I wasn't always the best of daughters. I hated moving, and once I hit my teens we argued about it often. But that's because I didn't know why. She always told me my father loved me and wanted to be with me, but that he couldn't."

"She lied."

She abruptly faced him with her head held high, her hands fisted by her side and fire in her eyes. "To protect me, yes."

"My father lied as well, but during a school vacation I researched the newspaper archives and learned the truth about my mama. She was a spoiled party girl always looking for excitement. Shopping. Drugs. Men."

The sympathy softening Stacy's eyes made him regret the confession. Confidences would lead her to expect more from him than he was willing to give. He was a cold bastard—or so he'd been told. Stacy would do best to accept his limitations and his money and move on.

"I'm sorry. I assumed living in a wonderful place like this meant you'd automatically have a happy childhood."

"I was not unhappy." And why was he sharing that? Because he did not want her pity.

"Are you and your father close?"

"When he is not enthralled with his latest paramour, *oui*. We used to go to the races together." She was getting too personal. He had to derail this tête-à-tête.

Franco approached her, pinning her in the window by planting a hand on either side of her. He leaned closer, inhaling her unique scent and aligning his hips with hers. Desire thickened his blood. "I have not made love in this room either and we have an hour before dinner."

That he considered sex less personal than conversation was telling, he realized. The understanding he saw in Stacy's eyes took him aback. She saw through his actions, but rather than call him on his evasive tactics, she smiled and cupped his cheek. "I'm all yours."

For two more weeks. Longer would be too dangerous. Stacy had a way of breaching his defenses. He would have to find a way to stop her before he crumbled like castle ruins at her feet.

Nine

Franco's laughter stirred something deep inside Stacy.

She crossed from the luxurious en suite bathroom to one of the tall tower windows of Franco's bedroom and looked outside. Franco and Mathé were kicking a soccer ball around on the lawn below. Franco's teeth flashed in the early-morning light as he laughed again.

He'd be a good father. The kind of father she wished she'd had. And his children would have all the things she'd lacked. History. Roots. Security.

According to Monsieur Constantine, this room hadn't changed in over two decades. Franco could have had something new with each of his stepmothers' re-decorations, but instead he'd stuck with the furnishings he and his father had chosen together. That told Stacy Franco liked stability. And he might even have a tiny sentimental streak. Like her.

She touched a finger to her watch and then smoothed

a hand over the scarred wooden headboard pushed against the wall between two windows. Last night she'd slept spooned with Franco on the narrow mattress. This morning she'd awoken alone, but surprisingly well-rested. Letting her guard down enough to sleep had apparently not been an issue after all. But then again, he had exhausted her before letting her sleep. Warmth rose under her skin and settled in her pelvis. The man seemed determined to make up to her for the mediocre lovers of her past.

"You are exactly what Franco needs, my dear," Monsieur Constantine said in heavily accented English behind her.

Startled, Stacy turned and found him in the open bedroom doorway. Hadn't Franco said he'd told his father the whole truth? "How can you believe that?"

The older man shrugged. "I am sure you had your reasons for agreeing to accept money in exchange for spending time with my son. But you are not like any…how you say?…gold diggers I have ever encountered. I have met many in my seventy-five years, and I have even had the misfortune to marry a few. Between my wives and Lisette, my son has become quite bitter and distrustful of women."

Stacy nodded. "He told me about Lisette."

Bushy white eyebrows rose. "That is surprising. Did he also tell you that he continued to love her until she admitted she had married him for his money, and that she had the abortion because she was planning to divorce him?"

Poor Franco. "Um…no."

"My divorce settlements put us in financial difficulties. Difficulties over which Franco eventually triumphed, but his wife did not have the integrity to lessen her expenses and stand beside him through adversity. When one truly loves one takes the good with the bad…as I did with Franco's mama."

He joined her by the window and looked down on Franco and Mathé. "He will not tell me what Lisette said to him in that Paris hospital, but it changed him. He is not the son I once knew. He keeps much locked inside now."

The weight of his gaze settled on Stacy. "My boy has a wounded soul. It will take a special woman to heal him."

What exactly was he implying? "Why are you telling me this, Monsieur Constantine? I'm not that woman."

"I believe you are."

A choked sound of disbelief erupted from her mouth. "I'm sleeping with your son for money."

"And the agreement troubles you, yes?"

"Of course."

"And that is but one of the reasons I know you are not like the others."

Keeping up with the bizarre discussion was beyond her. He might as well be speaking a foreign language. "One of the reasons?"

"*Oui*. If you cared only for financial gain you would be garbed in jewels and designer clothing instead of your inexpensive American pieces. Franco is a generous lover. Except in matters of the heart."

True. But his loyalty to Vincent and Mathé came from the heart, so he wasn't incapable of caring. "Dare I ask if there are more reasons?"

The older man smiled. "Only the most important one. When I gave you the tour of the chateau yesterday you asked many, many questions about the history of the house and furnishings. You never once asked the value of a single item."

No, she hadn't. She'd been more concerned with the

sentimental significance than the monetary worth. "I guess I never thought about the costs."

"*Exactement.* For a woman who claims to be motivated by money, it seems to have little importance to you."

Other than the security it represented, he was right. She didn't want to be rich. She just wanted a home. Otherwise, she would have sued her father's estate as Franco had suggested. Heaven knows the lawyers had aggressively solicited her and encouraged her to do so before she'd fled Tampa and started over in Charlotte. But she hadn't wanted to be tied to blood money. She'd rather be poor than feel guilty for profiting from her mother's murder. "Okay, you have me there, but I'm still not the right woman for Franco."

"We shall see, Stacy. I am hoping my son will see what a treasure you are before it is too late." He offered his arm in the same courtly gesture Franco often used. "Now come, breakfast waits and you should eat before you make the drive back to Monaco."

"And once every inch of your ivory skin is slick with the sun-warmed tanning oil I will thrust deep into your body again and again until you cry out as *le petit mort* overcomes you," Franco resumed his tantalizing tale after they crossed Monaco's border and turned toward the harbor.

Stacy's heart raced. She licked her dry lips and squirmed in her seat, attempting to alleviate the ache between her legs.

Franco had filled the past half-hour of their trip with a lengthy, detailed description of the sensual afternoon he had planned for them on his sailboat. His verbal seduction was a timely reminder that their relationship was all about sex. Only sex. Any emotional connection she might feel with him after the personal insights she'd gained into his character at the chateau had no place in the bargain they'd struck.

His fingertips trailed up the inside of her thigh. "And I will not stop until—"

An annoying sound interrupted him and dampened her arousal. A cell phone. Hers. Stacy blinked, exhaled and dug her phone out of her purse. "Hello?"

"Candace is having a meltdown," Amelia's voice said. "Madeline and I have tried everything we know to calm her down. It's your turn."

"What do you mean?"

"She's freaking out and talking about cancelling the wedding. We can't figure out why. You have to try. Tell her how much money she'd be wasting or something. Not that money would matter if she was really unhappy, but she's absolutely crazy in love with Vincent. We can't let a flash of panic ruin that. Please, Stacy, just get over here convince her to sit tight until rational thought returns."

Alarmed, Stacy glanced at Franco. "I can be there in fifteen minutes."

She disconnected and turned in her seat. "I'll have to take a rain check on the boat ride. That was Amelia. She wants me at the hotel."

"Something is wrong?"

"Um…Candace needs me." Because he was Vincent's friend she couldn't tell him why. But she wanted to. She wanted to ask him how someone as deeply in love as Candace could have doubts.

"And what of our plans?"

Stacy had never been on a boat, but that wasn't the appeal. She wanted to spend more time with Franco, wanted to learn more about him. She'd planned to ask questions during the car ride home, but his verbal seduction had waylaid that. Had he done it deliberately?

"Franco, I would love to spend the afternoon with you. And making love on the boat sounds amazingly sexy even though I'm not sure about doing it outdoors on the deck where we might be seen by anybody with a good set of binoculars. But when Candace needs me I have to go, and you promised our relationship wouldn't interfere with the wedding stuff."

His jaw hardened. "Vincent assured me your presence would not be required for several days."

She should have tried harder to check with Candace before leaving for Avignon, but the bride-to-be hadn't been in the hotel suite Sunday morning or answering her cell phone. In the end, Stacy had let her curiosity about Franco lead the way. "Vincent was wrong."

Franco turned the car away from the marina and toward the hotel. Moments later he stopped the vehicle outside the entrance. A doorman opened her door and helped her alight. She thanked him and joined Franco by the trunk.

She reached for her bag, but Franco held it out of reach. "I will see you inside."

Not a good idea since she had no idea what she'd be walking into. "No need. I'll…um, call you later."

He looked ready to argue, but instead he relinquished her suitcase and stroked her cheek. The passion simmering in his intensely blue eyes snarled a tight knot of desire beneath Stacy's navel. "Dinner tonight. I will send the car."

"I'll have to clear it with Candace first."

He nodded. "I will let you go, but first—"

Heedless of the hotel staff members and vacationers around them, he took her mouth. Hard. Hot. Intimately.

His tongue delved, stroked and then he suckled hers. By the time he lifted his head Stacy clung dizzily to his belt. "Do not keep me waiting one moment longer than necessary, *mon gardénia.*"

He stroked a thumb over her damp bottom lip and then left her standing in the driveway on trembling legs, torn between desire and friendship. She wanted to go with Franco, but Candace needed her.

Stacy shook off her indecision. Her friendship with Candace would continue beyond the next two weeks, but her relationship with Franco would not. And she'd better not forget it. Passion and profit were all she could expect from him. No promises, he'd said. And that wouldn't change no matter how well she understood him.

She marched inside and across the lobby. The elevator whisked her to the top floor. Stacy shoved her keycard into the lock and entered the suite in time to hear Candace ranting, "I can't believe he expected me to drop everything and spend three days in his bed."

Amelia spotted Stacy, grabbed her by the arm and dragged her into the sitting area. "Good. You're here. Tell her how crazy it would be to cancel the wedding at this late date."

Stacy let her purse and overnight bag slide to the floor. "What's wrong?"

Candace pivoted. A white line of tension circled her compressed lips. "I can't marry Vincent."

Stacy blinked. "Why?"

"Why does everybody keep asking me that?" Candace glared at them and then paced in front of the long window. "Can't you just accept I made a mistake and leave it at that?"

"No," Amelia and Madeline chorused.

"Don't you love him?" Stacy persisted.

"I wouldn't be here if I didn't."

And the love in Vincent's eyes at the ball had been impossible to miss. "Did something happen to make you no longer trust him? Did he scare you? Threaten you? Hurt you?"

"No." She sounded surprised Stacy would even suggest it, but then she didn't know Stacy's past. One day, Stacy realized, she'd have to tell her. But not today.

"Then I don't understand why you'd throw this all away. Do his scars suddenly repulse you?"

Anger flushed Candace's pale cheeks. "No. They. Do. Not."

"Then why can't you marry him? You love him and he clearly adores you."

"It's like you said. He's rich and powerful and I'm…not. I don't fit into his world. The balls, the limos, the designer gowns, they're not me."

"They're not any of us, but we've had fun faking it," Amelia said.

Stacy recalled Monsieur Constantine's words about Franco's ex. "Candace, would you still want to be with Vincent if he lost all his money?"

"Of course I would. I don't know what you're getting at, Stacy, but I am not marrying Vincent for his millions. I thought you knew me better than that."

"My point is, doesn't he deserve a woman who'll love him for who he is as a person and not for the penthouse lifestyle he represents? And doesn't the fact that you don't care about the scars or the superficial trappings and that you could live without the limos and designer clothes make you the perfect woman for him?"

And didn't Franco deserve the same thing? His father was right. It would take a special woman to appreciate the man beneath the glitz. Someone who didn't assign dollar signs to everything or mind slowly chipping away at his hard shell to discover his secrets.

Someone like you.

Stacy gasped in surprise as the thought sprouted and took root. It would be so easy to convince herself she was the woman who could heal Franco's embittered soul. But that would be foolish. Besides, he wouldn't be interested in a nobody like her when he had a continent full of glamorous, sophisticated women to choose from. And she…well, she couldn't risk it.

"Yes. No. I don't know." Candace sank onto the sofa and buried her face in her trembling hands.

Madeline sat beside her and passed her a tissue. "You have been happier this year than I've ever seen you. Do you really want to throw that away because of bridal jitters?"

"What I want doesn't matter." Candace blotted her tear-stained face. "Vincent's parents are arriving tonight. He wants to tell them about the baby, and once they find out they're going to think I trapped their precious son with a pregnancy to get my claws on their fortune."

Tension seeped from Stacy's muscles upon hearing the true reason for the panic attack. This was a salvageable situation. She glanced at her suitemates, but neither Amelia nor Madeline looked surprised about the baby news. Hmm. Maybe the baby wasn't a secret after all.

Stacy sat on Candace's opposite side and tentatively laid a hand over her clenched fist. "You're afraid to tell your future in-laws you're pregnant?"

"They're Boca Raton and I'm trailer trash. They're not going to want somebody like me raising their grandchild."

Stacy understood the feeling of not fitting in all too well, but running had never made it better. "Number one, Candace, you're not trailer trash. You're a registered nurse. Number two, I suspect the Reynards are going to want someone raising their grandchild whose love will stay strong through the good times and the bad."

"That would be you," Amelia said.

Stacy nodded. "Don't forget what you've already been through with Vincent. I'm sure they haven't."

After a moment Candace's lips curved into a quivery smile. She looked at each of them in turn and then took a shoulder-straightening breath and lifted her chin. "You're right. I am the perfect woman for Vincent, and if the Reynards don't agree, well…I'll just prove them wrong."

"We've got your back," Madeline vowed.

Stacy wished she had half as much confidence as her friend in matters of the heart. But she didn't. She was an emotional coward and probably always would be.

"Don't ever fall in love, man," Vincent groaned into his beer.

"That is not what you have been telling me for the past six months," Franco replied as he sat on the opposite end of the sofa from Vincent and pressed the remote control to his plasma television. He tuned his satellite dish into an American sports channel. "You have been singing the praises of a woman to warm your bed."

Vincent wore a besotted expression similar to the one Franco had seen on his father far too often—one Franco swore never to wear again. Lisette had cured him.

"It's more than regular sex. It's waking up beside her and watching her sleep. Or knowing she loves you enough to let you see her without her makeup on or to kiss her before she brushes her teeth."

The back of Franco's neck prickled. He shifted his shoulders to ease the uncomfortable sensation. He had watched Stacy sleep this morning at the chateau, but that had nothing to do with love. It had been lust. Nothing more. And the kiss on her brow had been an attempt to wake her and satisfy his hunger. If in the end he had elected to take a cold shower and let her sleep, it was only because he had driven her to orgasm so many times last night that he doubted her capable of coming again so soon, and he never left a woman unsatisfied in bed.

"Fifty bucks says the Marlins whip Boston," Vincent said, drawing Franco's attention back to the baseball game. "Women aren't logical. And they're full of contradictions."

"I agree, and I accept your bet." He had finally found Stacy's weakness. She could be bought but only if the gifts benefitted her friends. Such altruism had to be a pretense.

"Women are like a jigsaw puzzle with missing pieces. Frustrating. Unsolvable. And I ought to know. I must have put a hundred puzzles together during my hospital stay."

"You will get no argument from me." Each secret he uncovered about Stacy suggested she was not like the other women of his acquaintance, which only meant he needed a more complete picture to uncover her strategy. He glanced at his watch. When would she call?

Vincent had phoned immediately after Franco had left Stacy at the hotel ninety minutes ago. Watching baseball with his friend was not the sexually satisfying afternoon Franco had planned, but he could not concentrate on work, and he had been a Red Sox fan since his days at MIT.

Vincent's expression turned to one of bewilderment. "When I told you I'd keep Candace busy I honestly thought she and I would spend every spare minute of the next three days making up for four weeks' abstinence. But this morning I mentioned my parents were flying in today and that I wanted to tell them about the baby, and she freaked."

"Due to your parents' arrival or to revealing the pregnancy?"

"Don't know. That's the illogical part. Candace and my parents get along, and in another month or two she'll be showing. No point in trying to hide it. Besides, I don't want to. I spent years avoiding getting a girl pregnant, but the minute I found out Candace was carrying my baby I wanted the world to know. Candace is the one who insisted we keep a lid on it. Besides, my folks will be thrilled to finally have a grandkid on the way since my sister isn't anteing up."

Franco's father was impatient as well. Impatient enough to force Franco's hand. Franco's mind flashed back to the image of Stacy in the nursery rocking chair, her wistful expression before she'd known he was watching and the sadness in her eyes when she'd talked about her mother.

Stacy's life had been tragically difficult, but it had not broken her. He had to respect her strength even though he disliked her willingness to sell herself for financial security. How hypocritical of him, since he benefited from her mercenary streak.

Vincent swore as a Sox batter hit a grand slam. "If they keep this up I'll owe you for more than the tickets to the ball and that killer dress you bought for Candace."

"There is no need to repay me."

"Bull. You and Toby are babysitting these women at my request. I'll cover all the costs, and I'll grant you a year's lease on a Midas Chocolates location in the galleria of the Aruba hotel." He popped a handful of nuts in his mouth and washed them down with a sip of beer.

"The hell of it is, Franco, that when I was stuck in

labor negotiations, Candace is all I thought about. And I got pissed—not because the union rep was being a prick, but because he was keeping me away from Candace. It's hard to care about dollars and cents when I'm scared as hell that I'm going to blow it with her. She's the best thing that's ever happened to me, and if having my lady-killer mug back meant never having met her, I'd rather keep the face that frightens children."

Surprised by the emotional speech from a man previously not given to sentiment, Franco drained his beer. Stacy had invaded his concentration at work as well this past two weeks. No woman had ever done so—not even Lisette. The only positive in the situation was that his preoccupation would end as soon as she boarded the plane bound for the States. "The scars are less noticeable with each surgery and graft."

"Yeah, but unlike you, I won't win any beauty contests."

The doorbell rang, wiping the smile from Franco's lips. He was not expecting anyone. Normally, he would be at work on a Monday afternoon. *Stacy?* No, she would call and his cell phone had not rung. He had checked twice to make sure it was turned on. "Excuse me."

He crossed the entrance hall and opened the door. Stacy stood on the porch looking as delicious as a juicy peach. A wide-brimmed straw hat covered her chestnut hair and a pale-orange sundress outlined her curves. Her bare legs looked magnificent despite the bulky walking sandals she insisted on wearing.

The breath stalled in his lungs, but his heart raced. He caught a glimpse of a taxi's taillights turning out of the drive.

A tentative smile wobbled on her lips. She removed her sunglasses, revealing her azure eyes. "Is it too late to go boating?"

"Vincent is here." He found her fading smile and obvious disappointment surprisingly gratifying since it mirrored his own. He used his thumb to free her bottom lip from her teeth. "Come in."

"I don't want to intrude. I'll just call a cab." She reached for her cell phone, but he caught her hand.

"Non. Stay." He dragged his knuckles along her arm. She shivered, reminding him of last night, of tasting every inch of her delectable skin until she whimpered and squirmed. "You may sunbathe by the pool. I will drench your body in suntan oil, and when the game ends I will send Vincent in search of Candace and we will have the sybaritic afternoon we anticipated, but on dry land. My patio is private. No one will see or hear when I make you cry out in ecstasy."

Her breath hitched and her nipples pushed against her dress. "Okay."

He motioned for her to precede him. Stacy crossed the foyer and entered the den. Franco noted that she avoided stepping on the rugs. He filed the odd fact away for later.

Snapping his cell phone closed, Vincent rose. "Hi, Stacy. Rain check on the game, Franco. Candace called. I have to go."

Vincent shook his head when Franco smirked. "You're laughing now, but one of these days a woman will have you dancing to her tune."

"That will not happen, *mon ami.*"

"Just wait, bud. Your day will come. I'll see myself out." A moment later the front door closed behind Vincent. The engine of his Ferrari roared and then faded in the distance.

Franco turned to Stacy. "Remove your clothing."

She gasped and clutched her bag tighter. "Here? Now?"

"Oui." He tugged his shirt over his head and pitched

it onto the sofa. He retrieved the condom from his wallet before dropping his trousers and briefs and kicking off his shoes and removing his socks. Stacy watched wide-eyed and then licked her lips as she stared at his growing erection. The slow glide of her tongue over her rosy flesh made him pulse with need.

She turned her back. Franco swept her silky hair aside, unzipped her dress, flicked open her bra and shoved both to the floor. He dragged her panties down to her ankles, pulled her back to his front and cupped her breasts. For several seconds he fought the urgency to be inside her and simply savored the feel of her warm, soft skin against his and the weight of her breasts in his palms. He inhaled her scent and his control wavered. He stepped away. "Come."

He led her outside, dropped the condom on the table and then arranged the double-width lounger to his liking. He took the straw tote which she held in front of her like a shield and set it on the tiles. Despite Stacy's apparent shyness, her nipples were erect and desire flushed her face and neck.

"Lie face down."

She crawled onto the chaise, presenting him with her delectable bottom. He fisted his hands against his rampant hunger.

"You have suntan oil?" His voice came out an octave lower than usual.

"I have lotion in my bag."

"*Pas le même chose.* Not the same. I will return momentarily, and then, *mon gardénia,* I will make you moan."

An all-over tan had never been one of Stacy's goals. She didn't even have the courage to try on one of the thong bikinis so prevalent on the beaches here. And forget going topless.

She could not believe she was naked on Franco's patio. Glancing left and right, she verified that this spot was indeed private, thanks to the vine-covered trellises at each end of the house. The sun warmed parts of her it had never seen before. And then Franco returned, striding boldly, *nudely,* in her direction. He had a pair of towels tucked under his arm, a bottle of suntan oil in one hand and one of water in the other.

Her heart pounded faster. She dampened her dry lips. If anyone had ever told her a month ago that she could become a hedonistic creature she'd have called them delusional.

"Close your eyes," he said as he dropped the items he carried beside her on the chaise and straddled her legs. Stacy did so, admitting she'd probably brought this on herself by telling him his masseuse had not turned her on. What Franco had done after the masseuse left, on the other hand…. The memory sent a delicious tingle through her. Suffice to say she would never view the long wooden benches of a sauna in the same way again. If she ever saw the inside of another sauna.

Warm oil trickled over her shoulders and back, quickly followed by Franco's firm hands. The scent of coconuts filled her nostrils as he massaged her with long, slow strokes across her shoulders and down her spine. His fingertips teased the sides of her breasts, her waist. The occasional drag of his sex against her buttocks made her breath catch. He paused, shifted and then oil dribbled onto the small of her back and over her bottom. It seeped into the crevice and between her legs to her most sensitive spot. She squirmed on the chaise.

Franco's hands stilled her hips. *"Non."*

He alternated feather-light brushes with muscle-deep massages over her back, her bottom, down her legs and across the soles of her feet. Throughout the process the wiry hairs on his legs teased her hyper-sensitive skin. And then he stroked his erection between her slickened cheeks. Stacy yearned to rise to her knees and let him take her from behind as he had once before, but he moved away. The memory of that night in front of his bedroom mirror, the way he'd cupped her breasts and nibbled her neck, the undiluted hunger on his face as he'd plunged into her again and again made her shiver.

"Attente elle," he ordered in a gravelly voice.

Wait for it. One of his favorite phrases. But Stacy didn't want to wait. She wiggled impatiently, but Franco didn't quicken his torturous caresses. Arousal pulsed through her. She no longer cared about prying eyes, but focused instead on the man who seemed bent on driving her out of her mind with desire. He rose from the chaise and she tensed in anticipation.

"Turn over."

Stacy hastily complied. Franco's shaft glistened with suntan oil. She reached for him, but he shook his head and pulled the brim of her hat over her face. "No peeking."

She settled back into the cushion. Oil trickled over her breasts and slowly ran down her sides like tiny, warm fingers. He poured another pool in her navel and then drizzled more over her curls. His palms covered her breasts and she gasped. He teased and tweaked, rolling the slick tips between his fingers and buffing with the flats of his palms. She shifted her legs, but that only intensified the ache. His massage continued down her torso and her legs, skipping her neediest parts.

Stacy was ready to beg when Franco bent her knees, knelt between them and stroked his shaft along her soft, slick folds and against her center. A moan slipped from her lips as she rose swiftly toward the peak. She heard a snick of sound, and then icy-cold water splashed her nipple. She squealed and tried to rise, but Franco planted a palm on her breastbone and treated the opposite side to the same cold, fizzy bath. The carbonated water teased in an unbelievably sensual way, and then his hot lips covered a cooled tip. He alternated between icy baths and hot suckling until Stacy batted her hat away.

"That was sneaky."

He sat back on his haunches, his grin unrepentant. Two could play that game. She sat up, snatched the water from his hand and drenched his erection. His howl turned into a groan when she took him into her mouth.

Franco fisted his hands in her hair, but he didn't thrust or try to gag her the way her high-school lover had. Franco let her take the lead and as much of him as she could handle. Pleased and surprisingly turned on, she released him and showered him with another splash of water and then another deep kiss. His back arched. He hissed with each splash and muttered what sounded like encouragement in French each time her lips encircled him. She smiled and repeated the process until the bottle was empty.

She had never expected to like doing this, but the tendons straining Franco's neck and his knotted muscles attested to his enjoyment. And she liked pleasing him.

"Tu es une sirène." He tugged gently on her hair, but firmly enough to make her release him.

A siren? Her? She smiled.

He reached for the condom he'd tossed on the table earlier, tore the wrapper with his teeth and then sheathed himself. Stacy reclined and opened her arms. Franco guided himself to her center and plunged deep. The sun-warmed latex over his hot shaft added yet another new dimension to his erotic play. She savored the sense of fullness, rightness, and then tangled her legs around his waist the way he'd taught her and held on tight. He took her on a roller-coaster-fast ride to the top and then she plunged over to the sound of him calling her name as he climaxed.

Their gasps filled a silence broken only by the hum of the pool filter and an occasional bird call. Stacy stroked a hand down his sweat-dampened back. "Wow."

He levered himself up on his elbows. "You have hidden talents, *mon gardénia.*"

A blush warmed her cheeks. How could she still blush around this man? "I've had an excellent teacher."

"And there is yet much to learn," he said gently as he pulled away. And then he stilled and stiffened. *"Le condom, c'est cassé."*

Stacy's heart missed a beat. Her muscles turned rigid. She prayed she'd mistranslated. "What?"

Franco's serious gaze locked onto hers. "The condom broke."

A wave of panic seized her. Her gaze dropped to the damning evidence, and her heart nearly beat its way out of her chest.

Dear God, was she going to repeat her mother's mistake?

Calendars, dates and biology scrambled in her head, and then sanity slowly invaded, making sense of it all, but leaving her cold, drained and eerily calm. She exhaled shakily. "My…um, period is due in a few days. We should be safe. I'm…um…unlikely to conceive now."

"How regular are you?" he asked without blinking.

She flinched, and feeling exposed, dragged a towel over her nakedness. Would she ever get used to these intimate conversations? "Like clockwork."

"Bien. But to be certain you will visit my doctor

before you return to the States. I will make the appointment." As if that settled everything, he straightened, crossed to the pool and dove in.

But Stacy was far from settled. She pressed a hand to her chest. Close call. Too close. She wasn't prepared to have a baby or let a man into her life.

Or was she?

Ten

A baby.

And not just any baby. *Franco's baby.*

The words reverberated in Stacy's head as the taxi carried her back to the hotel. Guilt nagged her for sneaking out while Franco was in the shower, but she couldn't calmly sit across the dinner table from him or go back to bed with him until she figured out the chaotic emotions churning inside her.

Her chances of getting pregnant today were slim. And that was good news. Wasn't it?

Absolutely.

This was the wrong time, the wrong place and the wrong man.

But there was a tiny spark of something that felt suspiciously like hope glowing deep inside her. Illogical, foolish hope. The idea of having a baby appealed, even though she hadn't once thought about having children since learning the truth about her mother's murder.

Had being around Candace activated some twisted kind of approaching-thirty biological clock?

She pressed a hand to her agitated stomach. Franco had the means to buy and sell her a hundred times over, and after his painful experience with Lisette there was no telling how he'd react if Stacy turned up pregnant.

Would he want the child or tell her to get rid of it?

"Mademoiselle, we have arrived," the taxi driver's words jerked Stacy back to the present before she could pursue that disturbing line of thought. She blinked and saw the hotel entrance outside the car window. The ride had passed in a blur.

A uniformed hotel employee opened her door. She dug the appropriate money from her wallet, paid and tipped the driver and climbed from the cab.

Standing on the pavement, she debated going up to the suite. But Madeline was far too perceptive. She'd zero in on Stacy's disquiet in seconds, and as much as Stacy longed for a dose of the savvier woman's no-nonsense advice or the support she knew her trio of suitemates would offer, she needed to get her thoughts in order first.

Stacy stepped onto the sidewalk and headed toward Monaco-Ville with no particular destination in mind. She loved the old-world charm, the sense of history and permanence in the oldest part of the principality. That it happened to be in the opposite direction to Larvotto Beach and Franco's view was an added bonus.

For the past ten years she'd focused on her safety and her financial security, but she'd completely neglected the emotional component of her life. She'd been afraid to let anyone get close and had paid for it with loneliness. Not even the teens she counseled were allowed past her emotional barriers. She cared about them, but knowing they might pack up and move without notice led her to maintain a protective distance.

But she didn't want to be alone or afraid anymore. She liked having friends, liked feeling connected and wouldn't mind having a family.

If she were pregnant, she wouldn't get rid of the baby no matter what Franco said. With his million euros she could afford to keep it, and even without his money she could manage once she found another job.

But could she deny a father his child or a child its father, live life on the run, always looking over her shoulder and never set down roots or make a home? No. She wouldn't wish her childhood on anyone. Not unless she truly feared for her own or her child's safety.

She didn't see Franco as being that kind of threat.

Didn't your mother's diary and your father's actions teach you anything? Rich men can't be trusted.

But she'd seen no sign of Franco being power-crazed or bending the laws to suit his needs. Other than buying her, that is. But as he'd pointed out, mistresses were not unusual here, and he'd shown her nothing but respect. He'd made sure that each sexual encounter left her satisfied when he didn't have to. He'd watched over the bridal party for Vincent, and he took the time to play with a fatherless boy—almost every weekend, according to Monsieur Constantine.

From everything she'd seen, Franco was a good man, and she suspected he'd be a good father.

Oh my God. Are you falling for him?

The leaden feeling in the pit of her stomach said yes.

Her steps slowed and her internal warning sirens screamed.

Had she learned enough about her own strength and resilience over the past decade to lower her walls and let a man in? Maybe. The training she'd had before and since she'd begun volunteering with the teens had taught her what constituted a healthy relationship. Surely she could practice what she preached?

A child's laughter startled her. Stacy looked around, stunned at where her subconscious had led her. The Saint Martin Garden was one of several playgrounds Monaco had set aside for children. She'd walked past it the day she'd toured the Prince's Palace. Sinking down on a bench in the shade, she studied the happy faces of the mothers and children.

Monaco would be a wonderful place to raise a family. According to her stack of guide books, the schools were good and the police force was second to none. Education and safety had been her guideposts in recent years.

Whether or not today's encounter resulted in a baby, would Franco want more than the agreed-upon month? Would he be interested in her staying in Monaco to see if their relationship had a future after the other brides-maids flew home? She and he were both wounded souls who feared trusting and being hurt. Could she heal him and in the process learn to trust again?

Could he be happy with her? She couldn't compete with the elegant women at the ball, but the remarkable chemistry between them had to account for something, didn't it?

Confidence swelled within her. She could do this. She would face her fears and ask him to give their relationship a try.

Her cell phone rang. Stacy checked the number on the caller ID. Franco's. Her heart raced and her palms dampened. She couldn't talk to him right now. Her decision was too new, too raw, so she silenced her phone.

Tomorrow she'd be ready to take that colossal leap.

A baby.

The idea didn't repulse Franco as much as it should have. In fact, having a child with Stacy could solve many problems. If he provided an heir, his father would not feel the need to impregnate the tramp plotting to empty the Constantine coffers. And Stacy wanted financial security. They could each benefit from continuing their relationship.

He tried Stacy's cellular number again and once more received her voice mail. He disconnected rather than leave a third message. Why had she left without saying goodbye? And why would she not return his calls?

By the time he had finished working out his tension by swimming laps, she'd been in the lower-level shower. He could have joined her, but he had needed a few moments alone to consider the ramifications of their situation. In all his thirty-eight years he had never had a condom break. He had retreated to his bathroom, and when he had exited his shower Stacy had been gone.

Had Candace phoned? Had Stacy's wedding duties once more taken precedence over her agreement with him? Was she having a relaxed dinner with her suitemates at this very moment while he paced his living room?

He looked forward to his evenings with Stacy more than he should, and he would not mind spending more time with her. She was attractive, intelligent and an extraordinary lover. She did not cling or make demands on his time that he was not willing to offer.

She is getting too close. And if you do not quit focusing on her absence you will be no better than your besotted friend.

He turned on the TV, but not even a baseball game tied in the bottom of the ninth inning with bases loaded could hold his attention. His thoughts kept straying to Stacy, her belly growing round with his child. But he could not afford to be deluded by a woman's false promises again.

What if Stacy were pregnant? Would she, like Lisette, choose to abort his child? Could he stop her?

He wiped a hand over his face. No. He would not engage in a legal battle to force a woman to carry a child she did not want. His only options lay in convincing her she wished to continue the pregnancy and in coming to an agreement satisfactory to them both regarding the child.

Stacy could not possibly be as pure-hearted as she pretended. He would prove it. And once he did then perhaps she would quit monopolizing his thoughts.

"I want you to have my baby," Franco said Wednesday night.

Stacy's heart and lungs stalled at the bald statement. She stared into his somber eyes across the secluded table in Le Grill, the ritzy rooftop restaurant at the Hôtel de Paris.

Her heart lurched back into motion and she dragged oxygen into her deprived lungs. Warmth and cautious optimism trickled through her.

Franco must have spent the forty-eight hours since the broken-condom incident thinking about a future together—as she had. She'd barely been able to concentrate on her bridesmaid's duties. She'd lost track of the number of rehearsal-dinner place cards she'd messed up yesterday and how many times the seamstress had asked her to stand still during her final dress fitting today.

"Your baby?" The words filled her with a tingly sensation. He offered her more than she'd ever dared hope for. Financial security. A home. The possibility of a family. A man who would treat her like a princess the way her mother had promised.

"*Oui.*"

"I might not be pregnant."

"A circumstance we can easily rectify."

Was this a proposal? It had to be. Why else would he bring her to this romantic restaurant where the roof retracted to allow the patrons to dine beneath a blanket of stars? But Franco didn't pull out a ring or get down on bended knee. Maybe the French didn't follow that custom? "I've, um…been thinking about that too."

"You would have to leave your job—a job you claim to love."

She clenched her napkin in her hand, looked away from his intense gaze and confessed, "No, I won't. I was laid off the week before we left for Monaco. I didn't tell Candace because I didn't want her worrying about me when she had a wedding to plan."

Franco's jaw hardened. "You are unemployed? You said you would go back to work when you returned to the States."

"I plan to search for a job, but there are a lot of companies downsizing right now. Not knowing how long it would take for me to find another position is another reason I accepted your offer. But now I don't have to worry about that. I wouldn't mind working here until the baby comes. Afterward—"

"I will pay the expenses on your apartment in Charlotte until you return. And of course, you will be compensated."

Confused, she blinked and frowned. "What?"

"I will give you another million euros upon the birth,

and I will cover all the medical expenses you and the baby incur."

Dizziness threatened to topple her. She grasped the edge of the table and studied his face, but she didn't see any trace of emotion or romance. In fact, he looked as if he were closing a business deal. "A-are you asking me to marry you, Franco?"

He reared back in his chair. "*Non.* I need an heir. You want financial security. I am offering a solution to fill both our needs. A second million will give you the life of leisure you claim the first would not."

The delicious shrimp appetizer she'd consumed turned to molten lead in her stomach. Her chest felt so tight she could barely breathe. "You want me to have a baby…and hand it over to you? Gr-grant you sole custody?"

"*Oui.* As you have seen, I can provide many advantages for a child."

The horror of his words chilled her to the bone and pain speared through her like shards of glass. Oh my God. She'd fallen in love with the arrogant bastard.

Impossible. She hadn't known him long enough to fall in love with him. But merely liking him and being disappointed in him wouldn't hurt this much.

"You don't want me? You only want to buy my baby?" For clarity's sake she rephrased her questions. The words burned her throat. She had to be wrong. He couldn't be asking that.

"*Tu es très* sexy, Stacy. I will enjoy sharing your bed for however long it takes to produce a child. But I have no desire for a wife."

He had clearly stated that he would never marry again on their ride to Avignon. Why hadn't she listened? Franco was alone by choice. He would never allow a woman to get close to him. And he would never change.

She might be willing to lower her walls and risk her heart, but he wasn't.

How could she be so stupid? She'd been falling in love with him and he'd been setting her up. She shoved back her chair and stumbled to her feet. "No."

Franco rose. "I will give you twenty-four hours to reconsider."

Déjà vu. "Don't hold your breath. This time I won't change my mind. You can take your two million euros and shove them up your fine French a—"

"*Y a t'il un problème, mademoiselle?*" an anxious waiter asked.

"Yes, there's a problem. I feel ill. I'm leaving." She turned back to Franco. "I don't ever want to see you again."

"Stacy, if you end this now you will forfeit the money."

And she'd be right back where she started. Nearly broke and out of a job. Too bad. There were some things money couldn't buy.

"Your price is too high. I could never have a child and let it go." A chill swept over her when she realized what she'd said and that she meant it to the bottom of her soul. There was more of her father in her than she'd ever realized. She gulped down a wave of nausea. "And I could never respect a man who would ask me to do so."

She gathered her wrap and her purse and raced for the exit before her tears could escape.

"You were right about Angeline."

His father's voice drew Franco from his contemplation of the Fontvieille harbor far below his thirtieth-floor office window. He swiveled his chair to face the door and the desk and the profit and loss statement he had been neglecting. "What happened to her?"

"I told her I was considering transferring ownership

of the Constantine holdings to you and she left." Pain, disappointment and resignation deepened the lines on his father's face.

"I am sorry." But good riddance.

Armand sank down into the leather visitor chair. "She reminded me of your mother. They all do. Young. Vibrant. Beautiful."

"My mother was unfaithful. Why would you want another woman like her?"

"Franccsca was always faithful to herself. I made the mistake of believing my love would transform a party girl who needed to be the center of attention into a loving wife and mother. But true love does not require change. And giving her free rein in hopes that she would be happy and always come home to me was not fair to you. I should have put a stop to the drugs the moment I found out about her habit, but I was afraid doing so would drive her away."

Franco digested the surprising insight into his parents' relationship.

"You were right about Stacy," he admitted reluctantly.

He had waited eight days for her to call and tell him she'd changed her mind. Eight days of being unable to concentrate or sleep well. But the only communication he had received from her was a box delivered via courier containing the gifts he had given her—except for the watch band. She had kept the gift he could buy with pocket change.

Where was the greed, the sense of entitlement that his other lovers had had?

His bed was empty. And there was a barrenness to his days and nights that had not been there before. Even Vincent's bachelor party last night had not lightened his mood.

"Stacy refused the money?"

"She walked away from our agreement when I offered her another million to have my baby."

"I assume that was a proposal."

"*Non.*"

"You asked her to bear a child and then relinquish it to you?"

"*Oui.*"

His father shook his head sadly. "For someone who is worried about our liquid assets you are throwing around a lot of money."

An accurate charge. "It was a test."

"To see if she was…what did you say? Ah yes, a duplicitous and mercenary creature who would sell you anything you wanted to buy?"

Franco nodded.

"And she refused."

"She said my price was too high."

"That would explain why our employees have been ducking for cover for the past week." Franco arched an eyebrow and his father shrugged. "I may have retired, but I have my sources."

Armand tapped the file against the sharp crease of his trousers. "So you have finally found a woman you cannot buy. What are you going to do about it?"

Franco fiddled with his pen and remained silent. He did not have an answer. He'd had confirmation this morning from a physician that Stacy was not pregnant. The news did not bring him any relief from the edginess riding his back.

"Our agreement was that you choose a woman you would be willing to marry if she could not be bought. I will not hold you to that because a marriage should never be based on anything but love." His father stood and tossed the file folder onto the desk in front of Franco.

"The documents are signed. You do not have to marry to gain control of the Constantine holdings. It is yours. But perhaps you wish to marry to regain your heart."

Taken aback, Franco stared at his father. "I do not wish to marry again."

Armand planted his fists on Franco's desk and leaned forward. "She is not like Lisette, Franco. This girl cares nothing for your net worth."

No. Stacy was nothing like his selfish ex-wife. But opening himself up for another evisceration held little appeal. "I know, but the risks—"

"Bah. When did you become a coward? Love is a gamble, but when it is true the rewards far outweigh the costs. Being alone and right is a poor substitute for being happy and in love—even if that love is imperfect." He straightened. "What will it cost you to let Stacy get away? Can you live with always wondering who is putting the smile on her face? Who is warming her bed? Think about that, hmm?"

His father turned for the door without waiting for an answer, but paused on the threshold. "I will see you at Vincent's rehearsal-dinner party this evening. Perhaps by then you will have your answers."

After his father left, Franco opened the document folder. The signature on the bottom line made Franco the sole owner of the Constantine holdings, including the chateau and Midas Chocolates. He had more to lose now than ever before.

In two days Stacy would return to the States. A wise man would let her go. Only a besotted fool would beg her forgiveness and ask her to stay.

"He's here," Madeline whispered.

Stacy's stomach clenched into a tight knot, but she kept

her back to the entrance of the private dining room in the upscale Italian restaurant hosting the rehearsal dinner.

She'd known Franco would be here tonight, but that didn't mean she was ready to face him. Only Madeline knew the full truth of Stacy's situation, and that was because she'd caught Stacy in a weak moment, dragged her for another late-night meeting in the bar and pried the sordid story out of her. Stacy didn't want to dampen Candace's happiness so she'd sworn Madeline to secrecy.

"Want me to keep him away from you?"

A smile tugged Stacy's lips at the mother-hen tone of her suitemate's voice. "I don't think that will be necessary. But thanks."

If Franco had missed her or discovered any feelings for her at all, he would have called. But Stacy hadn't heard from him since she'd left him in the restaurant last week. She swallowed to ease the tightening of her throat.

She, on the other hand, kept second-guessing her decision. She loved him more than she'd ever thought she could love anyone, but he obviously expected every woman to leave him as his mother, his father's exes and Lisette had done. If Stacy stayed with him but delayed getting pregnant, could she convince him in time that she wasn't like the other women in his life?

Her gaze shifted to Candace and Vincent's love-struck faces. Franco had never looked at her that way—with his heart and his soul in his eyes. She yearned for him to.

Technically, the bride and groom had been married earlier this evening in a private civil ceremony the way French and Monegasque law required, but they were waiting until after the church service tomorrow morning to actually begin their lives as husband and wife.

"What's he doing here? He's not on the guest list," Madeline said in a panicked whisper.

"Who?" Stacy turned toward the door. Her gaze landed on Franco in a dark, custom-fitted suit and her heart ached. She quickly looked away before meeting his gaze and spotted the man who'd posed as Madeline's tour guide—a man who'd turned out to be anything but the humble tour guide he'd led Madeline to believe he was.

The color completely drained from Madeline's face. She squeezed Stacy's hand. "Stacy, I don't want to abandon you, but I cannot face him right now. Go with me to the ladies' room?"

Stacy squared her shoulders. She would not run. Her running days were over. "No. Go ahead. I'm okay. Franco is seated at the opposite end of the table from me. I can avoid him until after dinner. Longer, if I'm lucky."

If not, she'd survived her mother's murder and her father's betrayal. Facing Franco couldn't be worse than that. Or could it? She felt as if her heart were being ripped out all over again.

Needing a few minutes to bolster her defenses, she slipped out onto the colonnade. In forty-eight hours she would not have this magic view of Monaco, but no matter what happened she would always be grateful for her time here. She'd learned that despite her dysfunctional youth she could fall in love, but she could let go—unlike her father.

"Why do you not tread on my rugs?" Franco asked from behind her.

Stacy winced and wished she'd had a few more minutes to prepare for this encounter. She took a bracing breath and turned to find him a few yards away. He stepped out of the shadows and her lungs emptied again when she noted the lines of stress marring his handsome face. She shook off her concern. If he was stressed, it was no more than he deserved. He'd tried to buy her baby.

"I had to walk through pools of blood on our white kitchen floor when I found my mother and father. Your red rugs on white marble remind me of that night."

"I will throw the rugs out and replace the floor if you will come back to me."

Her heart stuttered. "What?"

He closed the distance between them. "I was wrong, Stacy. All the money in the world cannot buy the one thing I desire most."

"An heir? I'm sure you can find some woman who'll jump at the chance."

His unwavering blue gaze held hers and something in their depths made her pulse skip. "I desire you, *mon gardénia*."

His velvety deep voice sent a tremor rippling over her. She held up a hand to halt his approach. "Don't do this, Franco."

But he kept coming until her palm pressed his chest. His warmth seeped through his silk shirt into her fingers and snaked up her arm. She jerked her hand away and fisted it by her side.

"I was afraid to trust what my eyes—what my *heart*—told me. I offered to buy your baby as a test. If you had accepted the money, then I would know you were like every other woman I have known. But you are nothing like them."

She couldn't comprehend what he was saying, but that look in his eyes was beginning to fan that ember of hope she thought he'd extinguished. "Why me?"

A smile flickered on his lips. "Besides your incredible legs and the contradiction between the siren in your eyes and your cloak of reserve?"

"Huh?"

"Because my father challenged me to find a woman I could marry if she couldn't be bought."

Had someone slipped something into her drink? "I'm sorry?"

"Papa suggested I stop dating spoiled rich women and find someone with traditional values if I wanted to find a woman who would love me for myself and not my money. I told him I would prove him wrong by finding one of the mythical paragons he described and buying her."

Stacy flinched. She'd thought she couldn't possibly feel worse, but she did. Had she been nothing more than a bet? He lifted a hand to stoke her cheek, but she jerked out of reach. "So taking me to the chateau was just flaunting me in front of your father to show you'd won?"

"*Oui*. That was my original goal. But then you told me about your parents. You had compelling reasons for accepting my offer. Reasons which I could not condemn. And you refused to let me spoil you with meaningless gifts. I found myself falling in love with you." He extended his arms, palms up and shrugged. "I had to push you away."

Falling in love with her? She pressed a hand over her racing heart. "I would have slept with you without the money, Franco."

"And I would have offered you more." He stepped closer and trapped her by planting his hands on the railing beside her. "So much more."

He really had to stop doing that. She told herself to duck out of the way, but her legs seemed numb. He bent and teased the corners of her mouth with tantalizing, but insubstantial and unsatisfying kisses.

"*Je t'aime*," he whispered against her lips and her world stopped. Taking advantage of her shocked gasp, he captured her mouth in a deeply passionate kiss. And then he slowly drew back, his lips clinging to hers for a heartbeat longer.

The emotion in his eyes washed over her, but she was afraid to believe what she saw.

"I love you, Stacy, and if you can find it in your heart to forgive me, I want to marry you. I will add fidelity to my vows, because I never want you to doubt that my heart and my soul belong only to you. And whether or not we have children, the money I promised you is yours because you have given me so much more than money can buy."

Her eyes burned and her throat clogged. Happiness swelled inside her. Only a man who truly loved her would offer her everything she'd ever dreamed of and at the same time open the door to set her free and provide her the means to escape.

He loved her enough to let her go.

"You don't have to buy my love, Franco. It's freely given."

"Tout a un prix."

A smile wobbled on her lips. She cupped his cheeks and stroked her thumbs over his smooth warm skin. "Not this time. I love you, and if you lost everything today, I would still love you tomorrow and every day thereafter. Yes, Franco, I will marry you."

His chest rose on a deep breath. "I swear you will never regret it, *mon gardénia.*"

* * * * *

Don't miss the next book in the
MONTE CARLO AFFAIRS *series!*
Look for
The Prince's Ultimate Deception
by Emilie Rose
coming in June 2008 from Desire™.

UNDER THE MILLIONAIRE'S INFLUENCE

by
Catherine Mann

Dear Reader,

My current Desire story features a heroine under foster care who grew up in a Southern antebellum home – a subject dear to my heart. When my husband and I married, we planned on a large family and promptly had four children. We had long discussed the option of a foster child or overseas adoption, when lo and behold, our next very special child found his way to us during the string of hurricane disasters that struck the Gulf Coast in 2004. Now our newest but oldest son has joined our fold, and what a constant blessing and joy he is!

I would like to encourage those of you who also feel called to expand your family to consider programmes such as the foster care system, adoption, overseas adoption, Big Brother/Little Brother, Big Sister/Little Sister. There's a wealth of children out there waiting to be hugged and loved!

Thanks again for all your letters. I do so enjoy hearing from readers! If you would like to contact me, I can be reached at Catherine Mann, PO Box 6065, Navarre, FL 32655, USA or www.CatherineMann.com.

Happy reading!

Cathy Mann

CATHERINE MANN

RITA® Award winner Catherine Mann resides on a sunny Florida beach with her flyboy husband and their five children. Although after nine moves in eighteen years, she hasn't given away her winter gear! Since landing on the shelves in 2002, she has celebrated twenty releases and been a five-time RITA® Award-finalist. A former theatre-school director and university teacher, she graduated with a degree in theatre from UNC-Greensboro. Catherine loves to hear from readers and chat on her message board – thanks to the wonders of wireless internet, which allows her to cyber-network with her laptop by the water! To learn more about her work and her latest moving adventures, visit her website at www.CatherineMann.com.

To Jasen:
Our newest child, but also our oldest.
We love you, son!

One

Starr Cimino vowed to invest in new pjs, even though her love life was currently on life support.

Facing her arch nemesis in a threadbare Beachcombers Restaurant T-shirt before she'd even had her morning coffee just sucked. So much for armor to gird her five-foot stature.

Her steely spine and some wit would have to suffice. She braced her back and stood down the strong and vital force filling the door of her seaside carriage house in Charleston, South Carolina.

She didn't doubt her ability to deck anyone who threatened her. She'd learned young to take control of her life after all her crook parents had forced her to endure. But it just wasn't cool to take out a seventy-eight-year-old lady in a housedress. The mother of the man to whom she'd given her heart and virginity.

At least she could reclaim her heart.

Swiping the sandy sleep from her eyes, Starr forced a smile taught to her by her foster mother, "Aunt" Libby. "What can I do for you, Mrs. Hamilton-Reis?"

Other than toss some blue food coloring into her fish pond so the old bat's prize guppies would look more like a certain current cartoon fish. Okay, so Aunt Libby's training hadn't totally saturated Starr's conscience as a teen.

Grudges. Man they hurt the soul and she really should get over it, but this lady had treated her worse than the scum on her fish pond for right around seventeen years.

And God forbid Starr should date the woman's precious heir.

So Starr and David had met behind sand dunes and shimmied up the rose terrace to climb into his bedroom window during their teenage romance that had swelled and broken her heart in one tumultuous year.

"What do I want?" Alice Hamilton-Reis's voice rose and fell along with the rush of the waves along the shore. "I want your relatives to move their RVs out of my neighbor's view."

Her family? Here?

Prickles spread over her as she looked around and found that, yes, there were three RVs parked right on the grass between the Hamilton-Reis's historical plantation house and Starr's carriage house. The same RVs she'd ridden in before luck and an efficient social worker had intervened.

Crap.

She shoved her hands through her snarled mess of hair, as if that might somehow restore order to her rapidly tangling world. No luck. In fact…the worst luck sauntered into view with broad shoulders and serious temptation.

David. Her attention skipped off those RVs pronto.

He took the lengthy porch steps of his family's Southern antebellum mansion with the same confident strides he'd possessed even as a lanky teenager who'd sent her pulse skyrocketing. David made clothes look good, no question. He wore formal dark pants with loose hipped ease, a crisp white shirt contrasting against his jet-black hair and a tan that attested to time spent in the sun.

Her heart rate still doubled, but for another reason. Yes. Because of their history and how he'd so deeply bruised her tender feelings over ten years ago with his all-or-nothing ultimatums. He wanted her to give over her hard won control of her life, and heaven help her, he'd once truly tempted her. And when she'd seen him again a year ago, her willpower had been in the negative numbers. They'd landed in bed together in seconds flat. Then they'd found their clothes again, he'd stuck to his same, unflinching party line—pick up and follow him around the world, leave behind the only home she'd ever known. His way.

Not a chance.

She didn't want to think overlong on the fact that she hadn't been with anyone since then—thus her crummy lingerie and love life gasping for breath. She would hold strong this time, regardless of her body already tingling to life again.

Lord knew she had enough to think about dealing with her biological parents showing up—*don't look, don't look, don't look at those RVs yet*—and David's perfect-lineage mama staring her down.

David stopped on the bottom step and yet still he stood around the same height as the women on the porch, darn him. "Mother, you shouldn't be outside in the morning damp air." A hand towel draped around his neck attested his recent shave, yet he still looked totally calm and collected even though he'd obviously rushed out after his mother. "Your doctor said for you to keep your feet up until the new blood pressure medicine takes effect."

Great. She *had* to be nice to the old bat or she ran the risk of David's mother stroking out on the carriage house stairs.

Aunt Libby's voice echoed through her head. Manners. Manners.

Jeez. She searched for something to say. Seagulls and cranes swooped for breakfast along the shore. Distant church bells from downtown Charleston chimed seven.

Starr tugged at the T-shirt and pretended she wore her favorite form-fitting jean dress and wedge heels with ties that wrapped around her ankles. She was good at the princess pretense. She'd perfected it as a gypsy child on the road. She refused to let herself be ashamed for things they had done—the things they'd insisted she do. She reminded herself she was a businesswoman now. She and her two foster sisters had turned Aunt Libby's mansion into Beachcombers—an up-and-coming restaurant.

She sidestepped cranky Alice and faced her old lover who looked too darn good for this early in the morning, his dark hair glistening with water from a recent shower. Saints save her from her vivid imagination. "Hello, David, your mother and I were just discussing a better parking place for my, uh…" She couldn't bring herself to use the word *family*.

They'd given up that right when they'd left her in the foster child system for years on end. Doing nothing to bring her home, yet doing nothing to cut her loose for adoption.

Mrs. Hamilton-Reis turned to cling to her son's arm as if suddenly weak. "We need to get those recreational vehicles situated elsewhere. Surely it would be better for her business if they were over there on the beach rather than in plain view of her restaurant."

Of course his mother always put a better spin on things when he was around…not that she could really think much about his dear old ma when he was moving closer by the second and saturating Starr's senses.

Now that he was closer, she could see the monogram on the hand towel draped around his neck. The tangy scent of his aftershave wafted up the steps to tease her senses along with the salty scent of the ocean breeze. All of which stole her self-control much like waves stole sand from the shore.

And darn him, the way his eyes heated over her, it didn't matter what she wore.

Starr turned to Mrs. Hamilton-Reis, a hefty reminder of why she needed to keep her distance from David. "I'll talk to them about parking closer to the beach where the lawn's already patchy."

David's mother surveyed the lawn. "That'll be much better for business, my dear." Alice patted her son's arm. "Thank you for worrying about me. I'll be having breakfast on the veranda with my feet up. It would be lovely if you could join me."

He nodded. "I'll be in shortly."

The woman who'd once never passed up an opportunity to tell Starr she shouldn't hold David back from pursuing his dreams pinched a smile as she started her pivot away. "I'm glad we could work this out, dear."

Starr scrunched her eyes closed with a sigh. Still the tequila sunrise bled through her lids to sparkle through her brain. Or was that all the emotion bubbling through her?

David. Her parents. Alice Hamilton-Reis. All at once. Too much.

She'd forgotten how the woman would speak nicely to her whenever David was actually around. Not that she'd ever been outright mean to Starr, just coolly disapproving until icicles formed in the spiral curls of Starr's hair.

She shook free the insecurities of her youth and opened her eyes. Yep, David was still here and dear old mom was gone. Time to deal. Fast. Before the RV crew woke up and she had her hands more than full of frustration…*and pain,* a little voice whispered.

No. She was an adult, a businesswoman who currently had a hunky, tempting piece of her past standing on her porch. "So, you're back from…wherever it is you traveled this time."

Even though his inheritance enabled him to sit back and never work if he chose, David still served as a civilian employee for the air force's OSI—Office of Special Investigations. He traveled the globe, slipping in and out of countries often undetected, just as he'd always planned during their teenage years, dreaming on a beach blanket under the stars. Even back then he'd wanted her to come along when the mission permitted and even then her root-seeking heart had quaked.

Taking the rest of the steps to join her, he stuffed his hands in his pockets and hitched one shoulder against her porch post, close. *So* close. "I was in Greece working on a NATO counterterrorism task force."

"Wow, you can actually share what you're doing. That's rare." How many times had she wondered? Too many for her comfort level. "It sounds really awesome."

He stayed modestly—or covertly—quiet. The distant sound of waves and the breakfast crowd heading into the restaurant next door faded away as she couldn't help but focus on him.

Her babbling mouth ran away from her. "I imagine this is one of those missions you always talked about me coming along with you."

David cocked a brow, his head tipping to the side even if he still stayed quiet. Embarrassment heated through her with a need to fill the silence. God, he could still undo her thoughts as easily as he'd once undone her bikini top.

"But we both know that's old ground. Like I really could have picked up and gone to Greece now anyhow. I have a business to run, obligations to my business partners, my sisters. Still it sounds really exotic "

Her foster sister Claire would have relished experiencing the exotic foods. They served mostly down-home Southern cuisine at Beachcombers, but Claire still enjoyed adding something a little different every now and again.

Once upon a dream, Starr had contemplated taking a trip or two to study the great artists of the world. Except, bottom line, she didn't want to spend her entire life on the road. She'd done enough of that for the first ten years of her life with her gypsy family.

Now, she thrived on the security of waking up to the same gorgeous ocean sunrise every morning. Her little carriage house behind Beachcombers might not be much, but it was hers. A home.

"Exotic?" he quipped. "Time was you thought that sounded too far from home."

Suddenly she couldn't hold onto the fantasy any

longer. No princess clothes or armor. Nothing but old pain and a worn out T-shirt. "Do we really want to walk down that road again today, David?"

He plucked at the shoulder of her shirt and pulled off a crumpled bit of a tissue-paper flower. Great. The fates must be plotting against her. Not only did she look like crap, but she also had arts-and-crafts bits and pieces stuck to her like a third grader.

David held up the silvery flower she'd been using to make personalized wrapping bags for wedding-shower party favor gifts for her restaurant. One corner of his mouth kicked into that confident smile that never failed to flip her stomach into somersaults to rival her circus gypsy cousins' talents. David tucked the crackly bloom behind her ear.

His knuckles skimmed her cheek in a touch so soft but undoubtedly deliberate. She knew him. Knew his touch well from their high-school romance.

And yes, from their brief time together a year ago when she'd been unable to resist him. Heaven help her, she couldn't spend the rest of her life jumping into bed—or against a wall—with David Reis every time he breezed through the United States.

Starr stepped back. "I'll keep my eyes open for your mother. Leave your cell-phone number and I'll call if I see her wearing herself out."

"Thank you."

She thought about asking for more details about his mother's health, even sympathizing since it was his mother after all, but then realized that would keep him on her porch longer. And when they spent any lengthy amount of time together, they ended up arguing and he ended up kissing her silent. She mentally kicked herself and mumbled, "God, we're both such idiots."

He cocked an arrogant brow. "What was that?"

"We both need to get to work." She backed up to grip her door. "I really need to get dressed, so…"

"Drag my sorry ass off your porch."

A laugh bubbled before she could squelch it. She so enjoyed his dry sense of humor. She couldn't resist it, either. "You said it, not me."

Starr slid away and sagged against the door inside her carriage house filled to the brim with her arts-and-crafts supplies. Victorian eclectic. *Hers*.

She exhaled long and hard.

She'd held strong, gotten her way. She was alone in her little house. She'd kept her distance from David. *And* she'd managed to shoo him away before her folks made their morning showing.

Thank you, Aunt Libby, for putting in a good word with the Man upstairs on that one.

But she couldn't count on Aunt Libby holding back the tide forever. With her luck, her family would set up Porta Pottis and charge folks for using them. Her ma and da never missed a chance to make a buck, and if they could land a dollar without working, all the better.

Ma and Da. Why she couldn't distance herself enough to call them Gita and Frederick instead, she didn't know. She wanted Aunt Libby, her foster mother, Mom.

All a moot point and waste of time to consider at the moment. Gather up those scattered thoughts before David had a chance to slip past her defenses.

But she couldn't understand why the fates had been so vengeful as to send those campers full of ex-family, who'd rejected her, used her, stolen from her, at the very same moment that David had chosen to make one of his rare appearances in Charleston.

Two

"The way you wield that hot glue gun, it's no wonder you sleep alone. Men must be hitting the floor in terror."

Claire's words rattled around in Starr's head with a little too much accuracy. Nothing like a sister—even the foster sort—to put you in your place. Starr spread her gift bags, glitter and shells along the kitchen butcher block as she put together the tissue paper. At least the RV crew had decided to sleep in today and give her a couple extra hours to gather her thoughts after seeing David had rocked her balance.

She simply wanted a half hour of peace to pull herself together. Tough to find with such a perfect contrasting view of the three rickety RVs and David's Lexus right there, reminding her of so many painful moments in her past.

But damn it, she would put a time stamp on that segment of her life because her days of romance with David had expired long ago.

She stared out the open window at the three parked vehicles. Her sister worked by her side decorating a cake, while two part-time help gals took care of the remaining breakfast crowd. The gentle ocean breeze ruffling the lace curtains may have cooled the steamy kitchen, but it did nothing to cool the steam curling inside her after a simple encounter with David.

She might well need more than a half hour.

Starr globbed another dollop of oozing glue on the magenta bag. "I imagine you've waited a whole year for that payback line just because I teased you about the way you whacked around a swizzle stick when you were mad at Vic."

Her sister had fought hard against falling in love, even contemplating single motherhood, until finally the burly veterinarian had won her over.

Earth-mother-type Claire swooped her cake-frosting spatula through the air. "Aha! So you *are* mad at a man."

Had she really just jumped into that net because she was busy thinking of her sister's tangled love life from last year? "Don't you have a baby to nurse?"

The multicolored sling around Claire's neck held the

infant snuggled securely to her chest. "Little Libby is snoozing away, happy and fully fed."

No surprise Claire managed yet another addition to her life with ease. Her unflappable, organized sister always had. Even her silky blond hair cooperated to make a smooth look along with the clean lines of her conservative clothes. Claire would never put together mismatched designer-fashion finds Starr liked to scoop up at the Salvation Army. But then Starr couldn't quite stifle the colors in her wardrobe any more than she could quiet her bright artwork.

Claire gently patted her baby girl's bottom. Motherhood suited her well. She'd obviously taken on all the traits of their foster mother.

Aunt Libby had been an eccentric—amazing—woman. Having lost her fiancé in the Korean War, she'd never married, instead devoting her life to taking in foster daughters. Countless foster girls had channeled through her antebellum home, money in short supply, love in abundance. Most had either returned to their homes or found new adoptive parents. All but three had left—herself, Claire and Ashley, who'd just graduated from college with her accounting degree. Her graduation being the reason for their flurry of preparations today, to put together a surprise party.

Their shy younger sister would work herself into a tizz if she had time to think of an impending celebration, so they'd opted for low-key festivities as a surprise party. Ashley deserved to have her accomplishments lauded. A whiz kid, she'd been keeping the Beachcomb-ers' books since the doors had opened two years ago.

Starr brandished her hot glue gun, which of course made her think of all the times she'd seen David's gun tucked in a shoulder harness. So often she thought of the glamour of his world travel, but the danger sent a sliver of...*something,* something she didn't want to consider overlong because it traveled up her spine to sting her eyes. "Okay, so I'm armed and fearsome. Why does that have anything to do with a man?"

Claire brandished her own decorator gun, swirling Congratulations, Ashley across the cake festooned with pink roses. "It's the way you're wielding it, big hot globs that don't allow for anything to slip away."

So? "And that tells you what?"

"The same thing you've always wanted where David Reis is concerned." Claire set her frosting aside and pinned her sister with her ever-wise older gaze. "You want to glue his wandering feet to the ground."

"Or glue his arrogant mouth shut." Now that called for a huge blob.

Claire tapped Starr's toe with her flip-flop-shod foot. "But then he wouldn't be as fun to kiss."

Starr couldn't help but shiver in agreement at that. "You're a wicked woman."

"I'll plead the fifth." She winked as she topped off another cabbage rose on the cake. "How long is he in town this time?"

"I didn't ask." But yeah, she wanted to know. Not wise.

"You're kidding."

"His mother was there at first, and then my, uh—" she swallowed hard "—relatives could have stepped out at any second."

Claire's hand fell on her shoulder. Her sister always did try to mother the world. "Speaking of which, why are they here?"

"I honestly don't know." Starr eased out from under the comforting hand that could too easily make her go all emotional when she needed to hold herself together more than ever. She had genetics working against her when it came to being overly dramatic. It was one of the things that used to drive David nuts. "I haven't asked them yet, but I promise I'll get to it right away. I won't let them interfere with business."

"I'm not concerned about that, honey, I'm worried about you." She gripped Starr's shoulders again and turned her back around. "I don't want them to take advantage of you."

God, the truth still hurt because undoubtedly they wouldn't have shown up for any other reason. Bracing herself to hold on tight to her emotions, Starr wrapped her arms around her sister in an awkward hug, the snoozing baby between them.

Claire patted her back. "We're a team, sister. Don't ever forget it. You don't have to take them on alone. Say the word and I'll walk over with you."

Sniffling in spite of her best intentions, Starr leaned back and flicked her hair over her shoulder. "Thanks, but I'm a tough cookie in case you haven't noticed. I have my killer glue gun, after all." Bravado in place, she retrieved her gun and her resolve.

And darned if one of those RVs didn't start moving with the first signs of life from inside, shock absorbers obviously having long ago given up the ghost.

Ghosts.

She could talk about bravery and guns and time stamps all she wanted, but it would take a lot of stamping to eradicate all the ghosts clamoring around in her head.

David slid his arms through his suit jacket on his way out the front door. He needed to report in and sign leave papers to take the time off to make sure all was well with his mother's health.

And to figure out what the hell was going on with Starr's family.

Speaking of Starr, the gorgeous spitfire came charging down the restaurant back steps now. He'd planned to have a "discussion" with her parents before she saw them, but apparently he hadn't dressed fast enough. Now things would be more complicated. Par for the course around Starr since the first day he'd done a double take, realizing his impish neighbor had grown into a bombshell.

He should have had the conversation with her earlier, but the risk had seemed too high given they were both half-dressed. He'd been too aware of her in that whispery thin T-shirt while he'd stood there only halfway finished dressing himself. Too easily memories from a year ago slid through his mind, how she'd sat on the edge of the tub and watched him shave. Not long after, he'd lifted her onto the sink and plunged himself deep inside her, her body already damp and ready for him.

Hell.

Clothes didn't seem to help much now since the wind played havoc with her gauzy sundress, plastering it to her body as she made her way across the lawn, sandals slapping her determination. He'd always enjoyed all that spunk and fire poured into the way they came together in bed.

They'd never had much luck resisting each other, another reason it was damn wise to meet out here on the lawn in open daylight rather than risk stepping into her carriage house. His leaving had hurt her last year. But *she* was the one who'd turned down his offer to try again. She could have come with him and he would have given her the world—shown her the world. Made love around the world.

But he had more pressing concerns than sex right now. Evicting Starr's family topped his list. "Good morning, babe."

She stopped dead in her tracks, her dress rustling around her legs, her mass of curls a swirl of motion, but then nothing about Starr ever stayed still. Well, except for the stubborn part of her that refused to leave this place.

Her toes curled in her shoes. Just that small motion stirred him because he knew. He affected her.

Then she turned, her eyes a sultry, dusky view that always sucker punched him. "Good morning to you, too. I see you're ready for work now."

Starr's voice washed over him like a surprise wave from the shore. She'd always had that effect on him— the only woman who'd ever had the power to linger in his thoughts.

Except he couldn't let her derail him now. "Actually, I'm heading over to give your family a wake-up call."

"That's where I'm going. They seem to be already moving about."

"I didn't mean that kind of wake-up." He stepped between her and the RVs, determined those people wouldn't hurt her any further.

"David, you don't need to worry." A sad smile strained her face as she swiped her windswept hair from her face. "Your mother and I have already spoken. I'm going to ask them to move off the grass and over to the beach."

A beach three states over wouldn't be enough to satisfy him. "That isn't what I meant. They need to leave."

"It isn't your place to make that call."

"You can't actually *want* them to stay."

"I'll handle them." Her chin tipped with a bravado he recognized from the day she'd arrived in the neighborhood, a grubby scrap of a kid with a mop of hair that likely hadn't seen a brush in a week. "I always do."

He resisted the urge to gather her in his arms,

knowing full well she wouldn't welcome the gesture. But he wasn't backing down. "You don't have to. I'll take care of this today. Now."

Her pretty lips went tight. "You don't have to and in case you missed out on noticing, I didn't ask for your help."

She may have been standing there steely strong, but he remembered well the teen who'd cried all over his chest because of how much damage these people could do with even a token visit when they attempted to lure her into their world again.

"David?"

He snapped back to the present. "Yes?"

"Step aside, please."

"No." Not a damn chance.

"No? Who the hell do you think you are to tell me no?" Her amazing hair seemed to crackle and lift with the energy overflow, as if her short and willowy body couldn't contain it all. "I realize you're embarrassed to have them in your precious prestigious neighborhood, but this is my property and I will take care of the issue."

He started to explain to her…then stopped. He didn't want her softening because then he'd do something risky…like touch her.

"We can stand here and debate this all day, but you know me well and once I've made up my mind…" David began to say.

"You don't budge." She fondled a glue gun tucked

halfway in her pocket. "It's not an endearing quality, you know."

Perhaps not, but it was one that would keep her safe.

Problem was, this woman was almost as stubborn as him. Almost.

So where did that leave him? Much more of this and he would have to do something like toss her over his shoulder and pass her off to her sister. Claire was the most logical woman he'd ever met. Surely he could garner an ally in her.

Starr stepped closer as if to brush past. His hands itched to touch her, even if only for a fireman's hold that would no doubt inflame her. God, she was hot when her temper flared.

Her pupils dilated with an awareness that could well send them both dashing back to her place. They wouldn't even have to get naked. They'd done it half-clothed often enough, coming together in a frenzy, too impatient to wait.

Then had come the slow, leisurely sex…

His breathing went ragged. His whole body tensed, muscles straining to be set loose and take this woman.

His cell phone buzzed in his jacket pocket. Damn.

It could only be work. He didn't have anything else in his life. He usually lived for the thrill of his job, but right now the thrill of this woman…

Just damn.

Stepping back, he reached into his coat and pulled out his phone to check the number. It could wait until he got into his car.

He shoved his cell back into his coat. "Starr, none of this changes what needs to happen with your family."

"And none of this changes the fact that my business, my life is not your problem." Her stubborn jaw jutted.

Without question, he would have to carry her off the lawn and lock her in her house, not exactly legal.

And then it hit him. He had a better way to circle around the situation after all. His connections at work. Find something on her family, because his radar, honed from assignments around the world, blared that they were always up to something, something that would spell bad news for Starr.

He nodded. "Believe whatever you want for why I want them gone, but I'm not done here. I'll be back to settle this later." He had to add, "Be careful."

David thumbed the remote control to his Lexus. The sooner he got to work, the sooner he could put out feelers about the Cimino family.

Just because Starr was hell-bent on her independence didn't mean he would stand back and let anyone take advantage of her.

Starr plunked her butt down on the back step of the Beachcombers Restaurant and stared at the Cimino family RVs from the quiet retreat of the deep porch. After her confrontation with David, she needed a moment to collect herself before she could handle another face-to-face with anyone—especially the residents of those three crumbling RVs.

The front of the restaurant hummed with activity from brunch traffic transitioning into lunch. Ashley worked the gift shop while studying for her CPA exam. The back section, which they used as a bar, wouldn't stir to life until suppertime and into the evening when the weekend's live band cranked to life, so she soaked up the second's silence to watch the shadows moving behind the gingham curtains covering the RV windows.

Her time to gather herself had come to an end.

The larger RV—the one towed behind a truck as opposed to the other two that were single units—rocked with walking bodies. Her stomach clenched. She'd seen her family only five times in the last seventeen years—this would make number six. And during each visit, they made their displeasure known when she hadn't fallen into line by returning to the "traveler clan" fold.

Aunt Libby's stolen silver flatware.

Mrs. Hamilton-Reis's Dutch tulips smashed by RV wheels.

David's keyed Mustang.

They knew how to hurt her most, through embarrassment. What would they do this time? Hard won control inched away.

A door swung wide. Ma filled the opening.

Gita had aged. The notion stabbed through Starr with a sympathy she didn't want and outright feared because it made her vulnerable, seeing those streaks of gray in her hair, the wrinkles lining her mother's face. Her ma still wore her hair long and curly like Starr, gathered in a ponytail, her jeans and shirt with fringe in constant motion, giving her a hummingbird air as she raced down the steps. "Good morning, sunshine."

More like *good afternoon,* but Starr wasn't going to start off the conversation by being contrary. "What brings all of you to the area?"

"Our baby girl of course," her father answered, standing on the top step, stretching his arms over his head.

No denying her parentage. She'd inherited her mother's hair, and her da's face and slight stature, which gave her a clear view into their home on wheels. Over his shoulders she could see the standard assortment of purses. Not that her ma collected purses in the manner of most fashion-conscious PTA moms. Nah. Gita Cimino collected purses *from* PTA moms.

Currently visible—a black sequined bag with a cell-phone caddy dangling and an oversize brown leather bag with diapers sticking out and a couple of bottles tucked into pouches along the side. Starr's heart squeezed as she thought about the poor young mother reporting her bag stolen while she jostled a hungry baby on her hip.

Gita and Frederick Cimino were a match made in hell.

The other two Cimino brothers and their wives had their own scams of choice. The older brother special-ized in items bought in bulk on the Internet and sold door to door—magic sweepers, garbage disposals, dishes, vitamins, herbal remedies. You name it, Starr figured he'd scammed it.

The youngest brother specialized in out-of-court set-tlements—slipping on a sidewalk, breaking a tooth in a restaurant, the list went on. She'd been roped into those many a time as a child because an injured kid evoked major sympathy.

Was it any wonder she'd been so jaded when at ten years old she'd clutched the social worker's hand and stood in front of Aunt Libby's looming double doors?

"So hey there, Starr," her mother called, making her way across the lawn. "No hug for your ma?"

"If you need one, then I'm over here."

Her mother hesitated mid hummingbird buzz across the lawn and perched her hands on her hips. "Still carrying a grudge, I see."

Starr stayed silent even though she wanted to speak. Nearly being killed by the woman after being stuck in the camper all day in the heat? Reasonable grudge material so far as she could tell.

While a very, very wise Frederick headed for a walk along the beach, Gita skimmed her way across the sandy lawn and took the Beachcomber steps more slowly. Starr could feel her skin tightening in fear of the hug…. Then Gita dropped to sit beside her, no fake semblance of familial affection, thank goodness, which showed an understanding of Starr's position. In that moment, Starr forgave her a little—or at least eased up on some of the anger.

She hadn't even known how much rage roiled inside her until she opened the tap to ease a cup free, almost like working an overfull keg at the bar. Could the rawness of her emotions be blamed on David's return?

Might as well make conversation, and the obvious questions needed asking after all. Heaven knew she needed to deal with them before David came charging over like a bull on a rampage. "What time did y'all pull in last night?"

"Around 3:00 a.m."

So she'd been deeply asleep by then, dead tired after closing up the restaurant. Still, she wondered how she'd missed the arrival of the caravan. It was ghostly spooky how they'd sneaked up on her. And David's return, too. The cosmos was ganging up on her today. "You must have better mufflers these days. I didn't even hear you."

"Your uncle Benny picked up a few extra, dirt cheap off the Internet." She stroked a seashell-encrusted stepping stone at the base of the stairs and by the covetous gleam in Gita's eyes, Starr knew where to look if it turned up missing tomorrow.

"I should have guessed. He's always got his eye out for those bulk bargains." When she'd been around nine, she'd helped him hawk encyclopedias. No matter to Benny that they were a decade out of date.

"Of course you didn't guess. You're getting rusty since you've been away from the family for so long." Gita shook her head and tutted, loosening a gray curl from the band. "It's to be expected since you're not with the family anymore."

Implied guilt? She refused to accept it.

So why couldn't she find her backbone? Time to rectify that now, as she'd told David she would. Not because she saw David's mother peering around her heavy brocade curtains, but because Starr wanted to regain control of her business, of her life before she weakened and leaned on David again.

"Ma, you'll need to tell the family to move the caravan over to the beach, so it's not visible from the road."

"Ah, we're bad for business parking in the lot like that." She nodded with surprising understanding and not a sign of censure. "Gives off the air of vagrants."

She hadn't expected it to be this easy or for her mother to be this blunt—or honest. "I don't mean to be insulting." She fished in her pocket and pulled out a folded piece of paper. "I've typed up a list of some beautiful waterside RV parks in the area that will accommodate your needs perfectly."

Her fist clenched around the paper while she waited—prayed—that her mother would take the list and hit the road.

"Baby, I'm not insulted. I understand about doing whatever it takes to bring in the buck. We'll get off your lawn and onto the beach over there. No worries or need to waste money on one of those parks. You've got a great view there and we'll situate ourselves just right, now that we know the angle you want us to work. We'll have vacationers stamped all over us by sundown."

"Hey, Ma, wait—"

"Shhh. Just listen." Gita slung her arm around Starr's

shoulders and pulled her in for that unwanted hug. "We can play roles well. We'll even beef up business for your little artsy gift shop as a personal favor. You'll see."

Starr stiffened even as her arm automatically slid around Ma's waist out of habit. Already she was falling back into old habits even though she'd told David not a half hour ago that she had a spine of steel. David. Why did all of her thoughts have to cycle back around to him?

This wasn't what she wanted at all. She wanted them out of sight. Actually, she wanted them gone before their con games and get-rich schemes caused trouble in town. Aside from the fact that she couldn't condone their crimes, she also couldn't bear these reminders of the gypsy child she'd been. A member of a traveler clan not worthy of David. How had the conversation shifted from having them out of sight to them poking their sticky fingers into her business?

The metaphorical beer keg exploded and she didn't have a clue how to stop the spewing mess of her emotions.

Three

Standing in her parents' RV doorway with stars glinting overhead at the end of one of those endless days, Starr passed the bags full of chicken wings and everything else she could think of to feed the gang supper. Hopefully this would keep them happily settled inside for the night.

Her aunt Essie—Uncle Benny's wife—shuffled off the Styrofoam boxes of food to the mini counter by the sink, pushing aside a Crock-Pot.

"Come on in and join us," Aunt Essie offered in that fake Bostonian accent she affected in an effort to claim she was a down-on-her-luck member of *the* Kennedy clan. She actually thought a few touch-football games on the lawn would convince people. "We would love the chance to hear all about your fancy new business."

"Thanks, really, but I've already eaten...." Starr backed off the last step—into air. She'd been swooped off her feet by someone.

A man.

Her stomach lurched as her brain caught up to the fact that a muscular arm banded around her waist. The scent of salty ocean breeze, expensive soap and...exotic *man* wafted up to her nose.

One man in particular.

David hefted her closer against his chest, his breath hot and bearing a hint of toothpaste against her ear. "Good night, ma'am," he said nodding to the crowd snatching containers of food. "Starr has other plans for supper this evening."

Pivoting without waiting for a response, he charged toward the beach with long strides. Away from his house. From her house. Away from the people scattered along the dock pitching shells into the ocean or making out under the moonbeams.

"Care to clue me in on the other plans?" Starr wriggled in his grasp. He hitched her higher, up over his shoulder in a fireman's hold. "I'm not enjoying these plans."

Well, perhaps she was a little interested and fired up as she grabbed hold of his waist to steady herself. Then she figured she shouldn't let him know she'd given up quite so easily. She kicked her feet in midair and managed to land two good thunks that elicited a grunt if not a more satisfactory outright ouch. "David, put me down."

"No." He kept right on walking, hitching her higher.

She gritted her teeth against the image of her family crowding the door of the RV, Aunt Essie and Uncle Benny side by side, watching while others peered through the windows. Jeez. Couldn't they just eat their supper, for heaven's sake?

"This is not the way to win me over." The macho show of force should have torqued her off, and it would have if she could think through the haze of shimmering hormones. The fine weave of his cotton button-down rubbed against her bargain-bin buy. She'd never been a clothes horse—more of a sales-rack and Goodwill-find shopper—but her tactile artist's senses appreciated the decadent fabrics a man like David wore.

"Who said I wanted to win you over?" he asked without missing a step.

Now that landed an ouch to *her* ego—and momentarily stalled her kicking. "Will you please tell me where we're going and why you're doing this?"

"Soon."

His timing. Always on his timetable, all or nothing.

At least she would get to know where he was taking her. And if she was lucky, she would get to push him into the ocean right afterward as payback for these he-man tactics that—damn him—really were kind of turning her on as she thought of other times he'd carried her over his shoulder only to toss her on a bed, or down onto the sand. Then he would make his way from the foot of the bed paying passionate attention to every inch of her body.

His feet thudded along the pier outside his house, abandoned. Apparently he planned to have their late night conversation out here.

Alone.

She was in trouble. Maybe she could jump in the ocean if she didn't like the path of their chat.

David set her down slowly, sensually easing her body along his until he leaned her against the dock's railing, the bulk of his height blocking out everything but him as he stood in front of her. His pants had stayed perfectly pressed even after a full day of work. His cotton shirt she'd so enjoyed rubbing against bore the slightest wrinkle from the press of her body against him when he'd carried her. Something about the faint wrinkle hinted at an intimacy that tingled through her. Her gaze fell to his arms, his sleeves rolled up, dark hair along his forearms. Strong arms.

Ohhh-kay. Time to shift her attention elsewhere. She looked up to his face. The moonlight cast shadows over his scowl.

She wanted to kiss that grumpy expression right off his face…except…oh, yeah…she was mad at him. God, she forgot that so easily when the sparks started snapping between them.

Starr bit her bottom lip to keep her words and kisses locked up tight. He'd started this. She wouldn't give him the satisfaction of begging for an answer. She'd begged often enough around this man—in bed.

The pupils of his eyes widened. Could he read her thoughts now, too? Was he that good of an interrogator at work? Would she be allowed no secrets from him?

Finally, he blinked. She exhaled.

He tunneled his hand through her curls and cupped the back of her head. "Starr, babe, I thought we went over this earlier today. You've got to stay away from them."

His touch muddled her thoughts when doggone it, she had a list of things, logical things, she wanted to say, such as this wasn't his problem or any of his business, and instead she found herself babbling, "I've asked them to leave and go to an RV park. They refused. Short of siccing the cops on them, I don't know what more I can do to move them."

"Then call the police." His fingers massaged hypnotic circles beyond anything her ma could have set up in one of her psychic scams. "Or evict them. They have no legal right to be here if you don't want them around."

Starr chewed on her lip again. She really should tell him to get his hand off her, but it felt so amazingly good and she'd never been particularly strong when it came to resisting his touch....

The very reason she had to stop this. Now. She gripped his wrist. "David. Stop."

She held his gaze in a battle of wills, the heat of his skin radiating through even his rolled-up shirt cuff.

Finally, his fingers slowed against her scalp and he swung his arm away, to his side. She released his wrist—and the gulp of air in her lungs.

He tugged at his tie as if in need of air, too. "Damn it, Starr, they steal from people, they prey on the weak and they're undoubtedly trying to prey on you."

"I'm too strong to let anything happen." And she was stronger now, thanks to the self-confidence Aunt Libby had given her. "They'll hang out for a few days, realize I don't have any money to give them and then they'll leave. Just like always."

His eyes narrowed. "I can make it happen faster than that."

Too easily she could let him deal with her problems, but she couldn't tangle her life with his again. "No offense to your professional buddies, but don't you think that has been tried again and again? It never works. They always get away with whatever illegal or squirrelly scam they're running."

Technically not true, she had to confess, at least to herself.

The police had caught up with them one time. The summer they had found ten-year-old Starr locked alone in a boiling hot RV for eight hours while her parents had gone door to door collecting money for yet another bogus charity. She'd nearly died of heatstroke. Five days in the hospital later, the child protective services in Charleston, South Carolina, had placed her with Aunt Libby as a foster child.

At first she'd been wary of Aunt Libby. Nobody could be that nice. Slowly, Aunt Libby's maternal magic had worn through the years of neglect and abuse and Starr had begun to heal.

Then had come a new fear—that her family would try to take her back.

Thank God, Aunt Libby had always known just how to handle them on their rare visits to the seaside mansion, always with their hands out. And today, Starr followed Aunt Libby's model of brushing them off.

"Starr?" David snapped his fingers in front of her face, his voice urgent, a hint impatient.

"What, David? Can we make this quick? I need to get back to work." Actually back to Ashley's party, due to start up in an hour.

"Has your family ever been reported to *me*?"

"What do you mean?"

"Has anyone ever told *me* the specifics of their recent scams?" He thumped his chest.

"Well, uh, I guess technically not." She knew he was darned amazing at his job. Heaven knew his mother bragged about his feats often enough. The woman hadn't wanted the two of them together, yet she also hadn't been able to resist rubbing Starr's nose in what a "catch" she'd missed out on as he sent postcards from this country or that.

Little did his proud mama know those far flung travels only cemented Starr's resolution she'd made the right choice. Her connection to Aunt Libby's crumbling old antebellum home, this city, the sisters of her heart went deeper than David could understand.

"David, honestly, I'm not in their inner circle these days since they know I'm not into that kind of life. Even if I were in the know on their plans, they're so darn slippery in the execution."

"No one gets past me."

His confidence was unmistakable.

She couldn't resist jabbing. "Could that be because your enormous ego blocks the doorway?"

His mouth twitched. God, she loved his mouth, those perfectly full lips that brought such pleasure. His ability to laugh at himself made him all the more attractive.

"You always have been the only woman who wouldn't put up with my crap."

David smoothed his hand over her head again, his fingers tangling in her curls as he slid farther this time, down her neck, her back, free of her hair to palm her waist. He flattened her body to his in one of those masterful shows of gentle force that sent her senses tingling even as she longed to stomp on his foot.

He tucked his size-fourteen wingtip shoes gently over the toes of her feet in a preemptive move as if reading her thoughts. "You may be the only woman who doesn't put up with my crap, but you're also the only woman I can't seem to forget."

Darn him. He always did know what to say to melt her like the glue sticks in her arts-and-crafts gun. His foot slipped off her feet so she could arch on her toes to receive the kiss she could already sense coming.

No. She would hold strong against temptation.

She flattened her hands to his shoulders to stop his kiss, if not the embrace. Their chests pumped for air against each other in time with the gushing waves below the dock.

"I have to go," Starr gasped. "We're having a surprise graduation party for Ashley."

His arms stayed banded around her, his chin resting on top of her head. He stood a full foot taller than her, yet their bodies always seemed to fit. "No way can she be that old already."

"A lot of time has passed since you and I were together." Years that had filled his body with muscles and her heart with resolve of what she needed from life.

But oh, how she couldn't push away from this man just yet. She'd resisted the kiss. She could indulge in at least this much.

"A year."

She'd meant since their teenage time together, since they'd had a relationship. "Does that really count? That was just—" incredible, heart-searing "—sex."

That she could narrow down the experience to one word was truly an injustice to a weekend that had left her seeing stars for days.

"And your point is?"

"We don't have anything else in common." Her heart pinched tight at the minor lie. They'd had plans in common, once upon a dream ago. Of course, now they'd plotted their lives and their paths diverged. Still, pushing him away again was tougher than she'd expected. Damn it, why did this have to ache all over again? "I can't see past your eyes anymore but I'll be honest and lay it all out there and say you hurt me. And quite frankly, between you and the gypsy circus act parked on my lawn, I've reached my hurt quota for one lifetime."

If only he would step back and give her space, she could breathe. And yet that traitorous part of her craved his touch. All the more reason she needed to make this break fast.

"Well, babe, while I'm not sure I like being lumped in with a bunch of crooks, I get your point." His hands fell to rest on her shoulders, a warm and too-tempting weight that spurred her to press harder.

She inhaled a bracing breath full of his tantalizing scent. "So while I understand that you have to settle your mother's health issues, you will stay clear of me while you're here." She tipped her chin toward each of his hands still cupping her shoulders. "I don't want us to repeat past mistakes."

This was tough enough—having him touch her, here where they'd once made love under an eiderdown comforter he'd dragged down to the beach behind a dune, back when the place had been less populated.

He raised his hands and backed away. "No past mistakes."

Starr wrapped her arms around her waist to ward off a chill that shouldn't have stood a chance on such a warm spring night. As she watched him lumber away, she let herself take one final moment to enjoy the view before she shook herself back into reality, a reality that would not include him.

Except wait. A dangerous realization tickled up her spine.

He may have said no past mistakes, but Special Agent Word Craftsman had never once agreed to stay away from her.

He was ticked off.

David stood on the outer edge of Ashley's farewell party held in the Beachcombers Bar and watched as everyone celebrated the youngest sister's summa cum laude success. His hand clutched around the gift he'd bought, his mind locked on his earlier conversation with Starr. He'd been pushed for time to find Ashley a gift but being here was important for more than one reason.

How could Starr just call it sex? He might be arrogant...

Might be? He could almost hear Starr's throaty laughter in his ear.

Fine. He had his fair share of ego. He had to be confident in his job, believe in his decisions and forge ahead without hesitation because a moment's flinch could get him killed. Or worse yet, cost someone else's life.

But back to the original source of his frustration. It had never been "just sex" with him and Starr, otherwise they could have figured out how to be "just friends" a long time ago. Otherwise, he wouldn't make a point of avoiding her during times he spent at his condo in downtown Charleston.

Sure, he was gone on assignment often, around the U.S. and overseas, but he spent more time in the city than she knew. Because *he* knew the more they saw each other, the more he risked hurting her again.

Why hadn't some smart guy snapped her up yet?

Some smart guy David already hated with every ridiculous dog-in-the-manger fiber of his being. Hell. David planted his feet in the sawdust-covered floor to keep from barging ahead and claiming her now. He knew he wasn't right for her. She'd made that clear enough. That didn't mean he could stand the thought of her with someone else.

So if he was avoiding her, what was he doing standing on the outskirts of Ashley's graduation party with a present in hand?

Because he wanted to keep himself between her and her scam-artist family. A quick glance showed him that lights blazed inside all three of the RVs. He shifted his attention back to the party and saw only a cluster of around fifty people. The bar floor sported a mix of college students, Citadel cadets and some friends of Claire and Starr's from their clientele, most of whom came from the local Charleston Air Force Base.

David scanned the room and finally found Ashley parked over by the leaning remains of a hacked-up tiered strawberry cake. Starr must have made it specially for her little sister because Starr preferred mint chocolate. A part of him resented that he knew that and a thousand more details about Starr, minute facts that packed his brain and refused to fade.

He inched into the room, flattening his way along the wall until he made it over to the guest of honor, who seemed to prefer to take her congratulations one at a time rather than en masse.

Tall and willowy, Ashley leaned against a support pole, her ever-present long ponytail draped over one shoulder as if to hide the slight remains of her scoliosis.

"Hey there, little sister." He tugged the tail of her auburn hair, kid-sis style. "You're quite the queen of the ball, tonight."

"I would have just as soon gone out to dinner, the three of us girls, but you know my sisters."

"A bit pushy and a lot proud." He let go of her hair. "You're thoughtful to go along with their plan."

"I love them."

His mother would have been shocked to know he envied the camaraderie shared by a houseful of dirt-poor foster girls without a lineage paper worth speaking of between them. Granted, the loner quality had honed him into a stronger agent, but as a kid, he'd watched through his window for years.

Only one female had dared defy his mother and cross the boundary line between the houses to say hello to the boy next door. Starr feared nothing.

So why did she balk at sending away the people from her past parked outside? What hold did they have over her?

All of which he needed to stop thinking about for now. This was Ashley's night.

He started to congratulate the graduate on her summa cum laude grades, but she'd been lured away by someone else wanting to pass along good wishes. He simply set his gift beside the cake and headed back to his perch by the door—

And bumped into a burly blond wall of two men. He recognized Vic Jansen, a lumberjack-looking fellow in flannel and jeans, a veterinarian who'd married Claire last year. Having that big lug around provided an extra level of protection. David would do well to cultivate a friendship with the man.

Time to quit thinking like a lone wolf, a habit ingrained in him growing up as an only child. "Good evening. Sorry I haven't had a chance to come over and say hello since I got back in town."

"No problem. Between work and the baby, I don't see daylight in the yard all that much myself." Vic gestured to the blond giant next to him. "Meet my cousin, Seth Jansen. We finally lured him from out west to join the family here. He bought that small airport ten miles down the road."

"Really?" His curiosity upped a notch. "I hadn't heard it was up for sale."

"It wasn't. I closed on the deal a month ago." Seth Jansen had obviously come straight from work, still in his suit pants and white button-down shirt, sleeves rolled up his only concession for the casual party atmosphere.

"Welcome to town. So you'll be living here in one of Beachombers' B-and-B rooms?"

Damn, but jealousy chomped hard on a man's hide. David waited for the answer.

"Yes, while I finish building a place of my own out by the airport."

Vic hooked his thumbs in the back pockets of his jeans. "I gotta admit, I appreciate the extra set of eyes around here with our new residents parked out back. Seth and I are working swing shifts so one of us is always around to keep an eye on the women."

Of course. David resolved to put his libido on hold. He'd been glad to have Vic around, but then of course Vic would always have the safety of his wife and child first and foremost in his mind—as it should be. Adding Seth to the protective detail significantly increased their odds of keeping Starr safe. And now that Ashley had finished college, they had another female to worry about.

Hell, he needed to get rid of the Cimino squatters ASAP. He'd done all he could at work to set the investigative wheels in motion. Now he needed to create a protective detail on site. And these men were valuable assets.

Four

Starr wiped down the bar for the thirty-first time. The darn thing was clean and she knew it. The whole place was spotless and empty of guests, Ashley's celebration complete.

Vic and Claire were upstairs in their second-floor living quarters with baby Libby. Starr couldn't find it in her to begrudge them their happiness. Claire had struggled hard to learn to let down her barriers and embrace love. And poor Vic had lost a daughter in a drowning accident before he'd moved here. His first wife had blamed him for no good reason and divorced him shortly thereafter. But Vic was a great guy who deserved the happiness he'd found.

And Seth? The big lug was a hunk, no question. She would have to be comatose not to notice. However, even having him reside in one of the third-floor quarters didn't offer the least temptation. She simply wasn't attracted to lumbering blond guys. Or red-haired men.

Or even *most* dark-haired guys, for that matter.

Her attention seemed stuck on *one* particular man with jet-black hair and a mansion-sized ego. Starr hitched a hip against the bar and stared out past the porch to the dock where David stood silhouetted at the end of the pier, staring outward pensively.

She recalled from past conversations that he said the water offered him the perfect place for concentrating, sorting through problems. The water drew him. He'd sailed competitively throughout the U.S. and even in Europe—as long as it hadn't interfered with his soccer playing. He'd wanted to compete professionally but his mother had found that too plebian.

Off he'd gone to college on a joint soccer and academic scholarship to circumvent his mother's power and money altogether—and taken a public service job, his dream, not his family's. The house and half the money, however, had become his at twenty-one because of his father's will, regardless of his horrified mother's wishes.

Now David answered to no one.

Starr wadded the rag in her fist, clutching it to her aching stomach. No doubt, the complexity of this man called to her.

Her gaze drifted to wicker baskets filled with gifts for

Ashley. David's rested right on top. A satiny backpack in the bright pinks Ashley loved, but ergonomic to accommodate her spinal problems. Big purses and briefcases left her already-out-of-whack vertebrae aching. It took a man completely comfortable in his masculinity to pick out magenta anything.

And his present for Ashley meant more to Starr than if he'd bought her a hothouse full of roses or some hefty gift certificate.

He deserved a decent thank you.

Starr pitched the soggy rag into the sink behind the bar and made her way down the steps, across the lawn and along the planked dock. She couldn't help herself. She reached to pull free the hair band restraining her curls and tried, tried, tried to tell herself she shook her hair loose because her head ached from the tight restraint. But she knew deep inside, a part of her enjoyed the fact that David liked her hair down. And darn it, even if her clothes—shirt and a shirt made of many scarves—might be rumpled from the long party, she would indulge in this small vanity to look that bit better in front of an old boyfriend.

Each step closer to David pulled the tension tighter in her stomach, too much like the days when she'd watched from her room for him to step from his house and gesture for her to join him. An instant later she would slip free for a 2:00 a.m. walk along the shoreline while they shared dreams and kisses. She shouldn't still want a simple conversation with him so much.

But she did.

Starr slowed to a stop beside him, careful not to let so much as her flowing scarf top brush against his suit that cost more than she made in a month. "You're still here."

He shifted to face her, leaning back on his elbows. "I could have been anyone lurking around." His white shirt shone like a beacon in the dark, his suit jacket draped over the dock rail, his tie tucked in the coat pocket, his top two buttons open to reveal a patch of throat she longed to kiss—holy cow he was that much closer to out of his clothes.

David blinked, slowly, sensually. "You should be more careful. I don't like your being alone at closing."

"I'm not alone." She forced words past her lips only half-aware of what she said, her body more in tune with the angle of his legs, his arms, the rise and fall of his chest, the widening of his pupils darkening his eyes. "Vic's upstairs. Seth, too. They're a simple shout away if I need them."

"And does Vic walk you over to the carriage house after closing?" He paused for a slow blink, then angled closer, possessively. "Does this new guy—Seth?"

David couldn't be jealous, could he? "First off, I don't need a man to be my keeper. Second of all, I'm only walking across my own lawn. And third of all—"

"You run a bar and you're hot. What if some drunk—"

"I carry a can of Mace and I have taken a self-defense class—" Hey, had he just paid her a compliment in there? Something about being hot. She indulged in a quick shiver of pleasure before she continued, "You'll have to accept it when I say that I'm a careful adult. Thank you for being concerned."

"And butt out." His mouth tipped in a one-sided smile made all the more devilish by the stars glinting off his dark hair.

"I didn't say it." She shook her head, her curls teasing her shoulders.

"You didn't have to. I hear you loud enough." His smile faded "Where's your Mace?"

"Fine. I forgot my purse with my Mace tonight because you've shot my concentration to hell. There. Are you satisfied?" She hated the bobble in her voice. "David, I don't want to argue with you anymore. We're going to bump into each other for years to come—or until you sell your mother's big old house. Can't we find a way to be polite to each other without ending up in bed?"

That silenced him for seven sloshes of the waves against the dock. He reached, looped an arm around her waist and pulled her against his chest, holding her loosely, his chin resting on her head. "I'm not sure."

There was such a familiarity in the way he touched her. Could it simply be because they'd known each other such a long time? Each time she saw him, she resolved she would handle things differently, establish distance, and yet they fell right back into their old patterns of physical ease around each other. Time after time, she tortured herself by allowing touches that couldn't lead anywhere.

Except last year…

Starr stood still, their only contact his hands on her back, his chin on her hair, but ah, she could feel him catching her scent in a primal way. "It was considerate of you to bring Ashley a gift, and such a thoughtful one, too." Sure it was just a backpack, something that likely didn't put a dent in his abundant portfolio, but the time and thought expended were far more valuable.

"You taught me how to pick a gift that fits the person rather than something generic." A wicked smile of reminiscence creased his tanned features. "I never expected to have roses pitched back in my face."

Well, whoa. That tossed cold water on her kissing memories. She tipped back to smile up in his face and let her arms slide to loop around his back in return. "I did *not* throw them back in your face."

"No. Worse yet," he continued, oddly enough not seeming in the least angry. Rather amused. "You sent them to my mother with a card labeling them From a Secret Admirer. My poor mother freaked out thinking she had a stalker."

She settled into the memory with him. "At least you finally got that German shepherd you always wanted."

"Günter was a damn good dog." He paused for the first time with a sentimentality that caught her unaware. However, before she could reach out to offer any sense of comfort, he continued, "Then I tried again with those chocolates that cost my whole allowance because, contrary to popular belief, my mother didn't let me spend whatever I wanted."

What? She hadn't known that. She felt pretty bad now as she remembered passing out the Godivas like lemon drops at lunch at school. Except afterward he'd watched her more closely and *that* was cool. Then he'd figured out how much she'd enjoyed her art class. The tubes of paint made into a bouquet of flowers had totally won her over.

She'd pulled him behind the lockers and plastered a kiss on him that even the memory could have melted those paints had she been holding them today.

How could he be so Cro-Magnon and thoughtful all at once? That dichotomy had kept her in his bed far longer than had been wise for her heart. All the more reason to leave now because, heaven help her, her heart pounded in her chest so hard surely he could hear. Her quick breaths matched his and knowing he wanted her every bit as much as she wanted him upped the ante to sheer torture.

"Enough, David, that's all I wanted to say. Thank you, I mean. It's late and I should turn in. Morning comes too fast. I hope everything is okay with your mother."

"Fine. Good night." He slid one hand free to click off the dock light.

She should pull away before she did something silly like arch up to press a thank-you kiss on one side of his mouth and a goodbye kiss on the other. And hey, that felt so good open-mouthed kiss smack dab…

His arms were tightening around her and dreams had

somehow become a reality with his tongue sweeping a deep and strong possession, his hands palming her back to press her breasts against his solid chest. Always, always his touch worked a perfect blend of yes, just like that and please, please more…

Her hands crawled up his back, the thin cotton of his shirt offering too little barrier to keep out the heat of him. Too much barrier when she wanted to touch skin.

Bad idea. Bad idea. *Bad* idea.

But sweet mercy, she was going to do it anyway. Just a sweep of hard, muscular pecs to give her something to dream about. She skimmed her hands around front to find buttons and made fast work down them until she could touch his chest, feel the gentle abrasion of hair and skin. Muscles pulled tight under her exploration, answering her with an affirmation of want.

She'd been so busy indulging herself that she'd almost forgotten about David's hand. An oversight he fixed for her in a hurry as his fingers wandered down her leg with deceptive slowness. Long, lazy fingers. Her heartbeat quickened.

He slipped his hands under her skirt, up to cup her buttocks and lift her so she meshed torso to torso against him, her feet dangling in midair. He left her with no choice but to trust him, trust his strength to keep her safely in place while they kissed and writhed against each other. Her flesh heated unbearably, her whole body sensitized until she could even feel the kiss of saltwater on the breeze.

Heaven help her, it would be so easy to raise her legs and wrap them around his waist as she'd done often enough. And before she knew it, her legs locked around him with a sweet familiarity.

A simple flick of her hand would open his fly and release the steely length of heat she felt against her belly. She wore a thong, so it wouldn't take much for him to slide aside her panties and plunge inside. But she couldn't bring herself to take that step.

Even thinking of it though, her body throbbed—begged—for the release he could bring her. It had been so long. She needed this. Needed him. A whimper escaped her. A whimper that sounded remarkably like a whispered *please*.

Please?

That lone word brought her back to the present. She would never let herself be so swayed by this man or any man again. She'd grown up at the mercy of her parents. Control over her own life meant everything to her.

With more than a little regret and an ache clear down to her toes, Starr slid her legs from around his waist and down to the dock. Given their height difference, gravity took care of the rest, pulling her lips free from his. Too bad she could still feel the heat of him on her mouth, the taste of him swirling through her.

With shaking hands she straightened her skirt, fingers plucking at the fabric. Why did something so wonderful have to be so wrong for her? She *knew* that being with David inevitably led to hurt. What would make her think now could be any different?

Nothing. She had nothing to go on. And damn, but that made her want to cry, which was dangerous because she just kept picturing that thoughtful pink backpack present for Ashley.

Starr backed away. "Thank you for coming by the party and thank you for worrying about my parents. You're good at taking care of people. You're a good man. But really, we're okay. We three sisters have been looking out for ourselves for a long time. Granted, dealing with my parents can be tough, but I need to do this. You won't always be here. So where does that leave me if I only know how to lean on you?"

He stayed silent though she took some small comfort from the fact that he seemed to struggle for the next breath almost as hard as she did.

"Exactly," she said sadly, wondering why she'd almost hoped he would have a quick rebuttal. She backed another step on shaking legs and then another, none of them far enough to cool the heat still searing through her at just his simple eyes on her body. "Goodbye, David."

Starr's farewell still ringing in his ears two hours later, David dropped to lounge against the wooden rail of his veranda, a glass of Scotch in his hand—a poor substitute for what he really wanted to be holding right now.

The moon shot a road of light across the ocean, so straight and simple. He'd stared at that often as a teen, planning his escape from this place. But he hadn't bargained on leaving alone.

His gaze shifted over to Starr's carriage house, all lights off where she now no doubt slept.

Starr. In bed. Naked.

A recipe for his insanity if ever there'd been one. David scratched behind his ear as if to shake loose that thought enough so he could function better.

And all the things that came after.

Still, he had an obligation to see this through. Find out what had brought her parents here and see them on their way. Once he knew Starr was safe, he could return to his normal life. In fact, he had a kick-ass assignment in Turkey coming up within the next two weeks.

Too bad Starr was so damn resistant to travel after her childhood. The artist within her would really get off on the rainbow display of tapestries to be found even in a simple row of street vendors.

He even had the perfect means of transportation for private, personal use at his fingertips now.

Talking with the Jansen cousins at the party, he'd found out more about Vic's cousin Seth. Apparently the guy was a pilot, small craft sort, who'd invented a must-have security device for airports to help combat attacks on planes during take-off and landing. He's registered the patent and made a mint.

Gotta admire the entrepreneurial spirit combined with making a major difference for his country.

Now he'd bought a local airport to set up search and

rescue operation in conjunction with a retired Air Force Special Ops guy, Rick DeMassi.

An idea sparked in David's mind. Why wait? He'd been approaching this problem with keeping Starr safe all wrong. He eyed the RVs full of bloodsucking leeches planning God only knew what this go round. No question, he needed to put distance between her and her family. And if he couldn't uproot them in a timely fashion, why not move Starr?

What better way than to entice her to go away with him?

Already he could hear her shriek of outrage, but he could overcome that. He swayed the toughest of people for a living and, quite frankly, given Starr's response last night, she wouldn't take that much persuasion.

He couldn't keep his hands off her and the feeling appeared mutual. Maybe they needed to get this out of their systems once and for all. And if they managed that very far away from South Carolina while his people in the office did a little unofficial investigation of her parents, then all the better.

He had a line on a nurse to watch over his mother. Nothing held him here. Talking Claire into letting Starr take a couple of days off would be the easiest part of the plan. Mamma Bear Claire would want Starr away from the Cimino Caravan as much as he did.

So, now all he had left to do was figure out what place would best entice Starr to fly away from all her worries and persuade her to go for it. But surely someone with his skills wouldn't have a problem with one five-foot-tall artist.

A petite bombshell artist who'd evaded him for a decade.

Five

No worries, Starr reassured herself. It was a new day.

Kneeling behind the cash-register counter, she pulled out a stack of hand-painted T-shirts to restock the shelves and resolved to be more optimistic. She'd stood her ground with David. No more *falling* back into old habits of falling into bed. She would put him in the past once and for all so she could move forward.

Much like she needed to put the Ciminos in her past?

Starr thunked down on her butt with the stack of shirts in her lap, her hand sketching over the inventory for extra gift-shop goodies. She might appear busy to the casual observer, but man, she was way gone in daydream land.

She had to stop short at placing David in the same category as her unfeeling, thieving relatives because, truth be told, she shared good memories with David. Amazing memories.

He deserved a slot in the sentimental file, even if placing him there gave him sway over her emotions now. She refused to deny the happiness they'd shared. To do so would be unfair, especially after he'd made her feel special when she'd spent so much of her life feeling like not just a second-class citizen, but somewhere around seventy-second class.

She also had to give him credit for helping her possess the confidence to pull off this business venture when she'd first had the inkling to present the notion to her sisters after Aunt Libby's will had been read and they'd realized the old house was theirs. And wow, who would have thought three girls with barely a penny between them could have turned a crumbling old Southern beachside mansion into a booming restaurant?

Business grew stronger by the day. The traffic now buzzed past, shepherded in for brunch by the extra help she and her sisters had been able to hire in the past months. Their success had been a real coup for a restaurant and bar that had only been in business for a couple of years. They'd even had enough cashflow this year to renovate the third floor for boarders or vacationing guests.

Their lunch and bar crowd came mostly from the military base and college community. Their supper clientele and parties catered to the wealthy interested in having their event in a historic Charleston beach home.

Having the large marina next door helped, as well, although there were some who wanted to turn that marina into a more sleek venture. Beachcombers had survived a number of buyout attempts from people who'd wanted to turn the stretch of land into condominiums. She and her sisters could have made a mint. But this business was about more than just staying together. It was about holding on to the only home, the only real sense of family the three of them had ever known.

Being a part of a growing legacy totally rocked and she never intended to take that for granted. No matter that David had tried to lure her into roaming the world with him during some of his less classified gigs as an OSI special agent. The enticing offer warred mightily with her desire for roots. Why couldn't he compromise?

Starr tossed a couple of the painted seashell ornaments on top of the shirt stack and rose.

And froze.

She sniffed once, twice. And yes. Her senses were right on. She would recognize her mother's over-applied cologne anywhere.

Starr peered around the side of the hostess station and sure enough Gita was checking things out with an attention to detail that went beyond curiosity. She wasn't stuffing her pockets, so Starr kept her peace and just watched rather than instigate a conversation. She would find out more this way anyhow.

Gita picked up the debit card machine, played around with the numbers for a moment, not that it would make a difference since she hadn't swiped a card, then shifted her attention to swishing her hand along a dangling line of necklaces as if playing an instrument.

Apparently bored, she made her way back to the door to—omigod—the rest of the family

So much for positive thinking. What were the odds that her family and David's mother would all decide they wanted brunch at the same time? And did they all have to wedge themselves through the double doors at once while the waitresses were occupied? The towering lobby seemed to shrink, oxygen definitely in short supply.

She'd never had a panic attack before, but she suspected her first might be well on its way.

Then it hit her. They had different dining rooms downstairs. She would simply place David's mother in her regular area—yes, for some bizarre reason the woman frequented Beachcombers for meals—and pray she didn't hit the buffet at the same time as Aunt Essie and company.

Of course that meant Starr would have to talk to David's cranky, judgmental mom, while keeping her eyes on the line to stage the right moments to set her free to fill her plate without running into the Ciminos. This would be pretty much like the mini-circus act her uncle Hugo had tried to offer schools. She'd broken her wrist trying to learn to ride a unicycle.

But she wasn't a defenseless child now.

Starr dumped the shirts and ornaments on a shelf and sprinted for Ashley over by the kitchen door. "Please, please, please take care of my relatives. Seat them at table thirteen. And tell them that's the number. They'll love it. They're into spurning superstitions." Starr monitored the incoming guests' progress. "I'll take care of Alice Hamilton-Reis."

The older woman had a way of leveling those censuring sniffs and glares at Ashley that made the younger girl draw into herself. But not on Starr's watch.

Ashley swept her long red hair back into a scrunchie as if preparing for a sweaty ordeal. "Are you sure you don't want to swap? I'll be glad to take on the old bat for you."

Starr's heart swelled at even the offer and what it no doubt cost shy Ashley to make. Sister love was a special thing.

"No, really. I'm going to manage her so she's out of the flow of traffic." She felt a pinch of scruples, too—which really bugged her. "Besides, David's worried about her health and the last thing I want on my conscience is to have her stroke out in the middle of her hash-brown casserole because the Ciminos tried to snitch her wallet."

"I really can handle her," Ashley insisted with a thread of steel in her voice Starr had never heard before. Maybe she needed to take a second glance at her baby sister who'd just graduated from college, not so much of a baby anymore.

Later though and she wouldn't make a test run on the theory with Mrs. Hamilton-Reis. Old Alice had more steamroller impact than all the Ciminos combined when she wanted, and Ashley…well…she'd been fragile for a long time. "I appreciate the gesture, but this is one ghost I'll take on by myself. Okay?"

Ashley reached to hug her sister in a fast embrace. "Good luck."

"Thanks, sweetie." Hey, it wasn't as if she were going to the gallows. Was she?

Starr glanced over her shoulder and saw Mrs. Hamilton-Reis making her way to the hostess station, her gaze cutting ever so slightly toward the Ciminos straggling behind her. Time to make an end run.

Starr patted Ashley on the back and they charged ahead. She listened to how her younger sister's quiet voice somehow cut through the babbling mayhem of the mass of chatter as she guided them to the left, leaving Starr alone with her charge.

"Good morning, Mrs. Hamilton-Reis. Would you like your regular seat by the window?"

She didn't understand why the woman came over so often when she obviously disapproved of the place and constantly complained about the food—after she ate. It was an odd dance they did, the aging lady griping, Starr always giving her a complimentary twenty percent off in recompense.

"Of course." She hitched her purse into the crook of her elbow, the same designer black leather bag Starr had seen the woman carry for as long as she could remember.

As Starr wove her way around tables of diners, she

wondered what had happened to make the woman so sour. Surely something like that didn't happen in a vacuum. People had reasons for their attitudes.

And her parents? Aunts and uncles? That was a tougher nut to crack because of the way they skirted the law. At least Mrs. Hamilton-Reis wasn't a crook, and she had brought up a strong son.

"Here's your regular table. The flowers are fresh since the warm snap brought an early bloom to our azalea bushes," Starr offered up in an honest attempt to connect, since David's mother lived and breathed for her garden.

Now probably wasn't a good time to remember how she and Claire had sneaked out one night and trimmed—okay, mutilated—tea rosebushes into the shape of hooks and arrows because the woman had made little Ashley cry for snapping a bloom off her magnolia tree. The darn thing had been right on the property-line border after all.

"They're a lovely shade of pink," Mrs. Hamilton-Reis acceded, while straightening the silverware in subtle censorship, which totally negated the compliment. Not surprising. That was her way after all.

What had it been like for David to grow up in that kind of negative atmosphere? How odd she'd never considered that before, instead simply thinking of him as the pampered, beloved heir.

Mrs. Hamilton-Reis settled in her seat, arranged her napkin in her lap with exaggerated care, taking her time even to glance over the menu, though she always chose the buffet, and finally she set down the plastic-covered specials of the day. "So I see those people are still here in spite of my advice."

Reaching into the back pocket of her jeans, Starr gripped the tiny pad of paper and pencil for taking orders. Pencil poised, she tried not to snap it in two. "Yes, ma'am, they are."

She wouldn't give the woman the satisfaction of saying she wanted the people gone, as well.

"Have they said how long they intend to stay?"

How was this her business? But that answer would start sparks. "Don't worry. They never stay long. You'll have your view of the ocean back before you know it." Diversion needed now. "We have some new items on the brunch menu you'll want to try. Claire added a heart-healthy sausage and egg strata made with an egg sub-stitute. You'll find it on the buffet."

The woman sniffed. "Are you insinuating I'm at death's door? Don't bury me yet, young lady."

She couldn't win with this woman, no matter what was said. "David mentioned you have some health concerns that brought him home early from an assign-ment. I only wanted to be helpful."

There. Talk your way out of that one. If she denied the health issues, she would have to admit she'd tricked her son into rushing to her aid for nothing. Starr waited for a three count that certainly felt like a guilty silence to her before the conversational thread picked up again.

"I imagine I'll try your sister's new concoction over

on the buffet. It never hurts to be careful with our diet." She passed the menu back up to Starr. "Of course I'll take my regular pot of mint tea."

Hmmm… A crafty dodge if ever she'd heard one. Not that it mattered because she was staying clear of David now.

She turned toward the buffet ready to escort her cranky customer over to load her plate and, ah, no. Starr flinched. Apparently Ashley had been overwhelmed by the task of containing the Ciminos. Aunt Essie was busy making her way from one table to the next passing out flyers for heaven only knew what. She usually tried to hock cooking herbs. Weeds she grew in the back of the mini-hothouse window of her van.

Starr only wished she could split herself in half and keep Essie Cimino and Alice Hamilton-Reis apart.

Why had she made such an effort to keep the woman away from the Cimino crowd? It shouldn't matter anymore if David's mother parked herself on the RV steps every single day griping. It shouldn't matter at all what the woman thought…unless Starr cared about David's world.

Ah, rats. The pencil snapped between her fingers.

She was no more over him now than she'd been when she'd risked shimmying down the trellis to meet up with him ten years ago.

David carried a glass of sweet tea out onto the veranda and wished for something stronger, but he couldn't afford to water down his guard right now. Not until he had a few less Ciminos in residence.

At least he had his mother settled in with a nurse/companion. His mother had nearly argued herself into a heart attack, but he'd stood his ground. If she had health problems, then he wanted someone on hand to watch out for her. He had a job—and he wasn't a qualified health-care professional.

She hadn't been happy, but once she'd realized he didn't intend to head off to another continent right away, she'd calmed down. He settled in a lounger, tipping back his drink. Beach music from the bar next door tempted him to seek out Starr, say hello, tuck her against his chest and dance with her nice and slow, their bodies fitting against each other.

His gaze scanned the yard, over to the caravan to ensure they were all locked down tight for the night. Only to find instead they were in the midst of a late evening barbecue. They'd rolled out the cabana and a mini charcoal grill with… He caught the scent of hot dogs on the ocean breeze.

Lawn chairs littered the beachy scene. And in the middle stood Starr, silhouetted by a bug candle and a tiki torch.

From her stiff stance and hands on her hips, she didn't appear at all cheerful. Which meant David was far from happy himself. Protectiveness roiled through him. Staying put was not an option.

Setting his glass of tea aside, he surged to his feet.

He took the side stairs two at a time and made his way across the lawn not at a run, but at a determined walk that left deep footsteps in the sandy lawn.

Just as he made it to the first RV, a man stepped from through the door and stopped his progress.

"Whoops. 'Scuse me." Frederick Cimino, Starr's father, swung shut the door, holding a bag of marshmallows. "Hey, you're that neighbor cop kid, aren't you?"

David normally didn't trot out his credentials and he certainly didn't brag, but he absolutely wanted to intimidate the crap out of this man who'd made Starr's childhood a living hell. "Special agent."

"Ah, an agent." Frederick rocked back on his heels, his sandals digging into the sand. "All that money and still you decide to work. Gotta admit, I don't understand that."

"Gives me a reason to wake up in the morning." David kept Starr in his peripheral vision while taking this opportunity to find out more about her father. Knowing the opponent always offered an edge.

Starr's father grinned. "Who says a man needs to wake up early?"

"I imagine it's all about perspective." Exerting some pressure on the man could only benefit and it certainly couldn't do any harm. "From my perspective, you have a great deal of cargo stored in these RVs. I'm sure you have documentation for its purchase, and none of it just fell off the back of some truck."

"Why, Special Agent Man, you're lucky I'm easy-going or I could take offense at that." His eyes might be the same shade of brown as Starr's, but they held none of her giving honesty.

Bad karma for Frederick. David had stood nose to nose with some of the world's worst terrorists. This man *would* leave, sooner or later.

David lounged against the side of the RV, blinked slowly. Mostly to tamp down how much the man pissed him off simply by existing. "I imagine you won't take offense, because I'm not a man you want to anger."

Frederick was smart enough to nod an agreement. "Starr's enough of a Cimino to know a sweet deal when she sees it. So I kind of figured we'd end up family one day. Why would I want to piss you off? We're all about making the most of a good thing."

It was all he could do not to throw the man off the property then and there for talking about Starr, much less occupying the same piece of land. Good God, as if she should sell herself to the highest bidder. David vowed right there, these people would be gone before they had another week to so much as bother Starr.

But for some reason Starr couldn't bring herself to evict these freeloaders, which further emphasized his notion to take her away from here now. With her out of Charleston, he could work with his contacts at the local police department to keep the area safe—and make it clear to the Ciminos that all the security labeled this a no-scam zone.

For tonight, he would have to back off. But the

Ciminos' days here were definitely numbered and he would keep Starr out of their path so they could wreak as little havoc as possible over her psyche in the interim.

He now had a plan, all he had to do was get her to go along with it.

Starr stuffed her head under her pillow, longing to recapture the tingling sensation of her dream.

She and David. Together. Far away from here with no concerns but totally immersing the other in pleasure until they both couldn't contain the building cries of completion.

Instead the only sound she heard was that blasted ringing of the telephone. On and on it went with annoying persistence. She punched either side of the pillow, sealing it around her head until she needed to peek her nose out for air.

The phone rang again. Persistent person, whoever it was.

She flopped over onto her back and reached for the receiver. "It's not even eight o'clock yet, so if you're a telemarketer, I'm going to stick pins in a voodoo doll bearing your image."

"I hear it's your day off."

David's voice rumbled in her ear, rekindling the searing need through her veins coming so close to the explicit coupling in her dreams. She swallowed to clear her throat, and yes, steady her heart rate and breathing before she answered.

"You hear? You must mean you've been bugging my sister…. Let me guess which one." She tapped her temple, sagging back into her pillow and wishing she'd chosen to wear at least a T-shirt to sleep last night.

But it had been so hot and her air conditioner didn't work well, so she'd slept naked with only a sheet that now barely covered her since she'd tangled it around her legs in her restless sleep. "My guess is you went for Ashley since she was probably softened up from that thoughtful gift you gave her."

"Nope. Wrong guess. You lose the prize."

Her hand slid restlessly over her bare stomach, her skin over-sensitized. "If you're the prize then—"

"All right," he interrupted with a low laugh, "no need to get spiteful."

She stroked her fingers over her stomach in a light touch, back and forth, higher every time. "I thought we were bantering."

That stopped him short. His breathing went heavier on the other end of the line. "Bantering, huh?"

She hadn't meant to show her hand that fast. Verbally backtracking, she rushed to speak, her hand stalling just below her breasts. "So Claire sold me out."

"Claire let me know you've worked the past three weeks without a day off."

"That's none of your business."

"You're right. And somehow I managed to find out anyway."

Starr rolled to her side, gathering a pillow against her

chest in counter-pressure against the ache begging for fulfillment. "I imagine that's a great skill in your line of work, prying information out of people."

"Who said I needed to pry it out her? Maybe she thinks you and I have some things to talk about." His voice went low and intimate.

With the tenor of his voice now, just talking could well send her over the edge.

"Just talking? That would be a first for the two of us." Even though simply the sound of his voice turned her on, there was still some truth to the fact that they had spent precious little time conversing.

"Unless you're afraid to be alone with me."

Was she? She hadn't considered a confrontation with him after her realization that this attraction for him wasn't going away after all. But now that she knew that simple truth, maybe it was time to put everything out in the open.

God, this was scarier than she'd expected. It was one thing to think about the fact that she still harbored some kind of unresolved feelings for David. It was quite another to come outright and make herself vulnerable by telling him.

Her gaze strayed to her window, gauzy sheers puffy with gusts from the inefficient air conditioner. The beach stretched with RVs, reminding her of their differences. But she'd grown beyond her upbringing. Right? Made something of herself.

Oddly enough, her parents seemed to be awake unusually early today, as well. Their front door swung open, Frederick stepping out in his jeans shorts and a Grateful Dead T-shirt.

Then he held his hand out to help a woman leave.

David's mother.

Starr shot up straight in her bed. What in the world was she doing there? Gita followed. Starr sagged back against the headboard. Old Alice must be lodging her complaints early these days.

Starr punched her pillow, the air growing chilly without the least help from any decrepit AC.

She measured her words with the same care she put into mixing her paints to achieve just the right hue. "We have a problem that appears to be mutual. We don't want the same things from life, but there's this rogue attraction between us. Since I'm not leaving my house or business, and it seems the Hamilton-Reis Historical Landmark will be there until the end of time, we will be running into each other for years to come. We have to be able to move on with our lives. We can't be sneaking quickies at ninety years old."

That low and sexy laugh of his caressed through the phone lines and over her again. "I bet you'll still be hot as hell."

She couldn't contain her laughter in return, or the arousal their camaraderie brought. She squeezed her legs together against the tender ache and answered, "And you'll still be full of it."

"Don't doubt your appeal."

In that moment she felt the wide chasm of impossibility. "How are we going to put this past us once and for all?"

"That's what you want?"

"Yes," she lied to herself—and to him—again. "Don't you?"

"Of course I want the same thing you do," he answered in that damned evasive way of his that drove her crazy. "Will you trust me and let's try something we've never tried before?"

The possibilities shimmered through her until she couldn't keep her hand from traveling up to cup her breast so heavy and hungry from wanting him. But her own touch wasn't enough. She couldn't evade the truth. She needed him right now at least, consequences be damned.

"Okay. What's your new idea for us try out, David?"

Six

"David, are you going to tell me where we are going before we actually get there?"

Behind the wheel of his Lexus, David kept his eyes on the road, a much safer place to look than at the woman beside him. Soon enough he would have plenty of time to stare at her nonstop.

This outing had taken some fast maneuvering, but he'd come up with a plan he thought would entrance her. He'd also left the house well guarded through his connections at the Charleston Police Department, plus some privately hired guards. He had a good line on a possible debit-card snitching scam the Ciminos may have tried to run in Dallas, Texas, malls.

With luck, he could at least get the cops to arrest them and bring them up on charges. They might well get away with only community service and a fine, but he hoped the threat would be enough to let them know he meant business. Then they would stay the hell away from Charleston in the future.

It had been a near thing getting Starr to leave once they'd seen Frederick Cimino standing out front with his hand painted sign: two for one omelet special. The older man had vowed he'd only wanted to help—and make a little money if they didn't mind sharing a small percentage.

Claire in full fury stomping down the front steps had been enough to scare five Fredericks. Starr had reluctantly left once her father cracked the sign over his knee and made tracks back for the RV beach cabana.

Meanwhile, David could focus his attention on Starr for the next two days. It struck him how they'd spent a large part of their relationship trying to find time alone. Luckily, he had far more resources at his disposal than during his teen years. "Where do you want to go?"

When she didn't answer him, he glanced away from the road over to her sitting in the passenger seat in her low-slung skirt and double tank tops. The noonday sun shone through the window, glinting off the shell necklace that drew his attention to places he could linger for longer than was safe while driving.

She toyed with the larger shell dangling at the

center of the necklace, between her breasts. "Don't you have a plan?"

He dragged his attention back to the highway. "Of course I do, but if you have a preference, I'm always open to suggestion."

"I think for now, I'll see what you have in mind."

Starr giving over control so easily? That was rare. They usually played tug-of-war for a while, but he wouldn't question the victory, although the tussle was sometimes fun. Or rather the making-up had often been mind blowing.

He knew full well odds were strong that they would end up in bed together during these next couple of days. He'd come prepared. But he'd made reservations for two rooms just in case. The choice would be hers. However, once she made it, if she decided on them being together…

Adrenaline pulsed through him at even the thought. "I appreciate your trust. I promise you won't be sorry."

He *would* deliver. And this time, he had something more than sex to offer her—although he hoped they would end up in bed together. Still, in watching her with her relatives, seeing hints of that vulnerable girl she'd once been, he knew he needed to give her something more before he left.

Last year, she'd vowed he'd given her the confidence to open her own business. Having that kind of sway over her life had made his feet itchy then. Even now, a crick started in his neck. However, he knew he wouldn't be free to leave until he gave her one last piece he saw missing in her self-confidence—the strength to say farewell to her relatives for good.

David pulled the car off the main highway onto a two-lane side road, leading to the small privately owned airport.

He'd done further research on Seth Jansen and after a couple of conversations with the man, found him to be a savvy businessman with a keen entrepreneurial eye. Not to mention a helluva gut sense when it came to security. Jansen's airport security inventions had made him a millionaire. His joint search-and-rescue venture with fellow air force pararescueman Rick DeMassi would be a real asset to the community.

David couldn't help but admire a guy who, even after he'd made his millions, still sought ways to give back to the world around him. The privately owned airport sported two hangars, one for Seth's five planes to rent out—a couple of Cessna 152s used for flight training, a Cessna 172, a Cessna 182 and a twin-engine Learjet that he would be using to transport David and Starr.

In the other hangar, he kept his planes for fun—like a World War II Corsair. Jansen had an adventurous spirit, which would work well since David needed the man to be flexible about their plans today.

Starr twisted in her seat, pulling her sunglasses on top of her head as if to see more clearly. She tucked the glasses in place, pulling back her tangle of curls. "An airport? Uh, David, when I said I was up for whatever you had planned, I was thinking more in terms of Italian food versus Mexican food. I wasn't envisioning actually flying to the countries."

He drove the car into the small parking lot, tires crunching on gravel. Shifting the vehicle into park, he turned to face her, staring back at her through his own shades.

"Well, that would be a shame, because travel is exactly what I have in mind."

Starr watched David walk toward the tiny airport terminal while she waited in the running car, air-conditioning humming gently. She'd told him to go on inside without her.

She hadn't told him why.

Fishing in her canvas purse stitched with shells painted to match her necklace, Starr dug out her cell phone. She punched in the numbers for her sister's cell and waited for the pickup.

"Claire," she said without preamble, "I can't believe you told David I could leave for two days. You even went so far as to pack a suitcase for me." She double-checked to make sure David was still inside the terminal—yes—before continuing, "Are you *trying* to get my heart stomped?"

It was one thing to allow herself to spend time with David, talk to him, even sleep with him again. But leave Charleston with him? Be completely and totally alone together in another state? That darn near scared her flip-flops off.

Claire sighed on the other end of the phone with an

older-sister indulgence even though she was only a few years older. "I'm trying to give you a chance to figure out this thing between the two of you once and for all, away from here, away from his mother, your relatives, even this house and your stupid belief that you're not good enough for him."

"I never said that," she replied automatically.

"But you've thought it."

She hadn't bought into that line of garbage, had she?

"But what about my folks? I can't leave you and Ashley to handle all of that."

"What's to handle?" Claire asked with her usual brusque efficiency. "They're here. They eat. Vic's around if I have a concern. Besides, it's you they want to bother, not me."

"But they'll wonder where I went."

"I'll tell them you had a conference related to the business. You left early and you send your regrets, so on and so forth, blah, blah, blah…. What do you think you can do that we can't?"

Starr scrunched her toes into her flip-flops and studied the tiny row of shells painted along the straps. "That's not my point. They're not your responsibility."

"Starr, am I or am I not your sister?"

How could she even ask? "You know you are."

"Damn straight. I am more your relative than any of those people inside those dilapidated homes on wheels. You have done at least this much and more for me in the past. Let me give you a couple of days."

Starr clutched the cell phone, tears stinging her eyes. How had she gotten so lucky to land such an amazing family second go round? "Okay. You're really too generous, but I'll consider it if—and I do mean *if*—David's plans sound like something I can handle."

"Just remember, he's a *man*," Claire drew the word out with wicked intensity, "not a glue gun."

Starr sighed. "Not funny." But a laugh escaped anyway because it was a little funny, and then she sobered. "Promise me you'll keep the cash-register drawer locked tight."

"Sister, I may be generous, but I'm not a fool." Her ever-practical tone brokered no question on that one. "Don't worry."

"But I didn't say for sure that I'm going."

"Yeah, right. See you in a couple of days."

The phone line disconnected.

Starr stared at her silent cell. Was she that transparent? The notion made her want to shout for David and demand that he drive her back to her carriage house pronto. But being contrary wouldn't solve anything.

She had decided to try and work through her residual feelings for him and here was her chance. She just needed to be brave enough to take it. Given all the hardships she'd faced as a child, she was tough. Deep down tough enough to handle anything. She needed to call on that steely spine now to see this through, for both their sakes so she could go of him once and for all…or not?

The airport terminal door swung open. David stepped through, with the Seth at his side. Wow, David really had put some planning into this.

She reached to turn off the car and pulled the keys free. When her feet hit the gravel and she slammed the door shut behind her, David turned toward her, his gaze holding hers for one of those long, electrified seconds that made her remember what it felt like to be a teenager. Then he turned away, said something to Seth that made him nod and head toward the hangar alone.

David started toward her. Lord, he was hotter than the steam rising off the runway. She spent so much time avoiding the attraction, she rarely allowed herself the indulgence of simply looking at him. Today, he appeared so the wealthy Southern male heading for a golf course or on a vacation in his pressed khakis and polo shirt. But those muscles, they still caught her off guard since she'd spent much more time with the leaner teen than the adult male.

His dark hair glinted in the afternoon sun with just a hint of brown in the black. She'd once dreamed of the babies they might have, dark-haired angels with that hint of his devilish smile.

David stopped toe-to-toe with her, not touching. Not needing to. She felt his presence strongly enough.

He adjusted the briefcase he carried in his hand. "I assume this means you've decided to go."

"David, where *are* we going?" she repeated her question from earlier.

"Where do you want to go?" he repeated his same answer, except this time they were nose-to-nose and standing at an airport, so the possibilities were far reaching.

And okay, growing more enticing by the moment.

Except how could he not have a plan? That blew her away. David always had a plan. He was always in charge. He was letting her do the picking?

Her eyebrows pinched together. "Surely you can't mean that. Don't you have to file a flight plan or something?"

He held up the briefcase. "I already have a number of them worked up with Seth for a variety of options. What would you like to see? Shall we go to the lush Louisiana plantations in Natchitoches where we can see the folk-art murals of Clementine Hunter? What about R. C. Gorman's Navajo Gallery in Taos, New Mexico? Or maybe you prefer a trip up New England way to see the work of the eclectic sculptor Joseph Cornell."

How did he know of the assemblage sculptor who combined photographs and bric-a-brac, something so appealing to her own eclectic style? David had certainly done his homework in researching types that would appeal to her. Knowing he'd thought about her that much made her a little breathless.

"What is your point, David?"

"They're all famous self-taught artists."

"That's really thoughtful of you."

He stared at her and waited.

"You want me to make a decision…." And she sensed

something more. Self-taught. "Hey, not so subtle after all. I get it. I should value my art more."

"You said it—" he tapped her on the nose "—not me." He pulled his keys from her hands and thumbed the button to pop the trunk. He pulled out two small suitcases, one she recognized as her own. The things Claire had packed for her.

Hefting the suitcases and his briefcase, David strutted toward the hangar, leaving her to follow whenever she chose.

Lean hips showcased just so in those khaki pants. His polo shirt caressed shoulders so broad and muscular she could rest her hands on them and her fingers would lie flat. He might not need to work but he kept his body and mind honed for his job, a job that offered something of value to society and she couldn't help but admire that.

He made sure little old ladies didn't get scammed by people like her uncle Benny. Fewer mothers lost their diaper bags, forced to file a report while the hungry baby cried.

Sure he dealt on a larger scale, but she thought small scale. Day to day.

She frowned. Was that a holdover from her childhood when she could only think of surviving a day at a time? Something she could address later, because right now it sounded like a plan for the day. She would admire his cute butt and she would go with...

"All right," she shouted after him. "I want to see R. C. Gorman's art gallery."

Without breaking his pace, he held up his briefcase and continued toward the hangar. "Okay then. We'll go to New Mexico."

God, but it had been a tough choice because she would have liked to simply enjoy viewing them all, and she knew if she asked David, he would make that happen. He had always wanted her to do nothing but follow him around the world. And she could see herself enjoying that for a year or even two before she needed home, routine, a normal life he would consider boring.

But for today—or even the next couple of days, she would be the adventurous creature David always encouraged her to be.

And then the possibilities washed over her.

She'd just committed to going away for a weekend with David. Alone, to a hotel, where they would most certainly be doing more than "just talking."

Seven

He had Starr in the Learjet with Seth Jansen piloting them through the bright skies to New Mexico.

Still half-certain he was in the middle of one of his dreams about Starr, David stretched his legs in front of him, watching her stare out the window at the clouds puffing past. The gentle hum of the twin engines afforded them a sense of privacy from Seth flying the craft while they sat in the back of the six-seater.

Finally, he had her alone and away from those bloodsucking leeches she called relatives, thanks to the help of Claire. Her real relative, for that matter. The kind that counted, a person who had Starr's best interest at heart.

Just the two of them together to work through this

off-the-charts attraction that had dogged them through a decade. He couldn't put it off any longer.

Still, questions from home rattled around inside his brain, drowning out the soft buzz of the airplane's twin engines. If only he could figure out why in the hell her family had chosen now to show up. What did they want? Because the Ciminos always wanted something.

At seventeen he'd found Starr bawling her eyes out two days into one of the Ciminos' visits. She'd been terrified of what would disappear from Aunt Libby's house when they left. She'd been afraid that maybe this time she would leave with them to protect those she loved.

Like hell.

Starr rolled her head along her seat to look from her window to him.

"Thank you for planning this. I really haven't gotten away from the restaurant…" She plowed her fingers through those amazing curls, her cheeks puffing with her exhale. "I don't know how long. Probably since we officially opened Beachcombers' doors two years ago."

"It's hard work starting up your own business. You and your sisters have taken on a lot." The clouds broke, revealing the long stretch of desert below. Not much longer and they would be landing.

A smile tugged up her plump lips. "Aunt Libby left us an amazing legacy."

"That piece of land certainly is prime." He'd been approached more times than he could count with buyers for his family's house, but aside from the fact that he couldn't evict his mother, something inside him hesitated to part with the home his family had occupied for over two hundred years.

"I didn't mean the realty or bricks. I meant the concept of home. This was the best way we could think of to keep it." She waved aside the air in front of her. "That's all beside the point. I was thanking you."

"You're welcome." For what, he wasn't sure, not that he intended to admit it.

Her smile returned. "This brings back memories."

"Of?" he prodded.

"Senior prom. Except we're in a plane rather than a limo." She ran her hands over the leather armrests. "Everything's nicer than what I'm used to."

"Is that okay?" He tried to gauge her reaction. He never knew what to expect with Starr. Of course that was part of her allure. He couldn't help but think of that moment on the dock just a couple of days ago when they'd driven each other so crazy he'd nearly forgotten about everything around him.

She scrunched her nose and sank into the luxury of her seat. "I'd be an ungrateful brat if I say no. Besides, only an idiot wants to deal with layovers, security screenings and delays."

"Hey, I like chili dogs better than caviar." He covered her hand with his, his thumb rubbing along the inside of her wrist, as much seduction as he would allow himself for the moment. "It's not always about the money for me."

Her eyebrows rose in apparent surprise. "I'm glad to hear you know that."

He shifted to meet her gaze dead-on, finding it strange they'd never talked about things like this before. But then they'd never had this stretch of time before and it wasn't as if he could touch her the way he wanted while Seth piloted the plane a few feet away.

"The money *does* give me the opportunity to live my life exactly the way I want, Coney dogs in Shea Stadium if I'm in the mood. And not just self-indulgent choices, either. I can make morality choices at work purely based on what I think is right, no concerns about playing politics to get ahead and make a higher pay grade. I'm lucky as hell and I know it."

"And yet you continue to advance anyway."

He stayed silent, savoring the soft skin of her wrist. No need to acknowledge the obvious in her statement.

"This whole day is so surreal, just leaving everything behind." She glanced up at their pilot with the headset on and leaned closer to David. "I appreciate your organizing it for me, but I'm not sure I can guarantee the day is going to end the way I believe you want it to."

She couldn't be any plainer than that, and as much as he wanted her, he wasn't into coercion. She'd been pressured enough in her lifetime as a kid.

The trained investigator in him could see the residual impacts of her upbringing in her. The way she always expected someone to want something from her in exchange. Why hadn't he noticed that before?

Because he'd been too busy thinking with the other head, damn it. Something he needed to rectify now, even when the heat between them continued to flare.

"This is a no-strings offer. We're going to land, have a quick late lunch on our way to the gallery and then look at some artwork before supper. If after supper, you want to go straight to your room alone, that's your call." He meant it, no matter how much he wanted to be with her, it would be mutual or not at all. "We have enough history between us for you to know that I would never hold you to something unless you want the same thing."

She stared back into his eyes, holding for a long drone of the engines before finally nodding. "I trust you."

"Good. Good."

He was glad she did because staying strong against the temptation while sleeping in the room next to Starr would be total torture. All advances in the work world aside, he wasn't so sure he'd made the wisest move in his personal life.

Still questioning his own relationship IQ two hours after landing in New Mexico, David watched Starr's face as she strolled slowly through the gallery.

She wove around the sparse remaining tourists still hanging around in the final minutes before closing. He took note of even the slightest hesitation, searching for preferences of ceramics over silkscreens. Or paper casts over landscapes. She seemed taken in by *all* of it…studying the swirls and colors of each piece.

Finally she paused by a ceramic plate with a silly-looking orange cat on it. Seemed a rather odd choice to him, but then art was in the eye of the beholder and all that. This was her gig. "Do you want it?"

"No." She blinked fast as if pulled from a trance and glanced back over her shoulder at him. "No! Don't even go there, Agent Money Bags. Do not, under any circumstances, buy that for me. You're going to make it impossible for me to enjoy this if I have to worry about admiring any other pieces of artwork for fear you'll whip out your credit card."

"You could throw a 'thanks anyway' in there somewhere." He felt compelled to add. He had just offered to chunk out some serious cash for a tabby-cat plate.

"Your ego doesn't need it." She turned her back to him and returned to studying the array of artwork on the walls and in display cabinets.

"You're right." He closed the few feet between them until he was standing directly behind her. He kept his hands in his pockets even though he wanted to reach for her and pull her so she leaned back against him. He'd sworn there were no strings until she gave an indication otherwise and he was a man of his word. "Good thing I have you around to help me keep my ego in check."

"Yeah, well, since your ego's been deflated for the day, I guess I can give you that thanks for the thought—although I only hesitated because it reminded me of a pet I had for two weeks once when I was eight." She glanced over her shoulder at him; a whimsical smile lighting her brown eyes that shared the same color as her father, but none of the same sentiment, hers so sincere. "And thank you for the whole day. Seeing these in books is nothing like seeing them for real."

"There are two more artists on my short list. With just a simple call to your sister, we could extend the trip and see the works of both." He edged closer, hands still in his pockets, not that it helped *him* any. He could feel the heat of her radiating through the scant few inches between them. Nothing overt that any of the three people remaining in the gallery would see, but God, he couldn't miss it. "You should see the artists I put on my long list."

She licked her lips as if thirsty—heaven help them both if she kept that up much longer. "What about your mother's health concerns?"

"I've hired a nurse to stay at the house and keep watch over her. I couldn't hang there 24/7, and I'm not a health-care professional anyway. A live-in seemed the best solution."

"But you check with the nurse, of course."

"Of course," he repeated. He was a detail man and right now, nothing was more important to him than putting his situation with Starr to rest so he—and the Caravan gang—didn't hurt her again.

"What does the nurse have to say?" Starr's attention shuffled to a series of landscapes with a woman and flowers.

"You're actually worried about my mother even after

the way she's treated you all these years?" All the more reason to make sure he read the signs correctly with Starr and treated her right. He flattened his hands over hers on the glass of the display case, so cool after the heat of the desert sun.

"Yes, I worry about her. She's your mother. If she's deeply ill, I would hate to take you away from her bedside at a critical time, although, um, she looked healthy at brunch last week."

He had to agree that his mother seemed fine, which was a good thing. He suspected she'd wanted attention and things would settle down now. "Other than a slightly elevated blood pressure, she's actually healthy as a horse. I suspect she just gets lonely sometimes and feels the need to call me home."

"It would help if you had siblings. I don't know what I would do without my sisters to help me." Her eyes took on a dreamy look as she stared at the desert landscape of a woman at the waterside.

"They're lucky to have you, too." He finally let himself touch her again, just a hand on her shoulder, a simple, platonic-like squeeze. "Don't sell yourself short."

"Thank you, and I don't."

He kept his hand light on her shoulder, nothing sexual. Problem was his thoughts were anything but platonic. His imagination went into overdrive envisioning what he would do if they were alone in this position.

First, he would flatten his hand to the wall by her head and wrap his arm around her waist, lifting her, pulling her against him. Just a simple adjustment of their bodies and he would be able to slide inside her. Somehow his thoughts created a tangible heat of a full-body press swelling between them until he could almost swear she felt it, too.

Starr shuffled from foot to foot until she made it back to her cat plate again.

David kept his hand on her shoulder through the move. "So do you like that piece because it reminds you of your old pet?"

"Yes." Her answer slid from her lips a bit breathier than before. She paused, cleared her throat and continued, "I like it so much I want to leave it right here for other people to enjoy, too."

He gripped both her biceps and turned her around to face him, hands still cupping her upper arms. "Damn, you're good."

She swayed toward him, pupils widening in her dark eyes with a deep desire he absolutely couldn't misread. "And you're so very bad."

"Which is what makes us so incredible together."

"Ah, David," she whispered, his name drawn out on a sigh, a plea he'd heard often enough in the past to know what she wanted. "I thought I told you I couldn't promise this would end with us in bed."

She startled as a college-aged man walked by pushing a broom. The place was closing and time was nearing to head to the hotel for the night. If they actually made it to the hotel…

Thank goodness he'd made a plan for them to have a romantic getaway, just in case she changed her mind about the no-sex rule. It seemed his preparations would be implemented in mind-blowing, fulfilling detail very soon.

But first, he planned to draw out the pleasure with a tantalizing wait.

David dipped his head, his mouth near her ear. "I know what you said and I agreed things would only be mutual. And I would bet every last one of my training instincts that what I'm feeling right now is very mutual and you've decided it's fruitless to resist."

Eight

"Drive faster," Starr urged from her passenger seat in the Mercedes convertible rental, car top down.

Where had David made their hotel reservations? The next state over?

"You want me to speed up? No can do, babe. I'm already pegged on the limit and that whole law-enforcement official thing obligates me to follow the rules of the road."

He kept a steady pace with cruise control. The car lights beamed ahead, luminescent strips on the asphalt the only glow on the deserted back highway.

Again he delayed fulfilling her need for him, which left her fidgeting in her seat as she had all through dinner. The wind spirited into the neck of his polo shirt just the way her hands longed to do.

They'd been driving for at least forty-five minutes since they'd left the five-star restaurant he'd chosen for their supper. He'd even selected an establishment much like Beachcombers so she could gather work ideas about food—although he'd surprised her when he'd told her they wouldn't be staying there for the night.

Not that she'd been able to think about work or even sleeping. All she'd been able to contemplate during the interminable meal was getting him alone and naked.

Still, he'd drawn out the pleasure, making each bite an aphrodisiac moment. He'd been seductive from the start in everything he'd chosen in this outing. This man in full-tilt charmer mode was irresistible.

She tore her gaze away from him. Her eyes took in the endless stretch of rocky desert on either side of the highway. Nothing but telephone poles, scattered cacti and the occasional Joshua tree, the dry air so different from the humid beach climate she'd come to love at Aunt Libby's.

The gritty wind tore at her hair with a wild abandon that fit the moment, tugging at the scarf he'd brought along to tie back her curls. Eventually she whipped the silky length free and let the wind have its way with her locks much the way she'd given over control of this evening to David.

He obviously had somewhere out of the way in mind, which meant a long time for them to simmer in the car.

Might as well make the best use of this time. She had memories to store.

She slid her hand across the seat, teasing up the length of his thigh, enjoying the heat and ripple of muscle under the rough texture of khaki. "And there's nothing I could do to entice you to take a shortcut?"

Grinning, she squeezed his leg, high, just shy of his fly.

David clamped a hand around her wrist. "Much more of that and we'll end up in a ditch."

He had a point. She sagged back against her seat, resolved to wait.

Except then he turned off the road.

"David? Where's the hotel?" She didn't see any signs of civilization even on the horizon.

"Who said anything about a hotel yet?"

The smile returned to her lips and swirled around inside her, as well. No more waiting, and she did so approve of his plan. She'd always enjoyed the times they'd made love outside as opposed to times they'd sneaked around in his room or hers. Outside seemed so much more neutral. Not her world or his.

He shut off the engine then turned the key to keep the music going, low classical tunes to suit the romance of the moment. Reaching behind the seat, he tugged free an Aztec blanket that would undoubtedly ward off the chill of the desert night because yes, yes, yes she could see in his eyes that soon they would be shedding at least some of their clothes.

She hooked her finger in the neck of his shirt. "How

about you come over here so we don't have to deal with the steering wheel."

"Yes, ma'am." He cupped her waist and hefted her up, sliding into her seat as he settled her onto his lap.

David tugged the blanket around her, tenting it over their shoulders, their bodies already starting a furnace of heat inside. The dashboard lights shone along with the full yellow moon to cast shadows over his square jaw clenched in restraint as a lonely coyote howled in the distance. The breadth of his shoulders alone stole the air from her lungs, and yet this strong man had set her onto his lap with such gentle ease, held her now in such careful, seductive hands.

What a rush.

Her starving hands tugged his polo shirt free of his pants, whipping it over his head and onto the steering wheel.

He chuckled low. "I've always liked how you know what you want."

"You taught me to take what I need."

He growled his appreciation of her words, his hands making slow and tantalizing work of peeling each of her tank tops off, touching her, caressing her, teasing her until they rubbed chest to chest. "Feel free then to act on that now to your heart's content."

Heart? The word made her uncomfortable, so she focused instead on the heavy thudding of his heart under her hand and dipped to press her lips to the warmth of his skin, covering the pulse increasing by the second.

She nibbled along his shoulder, the salty taste of him sending an erotic surge through her. "We've done it in a sandy region before, but this is a bit different."

He nipped her ear. "I thought you might enjoy the wild abandon of the desert."

"The solitude, as well. Just the two of us." She slid her arms around his back, holding him, holding on to this moment as tightly. "No parents on either side of the property line."

No different goals and backgrounds dividing them just as tangibly.

"A definite plus."

The richness of the experience was only enhanced because of the richness of their day together, the fun of touring the gallery. She knew he'd only gone there for her and would probably have preferred one of those Coney dogs and a ball game, but that he'd found something to enjoy in her world, well, that turned her inside out.

And totally *turned* her on.

He traced along the edge of her ear, soothing the nip, his breath hot along with his words and the stroke of his hands. "I also liked the notion that the stars are so vibrant."

"I guess I never thought about that when we traveled this way when I was a kid."

"Whenever I come this way on business, it makes me think of you, because of all the times we made out on the beach."

"You said the constellations reminded you of my name."

"I was such a sap back then." He sagged back, shaking his head with a low rumble of laughter.

"Sappy's not so bad if you want to get a girl into bed." She cupped his face in her hands, her thumbs retracing the strong cut of his cheekbones.

"I got you here today."

"Maybe *I* got *you*." She rubbed her over-sensitized breasts against his chest.

"Damn, you make me hot. You were a handful as a teenager and you're all that and more now."

"Is that a compliment?"

His hands slid up between them to shape around her breasts, rubbing, tempting with just the right amount of pressure. "What do you think?"

How could being with him feel so wonderfully right for her and yet be wrong at the same time? He'd done this thoughtful thing in taking her to see the art display, and she'd enjoyed the time away from Beachcombers more than she'd expected. But to her, it was a vacation. She didn't want to live her life this way and David didn't want to live his life in one spot. A fundamental problem they'd never been able to overcome.

Yet the taste he'd given her today of travel had truly shown her how much she would be throwing away. My, how he tempted her. Always had.

Her hands skimmed over his body as if forming over a sculpture. She hadn't done much in that art form, but it was one that had always fascinated her. She would have enjoyed capturing him in clay, her hands recreating from memory the cut and feel of him. Except this was a new feel, this man she'd only had brief contact with a year ago.

She had to be honest with herself; she wanted more. More time. More of him. His chest in particular fascinated her. This adult man was all the more intriguing than the teenage boy she'd been with before. The hard sinew of honed muscles called to her fingers to explore.

They'd taken their time learning about each other's bodies before, out of curiosity, as well as passion. Now the same feelings tingled through her. Did the same things still turn him inside out?

There was only one way to find out.

Starr arched up, traced his strong jawline and pressed her mouth to his. Without hesitation, she opened to him and yes, he swept her mouth with his tongue in bold possession. But she could take, as well as be taken. She sucked with a gentle seduction that all too quickly had another yes rumbling in his chest, his hips rocking under hers. The steely pressure of his erection throbbing between them—even through their clothes—leaving her with no question of how quickly she could tempt him into total arousal. And she'd barely even begun.

He made short work of hiking up her skirt and skimming away her underwear—he'd always been adept at that—before sliding his hands to cup her buttocks, and holy cow there went her blood pressure. David ducked his head to her breast, sucking, drawing on her nipple, his kiss, even the gentle tug of his teeth on her tightened bud with an extra friction that threatened to drive her over the edge from just this one pleasure alone. Then he switched his attention to her other breast while sliding his hand to cup the breast he'd just abandoned, rubbing, plucking.

Her brain went on stun and she lost the ability to think altogether until she felt cool air over her heated flesh and realized he was working the rest of her clothes down and off. She helped wriggle them free while opening his pants.

Arching up, he reached for his wallet perched cleverly within reach on the dashboard and withdrew a small packet. *Condom.* Thank goodness he'd thought of it since she could barely remember her own name, much less how to supply birth control.

A memory flashed through of how they'd learned to use them together. In fact, he'd found great pleasure in letting her…

She took the condom from him and flipped it between her fingers. He stared back at her with his best wicked albeit indulgent—darn him—smile. She straddled his lap, giving as good as she got in the wicked-smile department. She wrapped her hand around him at the base and held on with a strong but tender grip. Letting her smile broaden, she swept her thumb up and down ever so slightly to caress him in the way she remembered he liked. He throbbed in her hand.

Her body pulsed in response. No more waiting. She fit the condom on over him.

He gripped her hips in a firm but gentle hold and lifted her. Sighing, she braced her hands on his shoulders and threw back her head. Ready. Oh, so ready. Still he drew out the moment until she finally realized what he wanted from her. She'd closed her eyes.

She opened them and stared at him, moonlight shimmering overhead and glinting off his clenched jaw. The restraint cost him as much as it did her.

"Now," she panted.

As soon as the word slipped past her lips, he surged upward, into her with a thick and wonderful familiarity that brought tears to her eyes.

"You okay?" he asked, not moving, so deep inside her she vowed she would feel him forever.

She could only nod.

He took her mouth and withdrew, slowly, then filling her, again and again as she reclaimed their skin-tingling rhythm. She lost herself in his strokes, in his kiss with his tongue that thrust in a matching boldness of his body. She clung to him, writhed against him, wrung as much from the moment as she could and tried to ignore the voice inside her insisting she ought to snitch as much from the moment because she feared there wouldn't be another.

Hadn't that always been how they loved? As if living for the last time. They didn't know any other way.

She continued to grip—even claw—at him, at fate, at her own inability to figure out a way to have more with this man than stolen moments. She felt even more the gypsy child filching what she could for herself because there was no one to look out for her.

Except she had this strong and amazing man in her arms. A man who'd thrown her life and emotions into chaos for years. She pulled her mouth from his and scattered kisses along his jaw before burying her face in the crook of his neck and surrendering to sensations.

She knew she spoke, but couldn't pull rational thought together enough to decipher her own rambling litany of want, much less understand his. But oh, she heard the strength of his desire in the tenor of his tone. Knowing she moved him as much as he touched her pitched her forward, over the edge of desire.

Her back arched with the strength of her release, and the sparkling lights above could have been the sky in a nighttime rainbow above or behind her lids in a palate of color. She wasn't sure and couldn't think of anything except the power of the pleasure pulsing through her. He gave her so much and she could do nothing but collapse against him, exhausted.

His rumbling groan of completion vibrated against her skin, jarring a second, echoing release from her sated body.

If only they could stay right here for the rest of the night, wrapped up in a simple Aztec blanket, under the desert's stars.

Tugging the eight ka-jillion thread count Egyptian cotton sheet around her naked body in David's hotel bed, Starr couldn't help but be glad they'd made love in the desert that first time, in the more neutral outdoors.

This high-class hotel with its expensive linens and hop-to bellmen only served to remind her of the chasm between her upbringing and his. She so didn't want to travel down that road of thinking, but couldn't seem to recapture an emotional detour to match the real one they'd taken earlier.

She gave up trying to get comfortable in the unfamiliar surroundings of crystal chandeliers and monochromatic creamy colors and sat, clutching her knees to her chest. "I'm sorry you had to pay for a suite of rooms when we're only going to use one bed."

"The money doesn't matter."

He rolled to his side, tugging a lock of her hair and looking supremely at ease in the monstrous wooden sleigh bed. A huge bouquet of imported tulips and lilies lurked behind him on the nightstand, filling the room with an elegant fragrance that struck her as all wrong for the desert climate outside.

"Money always matters." She yanked the sheet more securely over her breasts. She could get used to the sheets, though. They were truly heavenly. "It shouldn't be squandered."

"Consider that it helped someone meet their bills then. If you're really feeling guilty, then we can just be sure to make love in both beds."

"Oh, and both showers, too." She liked how he thought, the wicked, wonderful man.

"Now you're getting the right idea." He tunneled a hand under the covers to cup her hip, stroking gently, distracting her ever so slightly. "Let's not forget the sofa and there's all this carpet that needs breaking in, as well."

"You *are* an indulgent man. I'll bet you actually eat things from the minibar."

"Is that a trick question?"

She flopped back with an exasperated *argh*. "You are so totally from another universe." She tugged on his arm. "The minibar is always full of way overpriced stuff someone like me can't afford."

"Tonight you can." He swung his feet to the floor, a gust of cool air slithering under the sheets. "What would you like? Some twenty-dollar M&M's?"

"Okay, it's not that bad," she huffed. He didn't have to poke fun at her.

"Really?" His back to her, he continued to speak, irking her all the more with his lack of understanding. "I could have sworn…"

Or maybe he did understand. "Now you're just teasing me."

He turned back around, candy bag in hand and open. He upended it, pouring M&M's all over her torso.

"David!" she squealed.

How like David to ply her with M&M's rather than the champagne in the silver bucket beside the bed. And how wise of him to know this would tickle her funny bone and fancy far more. The thought of common ground intimidated her even as it held obvious appeal. What if he made steps to close the gap between them?

He straddled her. "Did I mention I like twenty-dollar M&M's eaten off a naked woman even more than Coney dogs in Shea Stadium?"

David dipped his head and found a piece of candy nestled in her belly button. He crunched on a couple more, popping some into her mouth, as well, while he feasted, before he rolled to the side, laughing along with her. Once her laughter faded, he gathered her close and oh, where had the tension gone? God, he was good at maneuvering her.

"So money was tight for you growing up," he said with a no-so-subtle probing intensity.

Really good at maneuvering.

"Not tight, so much as always the focus of every action they made." She traced swirls of hair on his chest. "And of course things were tight at Aunt Libby's because she always took in as many girls as she could possibly afford."

"You showed up when you were ten, right?"

"Yes," she slugged his arm. "You know that's right since I've told you before. You never get facts wrong. If you want to know something, just ask me." Although she had to be honest with herself that he had asked her in the past and she'd dodged his questions. She'd become good at that, manufacturing a history for schoolmates that wasn't humiliating.

"Okay, I confess, I'm curious about what brought

you to Charleston." He trailed his fingers along her side, down to her hip and up again to the curve of her breast. "I want to know more about you, something I should have asked when I was seventeen but I was too horny back then to think of anything but getting you naked."

"Yet, here I am naked now, too."

"I still want to get you naked, but I also want to know what happened to bring you here."

There was no mistaking the intensity in those beautiful blue eyes of his eyes she'd once dreamed of seeing in a baby boy they'd made together—silly teenage dreams. Starr tugged herself back to the present and dealing with how much of her past to share. She'd told him precious little as a teen, embarrassed by her parents' shady dealings.

Now, she figured it was probably best not to tell David the total story about how she'd ended up at Aunt Libby's or he might do damage to her family out on the lawn and end his illustrious career with the OSI. His imagination from years on the job could likely hazard a close enough guess.

Instead, she opted to share her early years with Aunt Libby. "The first few months were pretty rocky. I was certain she would boot me out, so I preferred to leave on my own terms. A week after I arrived—" once her ten-year-old self had recovered from her near miss with heat exhaustion in her parents' RV "—I stole a piece of her mother's silver flatware and hid it under my mattress."

He yanked a curl in gentle chastisement. "Sticky little fingers you had, huh?"

"It wasn't my first time. You should probably know I was picking pockets by my fifth birthday. Aunt Libby found it before lunchtime. Looking back, she'd probably dealt with far worse from other girls in the past. But anyhow, I thought for sure I was toast. Instead, I lost re-creation time outside and had to polish all her silver."

"She sounds like a savvy lady."

"It took me a few months of pranks to realize she planned to keep me around for as long as I needed her, but I wasn't going to get away with jack."

"I wish I'd spent more time with her."

Starr could feel the automatic retreat inside herself. Her gaze skittered away from his and she plucked at the sheet draped over her. "She wasn't on your mother's bridge-club list."

"That shouldn't have mattered." He rolled her to face him, his eyes holding hers. "And actually works in her favor."

"Whatever." Starr shrugged dismissively, unable to stop old defense patterns from creeping over her. "I kept pushing the boundaries until this one day when I really started to get scared because I liked it here with the sisters and the food."

The admission slipped free in spite of her defenses screaming at her to hold back, not to give away anything someone could use against her later. "And oh, God, how it felt to have a mother figure who fed me and cared how I did in school. Having good stuff in your life means you have something to lose." She swallowed down the lump of anxiety in her throat that still lingered even today. "So I broke her porcelain jewelry box."

"I take it you weren't normally a clumsy child."

Starr nodded. "I was usually very careful not to upset the grown-ups. Aunt Libby went real quiet as she scooped up the pieces. She wouldn't look at me or even scold me. She just left the room." That choking lump grew to tangerine size in her throat. "One of the really bitchy foster girls told me the box had been given to her by her fiancé who died in the Korean War."

"Ah, hell." He gathered her close for a hug, stroking her hair. "You had no way of knowing."

"I heard her cry." She stifled her own sniffle against his chest.

"Nearly seventeen years later and you still feel guilty." He tipped her chin so she could see him. "Babe, I make my living off knowing when people are guilty and when they're not. I'm telling you, you've got to cut yourself some slack or you're never going to get those people out of your backyard."

Her spine straightened and she shrugged free of his grip that urged her to see things in a new and uncomfortable light. "Could you ease off your high horse for just one minute and let me have my crappy-ass memory? I'm trying to share something with you, you thickheaded man. It just takes women more words to get there."

"Fair enough. I'm an interrogator. I should know better." Sitting up, he scooped her up in his lap as if she weighed less than a poodle. "Talk away."

Not exactly the sensitive acknowledgment of her individuality she was looking for…but close. And he smelled good and felt good and who really wanted perfect anyway? Perfect sounded boring.

"I gathered up all my money—none of it stolen because she'd broken me of that habit by then—and I bought a paint set, which pretty much depleted my funds so I couldn't afford a porcelain anything. I got a buddy of mine to build a wooden box with a leather thong latch and I painted it."

She sighed long and hard, remembering the feel and smell of those paints along with the rush of bringing the image in her mind to life…. "Man, did I paint it with a view of the ocean sunrise that blended realism and romanticism until… David, it was really beautiful. It may not have been the box she had but I found I had a talent, something special for just me." She smiled at the memory. "Aunt Libby and I cried together over that box. Then we laughed and celebrated. I had a talent, something that set me apart from all the other girls. Aunt Libby had a way of helping each of us find that something special about ourselves."

She relaxed into his chest as they sat leaning back against the sleigh-bed headboard with her draped across his lap—too comfortable. Too easy to stay this way. "I'm not sure I can fully express to someone like you how much that meant to us, finding out we were special."

"To someone like me?" He went still against her, his voice rumbling under her ear.

Oops. She'd stepped in it, but there was no back-tracking. "Someone born knowing his place in the world. Someone valued from birth. Someone encouraged to stand out…" She shook her head again, embarrassed, wary in a way she hadn't felt in a long time. Putting her whole self out there got tougher rather than easier with age.

He caressed the back of her neck in a gentle massage. "Don't stop there."

Apparently even if she'd stepped in it, he wanted her to keep on wading through. She swallowed down that darned persistent lump. "Why, Special Agent, that was positively sensitive of you, urging me to continue with this emotional discussion."

"I work to understand people for a living. It strikes me that understanding you should have been my number-one priority and yet I worked like hell to…"

"Keep your distance while getting me naked?"

He didn't answer, simply rested his chin on top of her head. An affirmation of sorts.

"So I'll talk." Because if she ever wanted to figure this thing out between her and David, they would have to stop hiding from each other. She wasn't sure where this would lead—to more closeness or the final heart-break—but this time, they would have to see it through. "Most of us came from situations where it was best not to be noticed. I had problems in my childhood, no question, but David, some of the things I heard from the other girls would break even your hard heart."

"Ashley."

"For one." She thought of so many others, ones who'd found homes, ones who'd gone to mended homes, ones who'd been forced to return home, even though nothing was fixed at all….

Starr blinked back the gritty craziness of the world and focused on what she could repair. "We couldn't exactly take out a hit on Ashley's heartless birth parents who gave her up rather than take on the cost and stress of dealing with her birth defects, but we've given her a family, a home, and we hocked ourselves up to our ears to give her the college education so she could achieve more."

"The education both of you wanted."

She shrugged, not ready to admit that yet, because heaven forbid Ashley should somehow even catch a whiff of the feeling radiating off Starr.

"Babe, you may be right that they could put a dent in my hardened heart." David swept her off his lap and onto her back beside him. "But right now, you're the one chipping away at that pounding rock in the middle of my chest."

Staring up at David looming over her, Starr wondered if she would be able to deny this man anything he asked of her right now.

Nine

David twined his fingers through Starr's hair and watched her sleep, in no real hurry to wake her and launch the morning. The day would start soon enough and he would resume his campaign to persuade her that following him around the world wasn't such a hardship after all. Convincing her wasn't going to be as easy as he'd led himself to believe setting out on this trip.

He thumbed the off button on his cell phone and rested it on the bedside table by the remains of their midnight feast. Thank God the call hadn't woken her because as far as he was concerned she didn't need to know.

Her mother had been picked up by local cops, questioned and ultimately released. There was a chance she was involved in a purse snatching, but Gita had spun the attempt to make it sound as if she was only trying to catch the real thief and—lo and behold—she caught him so she had the woman's stolen purse, which she turned over.

She'd waltzed out of the station on lack of evidence.

Already Starr carried such a chip on her shoulder. Hell, call it what it was—an inferiority complex. Damn. He just didn't get it, because she was the smartest, sharpest, most amazing woman he'd ever laid eyes on. Convincing her, however, helping her overcome the hell of her childhood and find an inherent new sense of self… He still had some work to accomplish in that arena.

He refused to doubt that he could win. But for now, he allowed himself a window of time to forget about the fact they had past problems or a future to settle.

The desert sunrise shone through the hotel skylights, glinting off her skin, reminding him of how he'd wor-shiped every inch of her through the night. Being with her that first time in the desert had been mind blowing, and damn near control shattering since he hadn't been with anyone else in the past year since he'd last left her.

Something he hadn't told her. Of course they always played these little games with each other, holding back pieces of themselves.

It didn't escape him that she still hadn't told him what had brought her next door to Libby Sullivan's doorstep. Starr was efficient at dodging questions, far better than anyone he'd ever encountered, and he'd interrogated the best. Of course, he didn't want her to feel threatened.

Still he couldn't escape the driving need to know more about her. And what better time than now to gather up as much info about her as possible to use in his quest to win her over? Winning her to his side grew more important the more time he spent with her.

Being with her—well, damn it all—he'd been deluding himself that a couple of days would be enough. So he needed to come up with a way to sway her into taking more time off from that business she loved so much. Why couldn't she see it was just a house? Bricks and wood and nails.

He'd hoped that the excitement of making love out in the open would give her a taste of what was out there to be experienced—beyond the limiting boundaries of home.

Starr sighed and stirred beside him, stretching. He slowed his strokes through her wildly tangled mass of hair, letting her find her own pace waking. Besides, he couldn't deny himself the pleasure of watching her. They'd woken together very few times, only last year the one weekend they'd spent together. While they'd slept together as teens, they'd never been able to share a night.

She kicked the covers, inching her feet free, curling her toes until a subtle *crack, crack, crack* echoed in the otherwise silent room. Turning from his side, she stretched, clutching the sheet to her chest—damn shame—and rolled onto her back, tucking her head into the pillow, her neck arching. Okay, only a saint could hold strong against this enticing goddess greeting the morning.

"Good morning, babe." He kissed the crook of her neck, the first of her erogenous zones he'd discovered in making out with Starr.

"Mmmmm," she answered with a groggy groan, reaching to stroke his chest while tipping her head to give him better access to her neck.

He definitely liked mornings with Starr. Sliding a leg over hers, he trapped her still and trekked toward her breasts. She fidgeted under his touch.

"Morning." She pressed a quick kiss to his shoulder and slid from beneath him. She rolled to her feet, gloriously naked. "Teeth. Gross. Gotta brush them."

From her brusque tone, apparently she wasn't much of a morning person. He grinned at the bit of knowledge and filed it away in his mind as she disappeared into the bathroom. David stuffed a second pillow behind his head and sat up, resting back against the headboard, staring at her stroll back to bed. She crawled across the sheets to rejoin him, pressing a proper good-morning kiss to his mouth before settling in beside him.

"How about room service, or do you want to compare their buffet to your own?"

"If I'm going to call this a true vacation, I guess I should forego the buffet in lieu of room service."

"That's my girl." He nuzzled her neck again before reaching for the phone and placing their order. He considered resuming their lovemaking, but didn't particularly want to be interrupted by room service. "You know, babe, as much as I'm enjoying this, I really don't want to stop halfway through to answer the door for your eggs Benedict."

"So we'll ignore it and order more."

As her hand made its way up his leg, he considered her proposition, seriously contemplated it, but then he remembered last night and how pleasure delayed was pleasure doubled. What better time to advance his goal of learning more about her?

David clamped a hand around her wrist with an inch to spare before she would have been hands on the target and able to talk him into ignoring food through the whole day. "Not yet. Soon though, and I'll make the wait well worth your while."

Starr eased away, studying him through narrowed eyes, crossing her arms over her perfect breasts. Her bottom lip jutted out in an honest to Pete pout. He couldn't stop his grin.

She grabbed a pillow and swatted him. "It's really ungentlemanly of you to revel in my pain."

"Your pain? You're actually hurting you want me so much?"

As he ducked the next swat of her lethal pillow, he couldn't stop the full-out smile that spread over his face. Call him a knuckle-dragger, but he liked that he had sway over this woman. Heaven knew she pulled him inside out with a look, a touch, a simple wish for a damn cat plate because he knew she still longed for a pet.

He let her rain her downy swats at him for another

couple of swings before looping his arms around her waist and pinning her to the mattress. Tickling. Laughing. And oh, yeah, kissing.

David eased his mouth from hers and brushed a kiss against her ear. "You've had the power to knock me on my ass since the first day I saw you."

She stilled under him. "You seem so self-confident. I didn't think anyone rocked you."

How could she not know? Of course he'd done his best not to let her into his head. Which brought him back around to his wish to crawl inside her brain. As much as he balked at ponying up facts about his life, sharing a piece of himself only seemed fair for what he expected from her. And it was a good interrogation technique. Right?

Whatever you need to tell yourself to get through the day, pal.

He twined one of her curls around his finger. "Actually, there was one other woman who could put the fear of God in me."

"Your mom?"

Staying silent, he shook his head. "Your aunt Libby."

"Why would she do that?"

The luxury sheet started to itch against his bare flesh. "Because she knew what we were doing."

"Aunt Libby *knew?*" She shoved him off her as if somehow the woman could see them now. Starr inched up higher against the headboard, sheet gripped to her breasts. "She knew I was crawling up into your room?"

How the woman had managed to mother anywhere from eight to eighteen children at once he would never know, but his admiration for her ran deeper than the dark Atlantic off Charleston. "She sure did, babe."

"Why didn't she talk to me?"

"Because you're as immovable as a tree stump."

"Why, thank you. I do believe that's the most romantic thing a man's ever said to me. How can I ever resist climbing onto your private jet for another getaway to an exotic locale?"

He considered apologizing for the statement and then figured he might as well opt for the truth. A relationship built on lies to make the other feel better wasn't worth a crap. "You grew up with bullshit flattery and downright lies. I figured you were a woman who would respect the God's honest truth."

She skimmed a finger along his collarbone in an innocent touch that shouldn't have had so much arousing power over him, but it did. He gripped her hand and brought it to his mouth, kissing her palm, more to give himself some distance, control over the situation.

A knock sounded at the door.

He pressed a final kiss to her wrist. "Stay put. I'll get it."

Rolling from the bed to his feet, he grabbed a pair of pajama bottoms from his suitcase and yanked them on before heading out to the sitting area. She was tougher to win over than he'd expected. But then when had anything ever gone the way he'd expected or wanted with Starr? Damn it, he wasn't a quitter. He'd vowed to make the most of these couple of days together and he would push it to the wall on all levels, if that was what it took. Even if it meant doing something far more difficult than staging impromptu cross-country trips. He would do that thing chicks seemed to want most—share feelings.

He shuddered even though there wasn't an air conditioner or fan in sight.

Starr slathered raspberry preserves on her whole-wheat toast, studying David across the small table the entire time. What was he up to now? She could see the wheels turning in his handsome head, although he'd been nothing but charming from the moment they'd sat at the romantic little table with its wrought-iron legs and seat backs shaped like hearts.

Adjusting a button on the pajama top she wore—his pajama top—she figured she would have to look into purchasing a table like this for Beachcombers.... But hadn't he done this a ka-zillion times? Chosen something in their outing that would speak to her and her life?

What about him? What did he want from these couple of days away? Besides the obvious naked time.

She swallowed down her toast with a swig of orange juice. "Okay, so back to the Aunt Libby discussion. I'm stubborn and sometimes I'm so focused on my goal I don't have time to weigh in other people's plans and opinions."

He nodded that blue-blooded regal head of his. "And

I have my own strong opinions. But when it came to you, your aunt Libby knew I had a…"

She'd never seen him wrestle for a word before. Did he not know? Or did he not want to own up? The possibility shimmered through her veins like the glitter spread out on her table in her studio.

"I could be less inflexible when it came to you, and that old lady knew it. She stood nose to nose with me."

Had he just admitted to vulnerability? He had. *Ohmigod.*

Starr set down her juice. His memory must be faulty, although Aunt Libby had had a larger than life quality. "She was a full foot shorter than you. How could she stand nose to nose?"

"Libby Sullivan was a savvy lady." He refilled his coffee, adding nothing else to the steaming cup of java. "She knew how to set the stage for her interrogation and made sure she stood a few porch steps up, on her turf, not mine."

"Did she threaten to tell your mother?" Obviously she hadn't, though, since his mother hadn't found out until prom night. The beautiful evening had been tainted by his mother's sniffy, haughty demeanor and yes, Starr still resented the old bat over a decade later.

"Like threatening to tell my mother would have made a difference to me. I wanted you and that's all that mattered." He shrugged with the easy attitude of a man who could have anything he wanted.

And he wanted her. The depth of that discovery made her forget to chew her toast for a full two seconds.

He wouldn't have cared what his mom thought? All these years she'd worried about his mother and he brushed aside her concerns with a simple sentence. Starr darn near went deaf for a moment as the notion settled and she faced the reality of her own insecurities and how she'd let Mrs. Hamilton-Reis play on them.

Starr shook herself free of the past and back into the moment. David was laying out some heavy stuff here and she didn't want to miss a word of it.

"Miss Sullivan told me I was hurting you by making you sneak around. That you had walked in the shadows and been ashamed too long. You deserved to be proud of who you are." He studied the handle on his coffee mug for an extended moment before taking a long swallow.

Aunt Libby's words had obviously bothered him.

It made total sense now. "That's why you asked me to go to the senior dance with you." It made total sense—and stung even now that he'd had to be pushed.

"No. I had already asked that."

Relief sluiced over her far stronger than she liked to admit. Something that had happened so long ago shouldn't have had this much power over her. But it did. *He* did.

"I'd already figured it was time to do the dating thing. We'd gotten things out of order because you made me so freaking hot I couldn't make it to dinner. I wish I could blame that impulsiveness on teenage hormones, but the hell of it is, I'm still as hot for you as I ever was."

Her skin heated all over at the admission. Did that make a second vulnerability he'd confessed? No. It didn't count when he knew full well she shared every bit of the impulsive, undeniable passion.

"We ditched our clothes pretty quickly around each other once you came back from that fancy boarding school of yours."

"You grew. God, did you ever grow up." His heated gaze scorched right over her, firing her up when her body should have been sated from their night of love-making. How could a woman with thighs that still ached be so totally entranced by a glance?

"As did you." She soaked up the hard-muscled look of him. Would she ever tire of simply seeing him? A scary notion because it scratched out the possibility of finding happiness anywhere else. "What did you do after Aunt Libby's big intimidating talk?"

"I asked you to come with me to college, to follow me around the world." He lifted a lock of her hair and teased it over the curve of her breast exposed by the gaping pajama top she wore, which made the satiny fabric feel all the more sexy against her skin because it was his. "I'm asking you again."

Why did he always have to try and distract her with sex? She only just now realized his every offer came with a sensual touch.

Starr met his gaze dead-on and tried her best to stifle the arousal zinging through her veins. "Nothing's changed, David."

"Sure it has. We're older. You can study the art you used to spend all those hours studying in pictures."

He really knew how to go for the jugular in a non-sexual way after all. She'd never been able to afford college, but had soaked up as much of art history as she could on her own. Still, growing up in a neighborhood of privilege, money, Ph.D. This and Dr. That, she couldn't help the occasional tweak to her self-esteem as she longed to go back to school.

Damn it, she'd made a successful business for herself and, while she made the arts and crafts for fun, her landscape paintings that she slid into the shop sold well.

David leaned closer in her silence, the heat of his body reaching to hers with a familiarity that never failed to stir her.

His mouth skimmed hers, his words heating her skin, as well as her desires. "We can make love in more exotic places than you can imagine."

She wanted. How could she not? His plan sounded enticing. But what about when she grew weary of travel and wanted to return home? She knew from David's infrequent visits that their timetables for travel differed by quite a few months.

And what about permanence?

Uh-oh. She was thinking that *L* word. They'd said it all the time in high school. But didn't many teens toss the word around with the frequency of their fashion changes?

Still, she needed to be realistic. This man had held a place in her thoughts, in her world, for over half her life.

She would be a fool not to consider the possibility that she might just love the arrogant bastard. And if she loved him, then someday she might want the whole shebang.

Marriage. Oh, God.

Kids. Oh, God, oh, God.

Matching rocking chairs and grandchildren. Where was a paper bag because she was going to hyperventilate any second now.

This time together hadn't helped her at all. They'd only complicated things more by opening up all the old wounds from the past. She still wanted him and he was still as committed to his plan to live his life on the road. His whole romantic getaway was nothing more than an elaborate plan to entice her over to his way of thinking.

Wait. Rather than getting all bent out of shape, maybe it was time to show him she wasn't the same vulnerable teen he'd been with before. He wanted to show the benefits of his way of living.

Well, two could play that game.

Ten

Striding up the steps to his house, David planted his hand firmly in the small of Starr's back, reminding himself to be patient. He'd negotiated localized cease-fires between warring militants in hostile territories around the globe. Surely he could talk one woman into giving him a second chance. In the middle of their conversation over brunch, Starr had insisted she wanted to put their discussion on hold until they returned home, and simply enjoy the trip as he'd planned.

Once they'd returned to Charleston, she'd overheard his mother was at her weekly doctor visit. Starr had insisted she'd wanted a copy of their high-school prom photos. She'd said the copies at Aunt Libby's house had been damaged when the roof had leaked during a tropical storm. Did he have any left?

Sure. He thought there were some in a trunk in the attic.

Time alone was fine by him since he'd already managed to log a quick call to the local police department to check on queries into the Ciminos and debit-card fraud. The mall video footage was on its way to him for ID. Meanwhile, he took comfort in the fact that Starr seemed intent on giving her relatives a wide berth.

He closed the door behind him and turned to find Starr staring up at the cavernous hallway. She'd been in his house before, but not often. He tried to see the space through her eyes, but could only pull up his own feelings about the place with his mother's brittle brand of love— her lack of warmth rooted in murky memories David rarely allowed. Echoes of his father's temper filtered through his head against his will. The reverberation of the slammed front door as his father walked out time after time. His mother's stifled cries.

Darkness. That's all he saw here. Even with all the curtains opened, the house held an innate gloominess he couldn't find the imagination to dispel.

Starr pivoted on her heels. "This truly is a beautiful mansion."

He grunted, resting his hands on an antique brass Chinese lion head. The stuff childhood nightmares were made of.

"You don't agree?"

"It's smothering." He patted the lion on the head, moving on to the lion's mate.

"That's only because your mother insists on staying with the over-cluttered decor theme of heavy velvets and dark brocades."

He frowned, reevaluated. She had a point but he still couldn't imagine a simple coat of paint could chase away his father's gloomy taint. "What would you do?"

Starr swept her hands through the air. "Take all those curtains down and replace them with white shutters over there and whispery sheers there. Let the light shine through. Why live on the water if you're going to deny yourself the view?"

She hesitated, stopping at a line of posed studio photographs along the mantel and the oil portrait above. More stilted framed pictures lined the antique grand piano that no one played yet his mother insisted made a pivotal focal piece of furniture.

"Don't stop," he said nudging her, enjoying the sound of her voice more than the words per se. He wasn't convinced the house could be saved, but if anyone could revitalize the space, Starr could. "What else would you do?"

She tugged one of her ever-present hair scrunchies out of her pocket and pulled back her curls as if prepping herself for the task. "You probably won't like to hear this but I would ditch half the furniture and recover the rest in a lighter color, stripes I think, rather than those dark cabbage roses."

"Streamlining life." David nodded. She could start

with pitching the lions off the dock if it wouldn't give his mother a heart attack on the spot. "Why wouldn't I like that?"

She tapped a finger along a line of photos. "I can't imagine someone wanting to get rid of their heritage."

"Maybe I don't think of it that way because I've always had it."

Starr lingered on a photo of him with his parents when he'd been in first grade. "I wish I'd been able to get to know your father."

He grunted, not at all eager to linger on this topic of discussion. "Come on." He gestured toward the lengthy hall, Persian rug running the length. "The attic stairs are this way."

"It must have been difficult losing him so young. That put a lot of weight on you to be the man of the house as a teenager."

Obviously he hadn't warded off the topic as easily as he'd wanted. "I guess you could put it that way. But seriously, there's no need to make a sob story out of it. It's not like I had to quit school and support the family. He left us with a fat portfolio and an honest executor to look out for things until I was old enough to take over."

"When was old enough?"

"Twenty-one."

She hesitated at the base of the attic stairs. "You took over the books on this place when you weren't even done with college?"

"I let the executor hang on for about eighteen more

months." He passed her and yanked the dangling chain to turn on the attic light. Three bare bulbs lit the dusty A-frame nook beneath the roof, light from outside streaming in through a circular window at either end of the room. "Then I took the guy to court once he and I started disagreeing on some investments. I felt he was too conservative."

"Conservative can be good though."

He stared her up and down as she followed him on the narrow staircase to the attic. "I can't believe I'm hearing that from a woman in a pink fringed jacket and purple jeans."

"I happen to be very frugal when it comes to my finances." She sniffed.

"That's good. Very good in fact. But there's frugal, and there's sluggish." He extended a hand to help her maneuver the last step around into the attic. "At the rate he was going, there wouldn't be enough to keep my mother in the style to which she'd become accustomed. For myself, I don't give a flying f—uh, fig."

He made his way around trunks and enough dusty furniture to fill another house. Passing a family cradle his mother had bugged him more than once about filling, he stopped by the trunk he'd been seeking. "I support myself and the trust fund is just a bonus I was born into but am fully aware I didn't earn. But I will make sure my mother is cared for. That's my duty. My old man owes her after what he put her through."

Damn, he'd said too much. He reached for the lock

and jimmied it with the special tool he kept on his key chain, a nice perk of his job. He held the door and gestured her inside.

"What he put her through?" She plunked down onto an old wooden rocking horse. "What do you mean?"

"Nothing."

"You meant something or you wouldn't have said it." She toyed with the dusty yarn-mane on the horse's neck. "I thought we were past holding back from each other."

He still wondered how she'd ended up at Libby Sullivan's. He knew he could find the information in a snap by checking out the Ciminos, but he couldn't escape the need to have Starr tell him.

"I just meant the long hours he put in at the office." David kept his head ducked down and worked the trunk lock even though he'd jimmied it free first twist through. "All the parties and support she gave him as he climbed the corporate ladder."

"Bull."

"What?" Startled, he looked up from the lock.

"Bull. You're lying to me." Her hand stroked absently down the horse's mane even though she'd long ago swiped it free of dust. "You may be an amazing inter-rogator. But you're a crummy liar."

"I am not." He was the number-one agent in his office, damn it. He swung open the trunk lid with extra force. "I can lie my ass off quite well, thank you very much. Many a time my life has depended on my keeping a cover."

"Then it must be that you can't lie to me."

That said too much about the two of them and why they always ended up like this, two very different people, working like hell to resolve their differences and beating their stubborn heads against the wall.

He tugged out a stack of envelopes from the trunk and smacked them on the floor in front of her. How ironic to see labels with his mother's scrawl indicating memorabilia from his parents' dating days. He couldn't envision his autocratic father courting anyone.

David thumbed through other folders until he finally uncovered the one he'd labeled as theirs after the prom. He passed it to Starr. Her hands shaking ever so slightly, she took it from him, twisted open the metal tines and pulled out a stack of photos with reverent slowness.

One after the other, she took her time with the candid shots Libby Sullivan had taken of the two of them together in their prom finery. How like Starr to totally ignore the formal portrait shot altogether. And how like his family to have a houseful of formal portraits.

He reached to gather up the extra copies of the posed picture under a floral arch, both of them so young. Starr's hair had been longer—he could still remember the thrill of it wrapping around him during sex for the first time. The white dress she wore accented her dusky skin, her dark eyes and hair. It could have been a wedding dress. In those days he'd dreamed of seeing her wear one.

And of course he wore the standard tuxedo. Had he really owned his own tux at seventeen? His folks had made their plans for him known. Follow in the old man's footsteps… Except his father had just died, leaving David with a boatload of unresolved feelings about his home life.

He plopped the prom shots on top of the folders. It was time to stop pounding his head against the wall when it came to Starr. Thoughts of his father made him realize he didn't want to perpetuate the Reis brand of autocratic coldness in his own life. "My father was a cold bastard. His banking job, the almighty dollar, his clubs and golfing with powerful senators, that's all that mattered to him. My mother's family name was merely a means to that end. I was nothing more than the heir to carry on the legacy. His legacy. His name living on."

She rested her hands on her knees and leaned forward with earnest intensity. "Except you threw it in his face and went your own way."

"Yeah, I did." He met her nose to nose, no dodging her eyes, no shielding his expression from hers. "He had all the paperwork laid out for his alma mater and just expected I would do things his way. We never really talked about anything in our house. Things just 'happened.' Except this didn't happen. I told him no and explained my plan for my life."

"What happened?"

"He backhanded me. Then put the pen in my hand."

She gasped. Her mouth opened and closed once, then twice. He waited for the platitudes that would help him distance himself from her…then she simply laid her hand on top of his. Damn it. Her silence and simple touch, the way she looked right into his eye connected in a way far more intense than any words.

His throat moved in a swallow and a slow clearing. "As I held that pen with my face stinging, I could only think that was the first time my father had touched me in as long as I could remember."

Tears streaming down her face, Starr's arms went around his neck as she slid from his childhood rocking horse into his lap. "Oh, David, I'm so sorry."

She pressed her mouth to his before he had time to come up with some lam-ass excuse about how it didn't matter even though they both knew it really did. Of course it did. How could it not?

Her tears seared his skin clean through, more leaking and falling until they mingled with the taste of her on his lips.

He slid his arms around her, gathering her closer and soaking up the familiar feel and comfort of having her close, her hands stroking his face, shoulders, chest with gentle healing. Thank goodness she seemed to have sensed he'd had enough of deep discussion for now. Maybe communicating on a sexual level might be shallow, but the connection offered a hotter forgetfulness he needed so damned much.

Starr kept exerting pressure with her kiss and her body until she realized she'd leaned him backward onto the floor. The unforgiving hardness of the wood should have bothered him, but with soft and oh-so-giving Starr above him, he didn't give a crap where he lay so long as she kept on writhing on top of him. Stroking him, murmuring sweet words of affirmation and want.

"How much longer until your mother returns?"

"She's gone shopping. Two more hours at least."

"Thank goodness."

And just that fast, she'd undone his pants, and he wasn't slow on the uptake, so he worked her jeans down while she kicked them off.

Glory be, he did so love the easy access of a thong.

"Birth control. Condom."

She held out his wallet.

He frowned. "When did you get that?"

"I'm a pickpocket from way back. Remember? Apparently the touch stays with a person."

That shouldn't have made him laugh, but somehow it did. The incongruity of them always had messed with his mind. He flipped open his wallet, pulled out a condom and sheathed himself.

Breathless, he thunked his head. "Damn it. I'm worse than a fumbling horny teenager. You probably want a soft bed and foreplay and—"

Starr clapped a hand over his mouth. "I don't want foreplay this time. We'll do foreplay next time." She panted, staring down at him with heated intensity. "I want you. Hard. Fast. Now."

She emphasized the last word with a wriggle of her hips, nothing more than the scant scrap of damp lace of her thong separating them. But not for long.

He swept aside the skimpy barrier and slid inside her,

where he belonged. Her fingers fisted in his shirt, clawing at his skin through the fabric as the wriggle of her hips urged him on.

Sure, she could say no foreplay but he had to touch her. His hands itched for the feel of her. His fingers crawled up inside her shirt to cup her breasts. She moaned a plea and moved faster above him, their bodies inching along the floor with memorabilia from their past scattered around them, prom tickets and pictures.

The moist heat of her clenched around him until his head thunked back on the floor and he clenched his jaw with restraint. Tougher and tougher to hang on by the second and not made any easier by the sweet feel of her soft buttocks, but he couldn't bring himself to let go. Instead, he gripped her tighter, guiding her against him in grinding rhythm that had her gasping and moaning in time with his own pounding pulse.

Not much longer. He couldn't last much longer. But damned if he would finish before she did.

He slid a hand around between them, finding her tight bud, teasing her for…ah, her tongue peeked out between her teeth in her telltale sign that she was close, thank goodness. Then, she gasped and he forced his eyes to stay open while he waited and watched the seductive vision of her completion wash over her.

The second she collapsed on top of him, limp, replete, he cut the bonds and let go, the power of his own release tearing a shout from him he couldn't control.

But finally he admitted it to himself, he'd never been

in total control of his emotions around this woman. If he thought so, he'd only been lying to himself. All he could do was ride the wave until his heart slowed enough for him to hear the sounds around him again.

Starr breathing against his ear.

The creak of the wooden horse moving because apparently one of them had kicked it as they'd writhed on the floor.

An air-conditioner unit kicking on below stairs.

And as he gathered Starr closer to him, David realized he'd been lying to himself in more ways than one. He'd been certain he could make it all work, his grand plan for her to follow him around the world. With her in his arms, he realized he knew her. *Knew* the essence of this woman and traveling the world wasn't what she wanted.

So where did that leave him?

Where did that leave *them?*

Because for the first time he had to admit the truth to himself. He couldn't give her up.

"I give up." Starr flopped back in her chair, ceding control of the remote to her sister. "There's nothing decent on television this time of night."

"Why don't you go to bed then? I have to stay up with the baby till she nurses again." She tickled her wide-awake daughter's toes as little Libby grinned in the swing. "But that doesn't mean you have to miss out on sleep, too. Catch an extra hour for me."

Starr shook her head. "I'm too wired."

"From your trip or from work this evening?"

From making love in the attic, but she didn't feel like sharing that intensely intimate moment with her sister. As a matter of fact, a big part of the restlessness stemmed from feeling raw after all the sharing with David.

No wonder he was distant so much of the time. He'd had precious few examples of how to be affectionate. Only a smothering mother—who wanted any part of that—and an emotionally sterile father. For so long she'd demanded that he give her more of himself and he'd been offering her everything he had to give.

She swiped her hand under her nose and glued another ticket to the memory book, mounting it on a decorative movie-strip paper.

Claire reached across the kitchen table. "What's that you're working on? Something new for the gift shop?"

"No, this is for me. I'm making a memory book."

"It's about time you did one of those for yourself. The one you started for baby Libby is gorgeous. You have such a great eye for colors. I'm envious of how you put those together."

Starr snorted in disbelief. "You're so organized I would think you'd be great at these."

"Oh, I have my photos in boxes, filed by date, but when it comes to the cutting and the arranging, that's beyond me."

"I imagine we have skills that match up, which is

why we make good business partners." Starr sifted through the photos, searching for just the right one to center on the next page, finally settling on one of her and David sitting together in front of a bonfire. "I was talking to David about how Aunt Libby had a real gift for helping us find our strengths. God, I couldn't believe how lucky I was to have landed here."

The photo called to her to linger. She traced her finger over the two of them, so young, so long ago. David had his lanky arms looped around her as she grinned. Only now did she realize how few photos captured him smiling.

Claire's voice slowly pierced her reminiscent fog....

"I loved Aunt Libby, make no mistake about it. That dear woman mothered me from the time I was six. But in those early years, after I got past the aching for my own teenage mama—as unfit as she may have been—I yearned for a family. The fact that my own biological mother refused to sign away her parental rights was a mixed blessing. I never had abandonment issues, but I never could be set free, either. I was terrified of losing control of my environment. It took me long time—and a stubborn man—to share control with him and make this family of my own I wanted so desperately."

Where was Claire going with this? Claire always had a reason for her rambles, so Starr settled back and waited for the moral.

"When it came to abandonment, Ashley had it in

spades. Her birth parents didn't want the financial obligations of her birth defects." Her hand grazed over her own infant's head as if to recheck the baby's health. "And neither did adoptive parents. At least as a ward of the state she had most everything fixed, God love our precious little sister."

A little sister whose willowy stature towered over both of her shorter older sisters now.

Starr couldn't help but think of her own trust issues and imagine how much more difficult it would have been had she been in Ashley's shoes. "It's going to be hard for her to trust enough to fall in love."

Claire pierced her with a pointed stare, staying silent.

Starr fidgeted in her seat, suddenly uncomfortable with all those pictures. She smacked the memory book closed. "Now that you've covered your past and Ashley's, I assume you want me to sort through my own non-adoptive issues."

Still, her sister stayed diplomatically silent, lifting her baby from the swing and settling her on her lap to nurse. Did Claire realize how lucky she was to have found such peace with her big hunk of a husband and the sweet baby? Even thinking about that kind of normalcy felt unattainable, larger than life somehow, swelling frustrated feelings inside Starr until she snapped.

"Fine." She shoved the memory book away. "Okay, my family would have sold me for a piece of pizza and that has left me with unresolved issues when it comes to relationships."

And just that fast, stalwart Claire's smile faltered, her eyes welling until two tears spilled over down her cheeks. "That should tell you what complete and total idiots they are because you are the most amazing and unique individual I have ever met."

"Thank you." Starr's eyes started to sting, as well, and she reached across the table to clasp her sister's hand. "I love you, too. So what does all of this have to do with why I'm still single?"

"Think back, sweetie. Make a memory book in your mind and let yourself remember. Couples wanted to adopt you, regardless of your age. You were cute as could be, so dynamic, everyone *saw* you. You draw people in, always have." Her smile returned with a nose scrunch as she shook her head. "And yet, you always sabotaged it at the last minute by doing something awful to the couple to scare them away. Why do you think that was?"

Starr shoved her chair away and made tracks for the industrial-size refrigerator. Opening it, she searched. Where was a good hunk of chocolate when a girl needed it? "Well, it wasn't because I was holding out hope of going back to hawking encyclopedias door-to-door."

"Starr, I'm being serious here. This is important. Really important." Her voice chastised until Starr finally turned around with a slice of cheesecake in a napkin clasped in her hand.

Starr made her way back to the table and stuffed an

oversize bite in her mouth so she wouldn't have to answer the increasingly uncomfortable questions.

"You probably realize the truth of why you sabotaged everything, at least subconsciously, and that's why you're avoiding answering. You've been avoiding this for a long time."

Chewing, Starr let the words shuffle around in her head until they settled like the photos in her memory book, finding the right background and framing. And in a beautiful rightness, it all made sense. "I didn't want to leave David."

Claire sighed. "Of course you didn't."

Her sister made it sound so simple, yet it had taken ten years to work out. "I thought I was the bartender who dispensed wise advice."

"I've been subbing for you enough to get the gist of how it goes."

"You're damn good." Better than she'd given her credit for. Why hadn't she taken the time to listen before?

Because she hadn't been ready to listen.

Claire stroked a hand over her child's head and smiled indulgently at her younger sister. "Maybe I can sub at the bar for you while you're on your honeymoon."

Honeymoon? Panic twisted Starr's gut tighter than her fist working the last remnants from a tube of paint. Honeymoons came after a wedding. A wedding came after declarations of love.

Love. The word settled in her mind with the greatest sense of rightness of all, providing the perfect framework for all the snapshots of her and David together. How could she have looked at them in any other light? Of course she loved him—with everything inside her.

But thanks to her abandonment issues bred from a childhood of neglect, she'd been afraid this man who traveled the world would one day never return to her. Yet, he'd proved to her over the past ten years that even without her giving him the least encouragement, he'd stayed steadfast. He might be a hardheaded man, but he was *her* man, with issues of his own.

And even as a part of her started to make plans to claim him as her own, she couldn't help but stare out the window at the trio of RVs parked along the beach. Shame prickled over her. What did they want? A rogue thought she'd never considered swept over her as she allowed herself to consider a life with David for the first time.

If she surrendered to her feelings for David, would that put him in the Ciminos' crosshairs forever?

Eleven

Parked in the stifling library with his mother, David couldn't help but see the room through Starr's eyes, envisioning the room with light and—what had she said?—white shutters and sheers. She'd also wanted to clear the place of clutter.

That struck him most of all. Clear the clutter. His gaze stopped dead on the mantel and piano filled with photographs—stilted, posed portraits. Not to mention the mammoth posed oil portrait over the fireplace. Nowhere could he find the kind of laughter ever-present in snapshots taken by Libby Sullivan.

For probably the first time in his adult life, he let himself speak first without thinking. "Mother, why did you put up with Dad's crap for all those years?"

His mother froze, her teacup halfway to her mouth. Three blinks later, she placed her china cup back on the saucer with exaggerated care. "I'm not sure what you mean, dear."

He'd had enough of the denial. Sitting here in this stifling room, he couldn't help but wonder if he'd used his only-child status as an excuse to be a loner all these years. It was far easier than putting himself on the line in a conversation like this. It was certainly easier than risking getting his heart stomped by Starr.

Except now the danger of losing her outweighed anything else.

"You know exactly what I'm talking about." Something niggled in his brain right now, a reason why he needed to figure this out. "Mother, I deal with people telling falsehoods all the time in my job. It may not be the profession you would have chosen for me, but I'm damn good at it, good enough to wave the BS flag here. No disrespect meant, but you called me home. If you want something from me, the least you can do is be straight-up honest."

His mother turned the cup around and around on the saucer, a nervous twitch of hers. "Your father wasn't an overly demonstrative man. That simply wasn't his way. It doesn't mean he didn't love his family."

Enough already. "The only time he touched me was to pose for a photo or to backhand me. There's not much affection between us to build a relationship."

Lips pressed thin, she folded her hands in her lap.

"You never met your grandfather. Your father came a long way from how he was brought up."

"That might explain things, but it doesn't excuse them."

"Or why I didn't step in?"

He stayed silent. He hadn't been headed in that direction with this conversation, yet he couldn't bring himself to redirect the path.

"I did what I thought was right, son. I did what I thought would keep this kind of life for you. You have no idea what it's like to grow up with people looking down their nose at you because you don't have money."

His mother's family had all died before he was old enough to meet them. He'd known they didn't have much money, but she hadn't mentioned any great hardship. "If you know how it feels to be poor, why do you treat Starr and all the girls next door like pond scum?"

"Because I want you to keep the stature I've worked hard for you to gain." An edge of panic laced her tone. "I don't want your bloodline to backslide."

"Whoa, back this up." His brain went into overload with all the info she tossed his way in a few short sentences. "I thought you disapproved because some of the girls had rough pasts with illegal activities. Not because of some ridiculous bloodline issue that doesn't even matter."

"That's easy enough for you to say since you've never had to prove yourself."

Her spine straightened and she smoothed her hands over her completely wrinkle-free powder-blue dress.

He couldn't remember a time he'd seen his mother anything but perfectly groomed, gray-blond hair turned under at the chin.

All of the things spouting from his mother's mouth should have made her more sympathetic to the girls next door and instead she'd hardened her heart. Money versus bloodline? David didn't much like the new image of his mother forming in his mind. And he definitely didn't like the notion that this image was far from complete.

He shoved up from his seat, turning his back on his mother long enough to rein in his anger. "Starr is a part of my life." He cupped a family picture of the three of them and wondered what kind of family photo Starr would envision. They'd never even discussed children before. He hadn't given her much to hang her dreams on, a mistake on his part, one he could see now he needed to rectify.

Setting the framed picture facedown, David pivoted to face his mother. "Where she and I take the relationship next is up to her, but I will not push her away just because you don't approve of her DNA."

His mother shoved to her feet, quickly, with none of the frail shaking she'd displayed in the past few days. "Have you seen her parents? Her aunts and uncles and their schemes? What if they get a piece of that property? I've heard them talking, you know."

She made her way across the hardwood floor with a rapid *click, click, click* of her heels, her face flushed with anger rather than inflated blood pressure. "They want a share in that restaurant. They could be here permanently and then all our property values will drop. They don't care how they make it happen. These are the sort of people she comes from. Time will tell. *Blood* will tell. Just you wait and see."

"If it's the truth that blood will tell, then things do not bode well for me, Mother, given the way you've treated Starr."

She snapped. "How dare you."

Her rambling speech shuffled around in his head with niggling persistence, but he was close; his instincts insisted that if he continued to push, it would all make sense. "I dare much. I am your son, after all, your blood, Father's blood, and apparently I have your strength when it comes to standing by my decision. The difference is my decision isn't to protect a piece of property. I'm protecting a person. The only person who matters to me right now."

His mother raised a shaking hand and for a moment he actually thought she planned to hit him—until she pointed out the window. "Look at them. Look. You have to see. I thought that if you really looked at them…"

The truth hit him with far more power than any hand. His mother's sudden illness that had vanished. Her insistence he come home. The puzzle pieces fell into a picture he wished he didn't have to acknowledge. "You brought them here."

Her shaking stilled. His mother's arm lowered and she clasped her hands in front of herself in a white-knuckled clench. "I don't know what you're talking about."

"You called Starr's family here and then summoned me home. You set up this whole volatile meeting."

She tipped her chin. "So what if I did? There's nothing illegal in that. You've been mooning over that girl for more than ten years. It's kept you from finding a nice young woman to settle down with and give me grandchildren. What's wrong with an old woman wanting grandbabies to hold before she dies?"

"You're nowhere near death, Mother, but if you're that lonely, I believe the time has come for you to consider moving to an assisted-living facility. You have begun wandering and falling under the influence of people of bad repute. I can't watch over you 24/7."

Panic laced her blue eyes. "Then we will hire someone to move in here permanently."

"Someone you can sway over to your side and manipulate. I think you misunderstand. There's not a decision to be made."

"You're not asking me?" She blinked back the tears.

He couldn't allow her to stay here, not when she had this obvious wish to rain heartache on Starr's head. No matter what happened between him and Starr, he would protect her. "Mother, we can make this transition with grace and dignity, or we can do this in a way that hurts us both."

"You own the house. You're not leaving me any choice." She tipped her head with the regality of a deposed queen. All her tears disappeared in a snap.

He wasn't sending her into exile, for heaven's sake,

just someplace nearby with her friends where doctors and nurses could keep a better watch over her health.

"I won't send you far away to a hovel. You are my mother and you will see me just as often as you do now. But I will not allow you to hurt Starr." He closed the six feet between them and rested a hand on her shoulder. "And Mother, I will not allow you to hurt yourself through a vendetta that eats you alive."

"I'm not a bad person. I didn't do such a terrible job bringing you up, after all."

"That's neither here nor there. So we have come to an agreement?" He gave her shoulder a gentle squeeze before stepping back. "One thing boggles my mind though, Mother. Why go to all this trouble? Starr and I resolved long ago we're not right for each other—for reasons totally different than yours of course. Why try to break us up when we aren't a couple?"

"Oh, my son, are you truly that self-unaware?"

He stared, unblinking.

"You've been obsessed with this girl since she pulled up in the driveway seventeen years ago, long before you even started dating. I don't know what kind of hold she has over you. Maybe it has something to with how these people are able to pull off such unbelievable scams—"

"Mother…" he growled.

She waved a hand in the air. "Whatever. The two of you play at this game and it doesn't seem to make you happy. I only want my son to be happy."

"Do you think being manipulated by my mother

makes me happy? Do you think being mortified by her family has made Starr happy?" He thought of her tears in the attic, her tears for him. He'd been a fool for leaving her behind all these years. She deserved better than she'd gotten from the people in his house. "I stand by my statement. Life moves on and it's time for us to make some adjustments. If you truly want those grandchildren, there's only one woman who will be their mom."

He'd made his point and she could accept it or not, he wasn't backing down. But since he'd won his point, he felt compelled to let her know something he'd perhaps forgotten to say often enough. He leaned to kiss her cheek. "I do love you."

"Thank you, son." She backed away toward the hall. "I believe I'll go call Bitsy from my old bridge club. I hear she's happy with the retirement home…."

Her voice faded as she made her way to the stairs.

Well, hell. She hadn't even bothered to say she loved him back. His parents really were a mess in the emotional department. No wonder he was so screwed up when it came to giving Starr what she needed.

What she deserved after being so horribly used by that clan of hers.

Except after her years with Aunt Libby, perhaps Starr had some things she could teach him in the emotional arena in exchange for the things he'd taught her in the bedroom.

What a sweet deal, now that he thought of it. It wasn't as if he were expected to be freaking Shakespeare shouting over a megaphone. These sorts of things were private. Awesomely private.

The time had come for him to accept the truth. He would take Starr any way he could have her, even if it meant curbing his travel.

Now that he'd made the decision, he didn't want to wait another minute in laying claim to his woman for life, and he knew just the thing to romance her artist's eye. Mind set, David reached for the family portrait over the fireplace, pulled it back to reveal a small safe and punched in the code. Making her happy would make him happy. She deserved that and more. He opened the creaking safe door to a small fortune.

He loved Starr. Always had, he just hadn't recognized the feeling since he'd had precious little example to compare it to at home.

But no more living in the dark, thanks to Starr. She'd thrown wide the windows to let in the light and he intended to do his best to persuade her they should spend the rest of their lives standing in the sunshine. Together.

But first, he needed to clear the beach of the traveler caravan, once and for all.

Starr juggled everything in her hands, wondering why she'd tried to carry so much at once. But then that was pretty much the story of her life. She always tried to take on too much, her eyes bigger than her stomach.

A big dreamer. Today, though, she hoped she could make all those hopes come true.

Under one arm, she carried a memory book she'd made, but it wasn't of she and David. In the stack of folders, she'd found an extra accidentally included one containing family photos of David as a baby. The photos of David's father were sweet, as well, the proud papa, a happy husband. Things may have gone bad in the Hamilton-Reis household later on, but at one time, they'd been better.

Starr couldn't help but think of how she'd been dating David as his mother had been grieving the loss of her husband. That couldn't have been easy. And in that little revelation, Starr was able to ease up on some of her anger. She might not like the idea of a clingy mother hanging on to her son, but at least she could understand on some level.

Under her other arm, she held the cat plate. She'd bought a reproduction for herself, doggone him and his gold credit cards. And finally, she held a cat carrier with an orange tabby inside.

For the first time, she trudged up the steps of David's house by herself.

She rang the bell and waited and waited. Nothing happened. She started to turn away—

Behind her, the front door creaked open. She spun around to find David's mother standing there, and surprise, surprise, the older woman looked rather rumpled, bringing to mind her front-porch visit of just a week ago. As much as Starr resented the way she'd been treated over the years, she had to get along with this woman. At least David would know Starr had tried.

Starr thrust the kitty carrier toward her. "I remembered you used to have a cat back when I first moved in. This one isn't all fluffy like the Persian cat you used to have, but pound pets are usually really grateful for the love. And it matches this amazing collector's item plate."

"Um, my dear, I'm not sure what to say." Alice Hamilton-Reis looked around her for others, no little surprise on her face.

"It's probably best you don't say anything. I just wanted to bring you a get-well gift since you've been feeling under the weather." Starr passed the album and took a deep breath since things were going to get a bit stickier now. "David gave me these photos to organize into this gift for you."

"*David* gave it to you?"

The pathetic hopefulness in her voice softened up a hard spot in Starr's heart. She figured David would forgive her the slight fudge with the truth.

"Yes, ma'am. You know that David and I have been friends—and more—for a long time now. He means a lot to me, which makes you a special person in my life, too. I hope that you will accept this memory album as a peace offering, a fresh start for a new relationship between you and I—for David's sake if nothing else."

The older woman took the album, staring at the wedding photo of herself with David's father. Mrs. Hamilton-Reis had clearly loved the man. Maybe the loss of that love had simply devastated her so deeply she didn't have much to offer anyone else.

Alice Hamilton-Reis's fingers shook as she traced the posed picture. "This is truly lovely, the way you've matted the portrait. Thank you." She smiled, albeit begrudgingly. "You have a good eye for mixing colors. I've always liked the flower bed you planted around the carriage house."

The woman obviously still adored her prize tea roses, but it was nice to hear she could see the beauty of a rambling cottage garden, too. Starr set down the cat and plate with hope in her heart.

A shriek sounded in the distance.

She pivoted, searched, finally peered around the corner of the house to find... Her relatives were all outside their campers, clustered around David—and a pair of police officers. Ohmigod. How had she missed that as she'd walked across the lawn? Likely because she'd done her best to keep her eyes averted from the problem.

Now she couldn't take her eyes off it. "Here, Mrs. Hamilton-Reis. You don't have to decide now about the cat. Just think it over. If you don't want the cat, I'll take it, but I really hope you'll enjoy her."

She'd read a lot about how much a pet could do to help alleviate depression in someone battling loneliness.

Starr charged down the steps toward the fray. "David? David! What's going on?"

Her petite mother ran to her, arms extended, flitting like a bird. "Oh, sugar, thank goodness you're here. You can straighten all this out before suppertime. Your boyfriend here thinks we're criminals. You know we would never hurt anyone."

Other than leaving a kid to suffocate in an RV. Or ripping people off with crap items. Or stealing from an old woman who took in cast-off children. Starr suffered through the hug before crossing to David. "What's the matter?"

He peeled her mother's hands off Starr's arm. "The police have questions about a series of debit-card scams in Dallas. They believe your family is responsible."

She didn't doubt for a second the Ciminos en masse could pull something like that off.

Frederick clapped a hand on David's back. "Young man, surely you can use some of your connections to help us out here."

David shook his head. "Actually, my connections are the ones who tracked this down and reported it."

Starr gasped. Gita grabbed her daughter's hand again like a last-minute lifeline. Starr had to look in her mother's eyes and deny the connection that had only hurt her. At least Mrs. Hamilton-Reis—in her own halting way—had admitted when she'd been wrong. Whereas Gita was still incapable of admitting she'd made mistakes. Starr turned to David and realized he was worried about her reaction.

His gaze met and held hers as if gauging her feelings. Did he really think she would be angry? Great gracious, she'd been waiting all her life for someone to help her take them on. Aunt Libby had tried, but she'd had so many children with problem families, there hadn't been much of her to spread around.

Heavens, she wasn't in the least angry. She hooked a hand in the crook of David's arm, physically choosing him over the parents who'd only hurt her. "I appreciate David's help. We don't want anything questionable going on around Beachcombers." She lowered her voice, but added a wealth of steel. "You lost me the day you left me to roast in the RV for hours on end until the cops finally discovered me and took me to a hospital. I almost died, you know. But I won't regret it, though, since your criminal carelessness brought me here."

She needed to vocalize her stance to ensure all the Ciminos knew where she stood, even as she felt the flex of muscles in David's arm under her touch at the mention of her parents' neglect. Essie scrambled away first, realizing the jig was up.

Gita and Frederick backed away more slowly, eyes and noses narrowed. Undoubtedly they would get away with community service hours. They were slippery that way. But they were also savvy enough never to pull a scam again in a town where the cops caught their scent.

Such as Charleston.

Relief flowed through Starr's veins as old worries slid from her shoulders. David had accomplished so much more than banishing her relatives from her land. He'd helped her see what she really wanted from her life. For the first time, she was brave enough to dream about a future that included love. Laughter.

Starr squeezed David's elbow again as she watched

her relatives load up in the Cimino gypsy caravan for what she felt certain was the last time she would ever see them. He looped an arm around her shoulders as the cop cruiser escorted the rickety vehicles onto the main road.

She tipped her face up to his, smiling. "Thank you."

"You're more than welcome. I'm sorry it took me so long to get it right, but I swear they will never hurt you again. I just wish I could have been there to help you when you were a defenseless ten-year-old locked in that damn camper." His embrace grew so tight it bordered on painful.

She hugged him back, realizing right now the event hurt him more than it did her. "It's okay, David. *I'm* okay. It's in the past and thanks to you, they are in my past."

"Damn straight," he rasped, his voice more than a little raw.

He started to lean down to kiss her when a screech split the air. He jerked upright. "What the hell is that?"

She fidgeted, embarrassed and grinning and so in love all at once. "Uh, I believe that's your mother's cat."

"My mother's cat?"

They both turned and, sure enough, there stood David's mother on the side veranda observing the whole ordeal—tabby cat in her arms, tucked under her chin. Alice showed that animal more affection than Starr had seen her give any human, but at least the woman was smiling for a change.

It was a start.

David tucked Starr closer to his side. "I assume it's

no coincidence that animal resembles the one in the gallery plate."

"You're an observant man. I thought she could use some companionship."

"I would kiss you senseless right now for being so thoughtful in spite of everything, but my mother's watching so that would be rather weird." He skimmed her hair away from her face. "Although that's a temporary situation. She and I had a discussion this afternoon about her going to a retirement village."

Shock rooted Starr to the spot. She couldn't have heard him right…. But searching his eyes, she saw that she had. There was more to this than he was saying, but regardless, she sensed that he'd done this for her. And from the way his mother held the cat that had come from Starr, maybe there was hope for all of them after all.

Starr settled deeper into David's embrace. "Well, from the look of things, I imagine you'd best make sure they take cats at the place."

"Money's no object, remember?"

"Of course, Agent Money Bags." She arched up to brush a quick, quite circumspect kiss across his lips. "Although if we're going to keep things low-key with your mother around, you should probably stay right here for a while until your body calms down."

"Those are just the family jewels in my pocket." He hugged her tighter with a secretive smile on his face. "Meet me on the pier at midnight and I'll let you check them out."

* * *

Music from Beachcombers drifted on the ocean breeze. Starr owed Ashley big time since she was closing the bar for her tonight. But her romantic younger sister had been more than happy to help her out. It felt strange to openly acknowledge the possibility of a relationship with David, but the time had come for them both to step into the light.

Speaking of which, he stood at the end of his family's dock, a lone bulb streaming light down over him. After all these years, he still stole the air from her lungs. Tall and dark and lean. As a scared, neglected gypsy child, she hadn't believed she deserved someone like him.

Now, thanks to his steadfastness, she knew she totally deserved his love.

"David."

He leaned back against the wooden railing. "Starr."

Just the simple speaking of their names carried a wealth of emotion. He extended a hand. She linked her fingers with his and stepped into his embrace.

For countless laps of the waves against the moorings, she stood in the warmth of his arms, enjoying the wealth of colors in the moonbeams streaking across the deep purple water.

She nestled her head under his chin. "What's this about family jewels?"

His laughter rumbled against her back. "I'll get to that in a minute. I have a few things I want to tell you first, things I should have figured out a long time ago." She felt his neck work in a long swallow. "I'm willing to cut back on the travel so you can have the home you need. You need those roots and I'm damn sorry I didn't see that before. The house is ours for you to bring light inside."

She squeezed her eyes tight against the tears threatening to pop free. She'd waited so long for this. She rubbed his hands over her stomach. "I'm not averse to taking a few road trips with you now and again. I think I would like to get an art degree and seeing the artists' work for real would only help my studies."

"I think that's an incredible idea. I've learned to see my home through new eyes because of you. Hell, I've learned to see life through new eyes because of you. Home has a definite new allure with you in it. And you'll be next door to Beachcombers whenever work calls."

She stared down at their clasped hands and let words slip free she hadn't dared share with anyone before, but then she'd never had David in her life for good before. "I have to confess to being a little jealous of Ashley when she graduated."

"Yet you still gave her the degree first." He turned her to face him and cupped the back of her head. "You're a helluva woman."

"She needed it more." The choice had been clear if not easy.

"Like I said, helluva woman. Is it any wonder I love you?"

"You love me?" She'd thought so, hoped so, but hearing him voice it meant more than she could have even imagined.

"Of course I love you. I asked you to marry me, didn't I?"

"Uh, no. You didn't. I would have remembered that."

"Damn, I'm messing this all up."

She rather liked jumbling the brain of this normally suave man, although it wouldn't hurt to give him some encouragement. "Feel free to try again, because I love you so very much this is something I definitely want to hear."

"You love me, too, huh?" Grinning, he dipped his hand into his suit coat pocket and pulled out a green velvet bag. "Hold out your hands."

She cupped her fingers and he poured out a hefty assortment of jewels—two necklaces, a bracelet and three rings with emeralds, diamonds and sapphires. "Uh wow?"

He laughed that wicked way of his. "Family jewels, remember?"

She threw back her head, joining in his laughter that tickled up her spine and always would. "And to think I had another sort of family jewels in mind."

David pressed a kiss to the side of her head. "You do make me smile, babe, and we'll get to those later if you're still of the same mind." He grazed down over her mouth, lingered for a sweep that had her toes curling in her flip-flops before he continued, "Seriously, these are just some of the heirlooms slated for my wife. I thought about the way you said you would redecorate the house and it occurred to me that you might have an idea for resetting some of these stones into an engagement ring. A one-of-a-kind look for the unique woman who stole my heart."

"Oh. Really wow. And holy cow, yes. Yes to your love and yes to making an engagement ring that showcases our very unique love." She looked down at the jewels in her hands and tears stung her eyes. He really was trying to meet her halfway, seeing who she was and accepting their differences. And it was working.

A sigh of relief racked through him before he smiled down at her again. "Thank you for those generous gifts you brought over for my mother. I'm not so sure she deserved them, but the way you compromised means a helluva lot to me."

"She brought you up." She stared into his deep blue eyes so full of love for her she knew she would never mistake it again. "That's gift enough for me."

"Like I said, you're generous. And about that cat plate, you bought it for yourself."

"I have my own money, buster." She slugged him in his muscle-hard arm. "You seem to have forgotten that along the line somewhere."

He locked those steely arms around her, where she knew they would stay forever. "Before we see it coming, you'll be the millionaire in our relationship."

"Bet on it." She savored his confidence in her.

He dropped kisses onto her face, along her jaw, accenting every word with the taste of his passion. "Either way, I'm totally and completely under the influence of your charms."

* * * * *

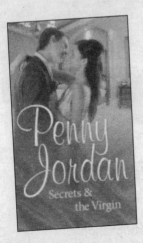

Queens of Romance

Uncertain Summer
Serena gave up hope of getting married when her fiancé
jilted her. Then Gijs suggested that she marry him instead.
She liked Gijs very much, and she knew he was fond of her –
that seemed as good a basis as any for marriage. But it
turned out Gijs was in love…

Small Slice of Summer
Letitia Marsden had decided that men were not to be trusted,
until she met Doctor Jason Mourik van Nie. This time, Letitia
vowed, there would be a happy ending. Then Jason got the
wrong idea about one of her male friends. Surely a simple
misunderstanding couldn't stand in the way of true love?

Available 1st August 2008

Collect all 10 superb books in the collection!

0708/25/MB150

Queens of Romance

Impulse
Rebecca Malone sold all her possessions and jumped on a plane to Corfu! So when sexy stranger Stephen Nikodemus began to romance her, all she had to do was enjoy it…

The Best Mistake
Zoe Fleming was a hardworking single mum looking for a tenant, not a lover, a father for her son or a husband. Then sexy, single, gorgeous J Cooper McKinnon turned up!

Temptation
When socialite Eden Carlborough came crashing down from one of his apple trees into his arms, wealthy bachelor Chase Elliot knew she was simply too delicious to resist.

Available 4th July 2008

Collect all 10 superb books in the collection!

Celebrate 100 years of pure reading pleasure with Mills & Boon®

To mark our centenary, each month we're publishing a special 100th Birthday Edition. These celebratory editions are packed with extra features and include a FREE bonus story.

Plus, starting in February you'll have the chance to enter a fabulous monthly prize draw. See 100th Birthday Edition books for details.

Now that's worth celebrating!

15th February 2008

Raintree: Inferno by Linda Howard
Includes FREE bonus story Loving Evangeline
A double dose of Linda Howard's heady mix of passion and adventure

4th April 2008

The Guardian's Forbidden Mistress by Miranda Lee
Includes FREE bonus story The Magnate's Mistress
Two glamorous and sensual reads from favourite author Miranda Lee!

2nd May 2008

The Last Rake in London by Nicola Cornick
Includes FREE bonus story The Notorious Lord
Lose yourself in two tales of high society and rakish seduction!

Look for Mills & Boon 100th Birthday Editions at your favourite bookseller or visit
www.millsandboon.co.uk

FREE

2 BOOKS AND A SURPRISE GIFT!

We would like to take this opportunity to thank you for reading this Mills & Boon® book by offering you the chance to take TWO more specially selected 2-in-1 volumes from the Desire™ series absolutely FREE! We're also making this offer to introduce you to the benefits of the Mills & Boon® Reader Service™—

- ★ **FREE home delivery**
- ★ **FREE gifts and competitions**
- ★ **FREE monthly Newsletter**
- ★ **Books available before they're in the shops**
- ★ **Exclusive Reader Service offers**

Accepting these FREE books and gift places you under no obligation to buy; you may cancel at any time, even after receiving your free shipment. Simply complete your details below and return the entire page to the address below. You don't even need a stamp!

YES! Please send me 2 free Desire volumes and a surprise gift. I understand that unless you hear from me, I will receive 3 superb new volumes every month for just £4.99 each, postage and packing free. I am under no obligation to purchase any books and may cancel my subscription at any time. The free books and gift will be mine to keep in any case.

D8ZEE

Ms/Mrs/Miss/Mr..Initials ....
BLOCK CAPITALS PLEASE

Surname ....

Address ....

....

....Postcode ....

Send this whole page to:
The Reader Service, FREEPOST CN81, Croydon, CR9 3WZ